A Matter of Temptation

By Lorraine Heath

A Matter of Temptation • As an Earl Desires
An Invitation to Seduction
Love With a Scandalous Lord
To Marry an Heiress • The Outlaw and the Lady
Never Marry a Cowboy • Never Love a Cowboy
A Rogue in Texas

Lorraine Heath

A Matter of Temptation

Doubleday Large Print
Home Library Edition

An Avon Romantic Treasure

AVON BOOKS
An Imprint of HarperCollins*Publishers*

This Large Print Edition, prepared especially for Doubleday Large Print Home Library, contains the complete, unabridged text of the original Publisher's Edition.

AVON BOOKS
An Imprint of HarperCollins*Publishers*
10 East 53rd Street
New York, New York 10022-5299

ISBN 0-7394-6078-1

First Avon Books paperback printing: October 2005

Printed in the U.S.A.

This Large Print Book carries the Seal of Approval of N.A.V.H.

This one is for you, Lucia,
because over the years you've often been
my personal Obi-Wan Kenobi,
drawing me back from
the "dark side" of my writing.

Thank you so much
for not only guiding me through
the complexities of this story,
but for being a remarkable editor.

Chapter 1

London
1852

Robert Hawthorne stared at a face he'd not seen in eight long years.

A face he hardly recognized. When last he'd looked at it, he'd seen nothing except the unmarred countenance of a life untried—features that revealed an absence of lines, character, and depth. A face that had yet to be written upon. Unfortunately, it now told an incredible tale of unbelievable cruelty.

The deep creases spreading out from the corners of the eyes and mouth had been shaped by agony, agony brought on not necessarily by physical discomfort, but rather by emotional upheaval—which could carve just as deeply, and in many instances, more so, leaving the mark of its visitation visible to any who dared to look. Yes, the physical and emotional torment suffered was as clearly evident as the passage of time.

Black whiskers that had been as fine as the downy hair on a newborn's head were now thick, coarse, and scraggly. The skin was pale to the point of almost appearing sickly, but then how could he expect it to look any differently when it had not known the direct touch of the sun in years?

That unhealthy pallor might cause a bit of a problem.

But in studying the visage before him, Robert decided it was the eyes that shocked him the most. Not the color, a blue that matched the hue of a deepening sky just before sunset gave way to night. No, the color remained exactly as he remembered, but the pathway the eyes offered to the soul had changed considerably.

They reflected a journey of devastating betrayal. And that, too, might cause a bit of a problem, because a man could seldom hide the truth of his character revealed by his eyes. Well, not a good man anyway.

Robert shifted his gaze away from the reflection in the mirror he held to the man he'd secured to the bed with silk sashes he'd taken from several dressing gowns hanging in the wardrobe. The man's eyes were the same brilliant blue, but they burned with fury mingling with hatred. He wondered why he'd never recognized the emotions before when he'd looked into those eyes.

And he *had* looked into them—for the first eighteen years of his life. Surely during one of those glances, he should have *seen* the monster who dwelled within.

"Why, John?" he asked, his voice scratchy from lack of use after years of not being allowed to speak. "Why did you have me locked away? What did I do to deserve such abuse?"

The monogrammed handkerchief that Robert had stuffed into John's mouth prevented him from doing anything more than growling, and perhaps that was a bit unfair, but Robert didn't want to risk his brother calling out and rousing the servants. He doubted John would provide a truthful answer anyway.

Yet the questions had haunted Robert for

more than three thousand days: while he'd paced his cell, while he'd lain in his hammock, while he'd listened to the screams of men as they'd succumbed to insanity's tantalizing promise of freedom.

It was frightening how often he'd been tempted to give in to the siren's call of madness himself. But he'd managed to escape, and there he was, at long last, facing a nemesis he'd never known he possessed until it was too late, now with only a vague idea of what he would do to regain what had been stolen from him.

He couldn't deny that John had always been a bit of a scamp, laughing gaily at his own delightful wickedness, his transgressions tolerated as harmless pranks. The man—in his youth—had fooled them all. But Robert drew no comfort from the fact that he hadn't been alone in misjudging John.

He tried to find satisfaction in his captive's attempt to escape the bonds that held his wrists and ankles secured to the four posts of the magnificent bed in which he'd been born, but all Robert felt was deep and resounding disappointment. As though he gazed upon his own soul and found it withered and empty, void of any worth.

"I thought we were more than brothers. I considered us friends. We shared confidences. I would have trusted you with my life. More than that, I would have willingly sacrificed . . ." Inhaling sharply through clenched teeth, he turned away, the pain almost too great to bear. He'd loved his brother—remarkably, he still did in that strange way that affected those bound by blood—and that unconditional love was the very reason that the betrayal sliced so deeply into his heart and flayed it raw.

If he couldn't trust John, then whom could he trust?

He knew a moment of gratitude because his parents were no longer living, would never know the truth about everything that had transpired, but his gratefulness was fleeting, like life, and he wished only that he could return to the wondrous days of his youth when his worries had consisted of nothing more than meeting his father's lofty expectations—something he'd achieved with amazing regularity.

If he thought too long on his present circumstance, he began to feel adrift, losing his sense of purpose. Regaining what was his by right was crucial, not only on a personal level, but on an ancestral one as well. He couldn't turn his back on what duty, honor, and those who'd come before him demanded was not only his due but his obligation to set right. He owed the past as well as the future to stay on course.

Drawing on a reserve of strength he'd not known he possessed until everything had been stolen from him, he concentrated on the immediate task facing him, knowing it was imperative that he complete it as quickly as possible.

"Stop thrashing about, John. You'll only hurt yourself, and trust me when I offer you this bit of advice born of experience: you don't want to be in a weakened state when you receive your just reward. Rest assured that I plan to grant you a bit more mercy than you showed me, but I must take steps to protect myself, my inheritance, and my heirs."

He shook his head with a mixture of sadness and disbelief. After all this time, he still couldn't comprehend how it had all come about. "I can't fathom how you managed to pull off your deception. How long did you plot to dispose of me and take my place? The planning alone must have been extensive, the details numerous. I almost admire your cleverness."

Setting the mirror on the bedside table, Robert leaned it against a stack of books his brother had no doubt taken joy in reading before he drifted off to sleep; both joys—the reading of any books he desired and the peaceful slumber—would soon be denied him, along with many others.

Robert adjusted the mirror's angle so he could view his reflection clearly while he sat in the high-backed burgundy velvet-covered chair he'd dragged over and placed beside the bed. He wondered briefly when exactly the house had been modernized with gas lighting, wondered what other changes he might find. It was unsettling to realize that life had gone on as though nothing were amiss. And in the next instant he was comforted with the same thought.

Because it meant that it would again happen: life would continue without anyone other than the twin brothers realizing that an incredible change had taken place.

With scissors he'd located in the dressing room next to this bedchamber, he hacked away his stringy black hair until it followed the outline of his ear and the nape of his neck.

"No lice," he murmured. "The whole purpose behind isolation, I should think. Keep men isolated and they can't spread disease or rebellion. It has its advantages."

And a whole host of disadvantages few men could endure for long. How he'd managed to maintain his sanity remained a mystery. He didn't want to contemplate that perhaps he hadn't, that his escape was merely an elaborate illusion and that he would awaken to find he was still a prisoner housed in corridor D, gallery three, cell ten.

Forcing the unsettling thoughts away and concentrating on what he knew to be real, he gazed intently in the mirror and studied his shortened curling locks. His hair was far from perfectly cut, but he wasn't overly concerned. He'd have his valet trim it up nicely in the morning. He doubted the servant would say anything if he thought his master's hair seemed more unruly than usual.

After all, one didn't question a duke.

Next, Robert used the scissors to shorten his long beard until it was manageable, then he picked up the shaving cup, whisked the brush around, and began applying the lathered soap liberally. Inhaling the fragrance brought back memories of the first time he'd sat so his valet could shave him while his father looked on with pride.

"You're well on your way to becoming a fine young gentleman," his father had said. Robert had shared his father's assessment, not with conceit, but with a quiet acceptance that he'd worked hard to gain that regard and was succeeding.

He didn't recall his father saying the same to John when he'd sat for his first shave. Perhaps that had contributed to the problem. John had always been second: second at birth, second in his father's eyes, second in line.

Robert peered over at his younger brother, younger by less than a quarter of an hour, yet born not only a day later, but in a different year entirely, with Robert arriving before midnight on the thirty-first of December, while John arrived on the first day of the new year. But when it came to primogeniture, minutes held as much weight as years.

"Can't say I care much for your side whiskers, all bushy and long like that. Are they indicative of the latest fashion or are you still a rogue, doing things your way and to hell with what is proper?" He leaned over and ground out, "Or legal. But how to prove the truth of the matter when it will be your word against mine? Therein lies the crux of my dilemma and the reason that I must originally treat you as unfairly as you did me."

Ignoring John's groans, Robert returned the cup to the table, snatched up the straight razor, and very carefully began to scrape away what remained of his beard, leaving side whiskers that closely resembled John's. After taking a good look around London in the next day or so, he'd change them to a style he preferred. He didn't want too much difference in his appearance in the beginning for fear people would begin to suspect something was amiss. Although he would actually be righting what had been amiss for years.

He was desperately in want of a warm bath with scented soap, but that indulgence would require the servants bring up hot water, so he'd have to postpone the much anticipated luxury until morning. Tonight he would simply clean up as best as he could with the water he found in this bedchamber and the changing room.

"To explain my pallor, I shall have to say that I'm feeling a bit under the weather, I think. That should do it until I can get out in the sun. I must say that you look as though you've been enjoying robust health. That will soon change, though, brother."

He finished his task and laid the edge of the razor beneath John's chin. He wasn't exactly sure what reaction he'd hoped for: fear, remorse, regret. Instead, John looked merely more rebellious—as though he were the one betrayed.

"Why didn't you simply kill me, John? Was it that you couldn't look into a face that resembled yours and watch as you snuffed the life out of it? Or was it sentimentality over our sharing the womb that stopped you? Or something else entirely?" Saddened beyond belief, he took the razor away from his brother's throat. How had it come to this?

He moved away from the bed and began preparing himself with more haste. He had much to do before dawn and not much time in which to do it. John had been asleep when Robert had sneaked into the London town house and into this bedchamber. He would now have to do to John what John had done to him.

He turned toward the bed.

"Why did you drug me and have me imprisoned? A silly question. You did it so the dukedom would fall to you."

England's history was rife with tales of men who had killed those who stood between them and the crown, murdering nephews in towers and brothers on the battlefield and fathers in their sleep. For some, a title was as coveted as a crown. As long as a man's deception wasn't revealed, what did it matter how he came to be next in line?

"But how in God's name did you manage to pull it off? Did Mother and Father not suspect? What of the servants? My friends and acquaintances?

"Surely someone must have realized you were masquerading as me. And how in the devil did you ever explain only one of us returning from a night of revelry?" They'd gone out to celebrate their eighteenth birthday. Robert remembered drinking, the scent of a woman . . . and waking up alone, imprisoned. Anger at first, followed quickly by desperation. Until he learned the truth of the matter . . .

"What luck for you that Mother and Father succumbed to illness shortly after you'd dispensed with me. I pray it was as reported and not poisoning, because, dear brother, I fear I could never forgive you if you were responsible for shortening their lives.

"I must say I appreciate the fact that you had the newspaper announcing their deaths slipped to me, along with your succinct note. Otherwise I might have wasted time searching for them here, rather than coming straight for you."

An envelope had sailed through the bars on his door. Hardly able to believe he was receiving a scrap of communication—unaware that anyone except his jailer knew where he was—he'd watched it flutter to the ground.

Inside he'd found a clipping from the *Times* announcing the unexpected deaths of the Duke and Duchess of Killingsworth. The cause of their demise was reported to be influenza. Still struggling with his plight, unable to determine how he'd come to be where he was, he'd read the article three times, dispassionately, as though it discussed people he barely knew.

Then he'd unfolded the letter that accompanied the article.

Thought you should know.

—Robert Hawthorne, the Duke of Killingsworth

He'd stared at the words until they blurred, trying to make sense of them. And when understanding finally dawned, he could hardly believe the implications.

"I must give some credence to the brilliance of your plan. Much easier to have John disappear than Robert. No one would search for John, would they? After all, he wasn't the heir apparent. That must have irked somewhat. To know that John's disappearance would cause no ripples. But Robert, should Robert disappear, well, then that would be an entirely different story, wouldn't it? Would have required absolute proof of my demise before you could step into my shoes.

"So although you managed to rid yourself of me, you couldn't very well remain John. It would have complicated your little scheme, because only my death would give you the dukedom. And as we've discussed, you seemed unable to bring yourself to kill me. For which I suppose I should be eternally grateful. I hope you'll forgive me if I don't show excessive gratitude."

He reached inside his shirt and pulled out the brown scotch cap he'd been wearing when he made his daring escape. It was designed so that when a prisoner placed the cap on his head, its large peak dropped down to his chin, hiding his face and identity completely, hiding everything except his eyes, which peered through two holes.

"By now they'll have discovered that Prisoner D3, 10 escaped. Do you remember when we toured the facility with Father, right after it was built, before it began housing prisoners? Of course you do. Is that when you began scheming?"

He pointed to the brass badge on the front of his shirt—both of which he would soon give to his brother. "A man loses his name in prison. Without a name, a man is nothing. Simply nothing. Except a number. Prisoner D3, 10. Prisoner, corridor D, gallery three, cell ten. And now that prisoner has disappeared.

"Will the warder you bribed come to tell you—for I'm certain you must have paid someone off in order to achieve your end—or will he run away in fear of his actions being discovered? Either way it matters not to me, because you'll find yourself at Pentonville before dawn, with this over your head." He shook it.

"I know what you're thinking. They'll know

it's you and not me." He laughed for the first time in years, but it was a sound void of warmth or merriment, and he wondered if it sent shivers down his brother's back the way it did his own. If he was standing closer to the edge of insanity than he realized. "That's the beauty of my plan. They won't know, because they don't know what I look like. They won't know that this morning my hair was longer, my face bearded. Because the only time prisoners don't wear the hood is when they're in their cell, alone. Alone, constantly alone. We work in our cell, we sleep in our cell, we eat in our cell.

"England's innovative separate system for reforming criminals is hell on earth, John! And you shall soon bear witness to its inhumanity. Even when we're allowed to walk in the exercise yard with our caps covering our faces, we're not allowed to speak. Separation and isolation are the order of the day and must be maintained. Do you know what it is to never be able to share your thoughts with another? To never share a joke, a concern, a fear, a smile, a laugh?

"I'm sharing with you the benefits of my experience. Wear your cap and hold your tongue. Don't even attempt to tell them that you're not supposed to be there. They won't listen. Don't tell them there's been a mistake. They won't listen.

"The only time you're allowed to use your voice is when singing hymns in the chapel each day. Men weep at the chance to raise their voices in song."

Robert looked at the hated cap that matched the brown of his tunic and trousers. It was during his time in the chapel that he'd managed to escape. The pews consisted of high-walled stalls, each man assigned to one. One evening Robert noticed that during prayer, when he bowed his head, he could no longer see the guards, and if he couldn't see them . . . he reasoned that they could no longer see him. During those few moments, he became invisible. For weeks, he had patiently used that time to work loose the boards on the floor of his individual stall. Today he'd finally succeeded at working enough boards free that he created a small hole through which he'd squeezed himself. He'd crawled beneath the chapel until he reached the main building. There, a narrow opening for ventilation had led him to the outside and freedom.

He looked at John and again waved the

cap. "You will wear it, brother, because if you don't they'll beat you until you put it on. Then you put it on to hide the shame of your beating. You'll be completely alone, wondering when I'll come for you.

"Rest assured, brother, I'll come as soon as I determine how to prove that I am Robert and you are John. Pray that I come to a resolution quickly."

A knock sounded on the door. Robert's heart hammered unmercifully, almost painfully, against his ribs, while John began to struggle in earnest against his bonds, his cries for help muffled by the handkerchief. Robert silenced him further by pulling the pillow out from beneath John's head, dropping it on his face, and pulling closed the thick velvet draperies that hung down from the canopy.

He walked to the door and spoke through it. "I am indisposed. What is it?"

"I'm sorry to bother you, Your Grace, but a Mr. Matthews has only just arrived and is in quite an agitated state. He insists he must see you immediately regarding an urgent matter involving Pentonville Prison. He is quite adamant—"

"Tell Mr. Matthews that I'll meet him at the

back doorway, and see to it that no servants are up and about in that section of the house."

"All the servants are already abed."

Except for the man standing at his door. Good.

"Then deliver my message to Mr. Matthews and take yourself to bed as well."

"Yes, Your Grace."

He listened as the butler's footsteps faded away. He returned to the bed, opened the draperies, yanked the pillow away, looked at his brother, and smiled. "I say, John, you have a most loyal ally in Mr. Matthews. What did it cost you to hire him to ensure Prisoner D3, 10 was never given freedom?"

Looking at his brother, during that moment, he almost changed his mind. He almost said, "Let's talk, let's work this out. I am the rightful heir, but I will take care of you. I'd always planned to see to your needs without question."

But then he caught a glimpse of his reflection in the mirror. His brother had taken eight years of his life. Robert had no plans to be that cruel, to leave his brother languishing in hell for that long.

But what would a few weeks hurt?

* * *

Several hours later, Robert awoke with a start, disoriented, his heart thundering. The bed was too soft, the room too large. Slowly, it all came back to him.

His escape.

His hiding in the shadows.

His creeping into the house.

His finding John, asleep, unsuspecting.

The warder arriving just after midnight to let the duke know that Prisoner D3,10 had escaped. Knocking John unconscious with a good solid punch had gone a long way toward appeasing his anger at the time, but now the fury was roiling through him again, and he worked hard to squash it. It had been festering for far too long. He'd used it last night, used it to exact his revenge.

He'd always thought revenge was supposed to be sweet. He was surprised to discover that it tasted bitter. He shook off the guilt. He'd given John what he deserved. It was only fair, and he'd be damned before he'd feel guilty about the actions he'd taken—although truth be told, he'd already been damned, twice over by his brother's cruelty.

Lying still, he listened to his own rapid breathing, his heartbeat thrumming between his ears. Then the sweet song of a lark. Outside the window. Was that what had awakened him?

Relaxing his taut muscles, he inhaled deeply, a fragrance so pure that if he were a sentimental man he might have wept. But he feared whatever tendency toward sentiment he might have once possessed had been brutally stolen from him.

Still he could appreciate the scent of cleanliness and the comfort brought by a soft, feather mattress beneath his back. Tonight he intended to enjoy the feel of a soft, warm woman beneath his body. Tonight he would indulge in all the vices he'd been denied by his brother's calculating schemes. Denied through no fault of his. It was an aspect of this entire untenable situation that nagged at him.

Had he done something to deserve his brother's unjust treatment? He'd committed no crime, harmed no one. He'd gone to school, studied hard. He'd learned manners, etiquette, and protocol. He'd been prepared to step into his father's shoes when his father left this earth—which he'd assumed would be after a long life—but until that precise moment he carried out his duties and responsibilities with the proper decorum expected of the heir apparent.

He'd been an exemplary firstborn son. Was it his striving to make his parents proud that had turned John against him? Or was it simply his entry into the world first? It was hardly something over which he'd had control. Come to think of it, he'd had no say in a good part of his life. Obligations were thrust upon him, and duty dictated that he accept and meet them head on, never shirking his responsibilities.

And yet he'd been unjustly punished and found himself in the untenable position of having to prove who he was and taking some recourse to ensure that he managed to hold on to the dukedom. He had little doubt that John would attempt to usurp him with some sort of treachery, and the next time he intended to be prepared. He'd not be caught unawares again.

He stretched his muscles—relishing the luxurious sensation of silk gliding over his skin—shoved his hands beneath his head, and stared at the canopy above his bed while the first fingers of dawn spilled into the bedchamber. He'd left the draperies at the windows and those around the bed pulled aside. He wanted nothing denied him. And he had such grand and self-indulgent plans for his first day and night as the Duke of Killingsworth.

A steaming hot bath with sandalwood soap. Followed by warm towels rubbed briskly over his entire body.

Clean clothing.

A hot, hearty breakfast while he read the *Times*.

A leisurely walk through London.

A brisk horse ride through Hyde Park.

A carriage ride.

Another meal.

Another bath.

More clean clothes.

And then a night of revelry to celebrate his newfound freedom.

A bottle of the finest wine.

A cigar. Perhaps a hand of cards.

And then a woman. A beautiful woman. With voluptuous curves and hair like satin. He would know at last what it was to bury himself deeply inside a woman, to become lost in her warmth and softness as his body reached for release.

Tonight he would have it all, after being denied everything for so long. He would take her again and again and again, until he was replete, exhausted, unable to move.

He would do the same tomorrow night. And the next. He had a youth denied to make up for. And then he would see to his dukedom.

But first he would see to his manhood.

He'd known a moment of worry that his plans would unravel when he'd carried his unconscious brother to Mr. Matthews. He'd recognized the warder as one of the more brutal ones. The guard had recognized him only as the man who had paid him. Matthews's fear had been palpable as he'd stammered his profound apologies for the prisoner's escape, and Robert was left to wonder if it was more than coins that had made the man serve as John's henchman. Matthews had been only too willing to accept Robert's explanation that the prisoner had come here to cause him harm, and once again he was to be returned to Pentonville and held as before.

A prisoner without the promise of freedom.

Another niggling of guilt pierced the contentment of the morning, and Robert pushed it aside. He'd not be denied this day, no matter how selfish. He deserved it: the drinking, the womanizing, the sating of his long-denied body, the self-gratification. As long as John kept his mouth shut and his cap covering his face, he'd survive exceedingly well until Robert determined the best manner in which to prove the truth of what had transpired.

The door leading from the bathing room into the bedchamber opened, and Robert held his breath. His next test was descending upon him with rapidity. He'd once theorized that servants didn't truly look at their masters, but kept their eyes averted or downcast. If his theory was proven correct, he would be fine. If false . . . well, he'd had worse things to worry over.

The servant quietly entered the room. His valet. Or more precisely, his brother's valet. And he suddenly realized that he was in a spot of trouble because he didn't recognize the man. He was tall, slender, held himself well, and while he appeared to be relatively young, he was balding, the top of his head reflecting the sunlight streaming into the room.

Robert had expected Edwards, who had once been his loyal valet, to still be serving his brother, but as he pondered the situation it made sense that Edwards had been let go. The man might have had the ability to detect subtle differences in the heir apparent, and while he might have held his doubts to himself, it was probably a chance John had been unwilling to take.

And this unknown valet might notice subtle differences in today's duke as compared with yesterday's. Mainly that today's duke hadn't a clue as to his valet's name.

"Good morning, Your Grace," the man said as he crossed the room.

"Good morning." Robert cursed beneath his breath. The words had come out hesitant, unsure, not at all the tone usually rendered by a man in control, a man to whom deference was given by virtue of rank if nothing else.

The valet suddenly stopped in the center of the room as though aware that something was terribly amiss. He looked at the bed—not so much the man lying in it—the windows, then quickly at the walls, the ceiling, the floor, and Robert wondered if the servant was feeling the room close in on him as Robert was. Robert should have held his tongue, kept his silence.

"I'm not accustomed to the draperies already being pulled aside," the servant said. "You must be anticipating the day."

"Indeed I am." The truth was easily spoken. It was the first time in years that he'd awoken and actually looked forward to the day ahead.

"I've had your bath prepared." The servant walked to the wardrobe, opened the doors, and began gathering items.

Robert contemplated lying abed a bit longer, perhaps even having breakfast brought to him on a tray, but the amount of food he planned to eat was best handled by a sideboard. He slid out from beneath the covers. Standing in a nightshirt he'd confiscated from a drawer, with his bare feet on the floor, he suddenly felt exposed.

The servant had yet to take a full measure of him, and when he did . . .

He was a duke now. Closing his eyes, he drew on the memories of his father's commanding voice. His father had never left any doubt as to who was in charge, even before he inherited the dukedom from *his* father. Self-assured, confident. Robert simply had to follow his father's example and teachings now. He felt calmness descend over him. He could do this. He *would* do it. He opened his eyes.

"I should like to take a ride in the park this

morning," he said. "See to having my horse readied."

The servant turned slightly, his brow creased to such an extent that it seemed to roll his balding pate forward, and Robert easily determined that he was hesitant to speak.

"What is it, man?" he demanded to know—impatiently, as his father had when a servant was slow to respond.

"With all due respect, Your Grace, I'm not certain you have time for a ride this morning."

"Whyever not? Is there some pressing appointment that can't be put off?"

"Only your wedding, Your Grace."

Chapter 2

Now that the moment had actually arrived, Torie Lambert wished that it hadn't. An unfortunate realization that she could hardly reconcile with the excitement she'd felt only last night as she'd prepared for bed. For months she'd been eagerly anticipating her wedding to the Duke of Killingsworth. The problem as she saw it now was that she was no longer certain she was anticipating the marriage. A strange notion indeed, but there you had it.

With a sigh, she stared at her reflection in the cheval glass while her lady's maid fluttered around her like a butterfly that couldn't quite determine where to alight, touching up

Torie's dark brown hair, adjusting the wreath of orange blossoms that held the veil of Honiton lace in place, tittering about how lovely she appeared on this most special of all days.

Torie couldn't deny that it was a special day, which was the very reason that it seemed incredibly odd to find herself suddenly filled with such doubt. Her engagement and the upcoming wedding were the talk of London: how she, an untitled landowner's daughter, had managed to snag the most eligible—not to mention very nicely titled—bachelor among the peerage. They gossiped about the affair as though she'd done something special, and for the life of her, she could think of nothing exceptional she'd done other than smile at the duke and carry on conversations that, for the most part, seemed to delight him.

She was incredibly fond of Killingsworth, but what did she truly know about him? He was exceptionally good at charades, was a fine dancer, and enjoyed long walks. Ah, yes, and he was undeniably handsome. Not that she thought a gorgeous face was a quality to take into account when selecting a husband, but it certainly didn't hurt matters that he was incredibly pleasing to gaze upon.

He had the most astonishing blue eyes, and while they seldom sparkled with merriment, as he was a decidedly serious fellow, they did make her feel special when he gazed at her with such intensity that oftentimes she would blush beneath his scrutiny. He never revealed what he was thinking at times such as those, as if he might be embarrassed by his own thoughts, and she often wondered if he was thinking about the same thing as she: what it might be like to truly kiss each other.

He was so terribly proper, had never kissed any part of her other than her glove-covered hand—not even when he'd asked for that very hand in marriage—and yet tonight . . . well, tonight he might very well kiss a good deal more with no material to separate his lips from her skin.

She warmed at the thought of such intimacy and wondered if perhaps that was the source of her unease. The realization that very soon she would become embarrassingly intimate with a man she liked extremely well, but didn't love. Or at least she didn't think she loved him. Shouldn't love be all-consuming?

Of course, she'd been thinking of her wedding every moment of every day for the past six months, but she hadn't truly been thinking of her betrothed. Had she?

She'd thought of gowns, and petticoats, and veils, and invitations, and her trousseau. She'd been so overwhelmed with the details of the wedding that she'd given hardly a thought to the particulars of her marriage or her wedding night. And now that the moment she'd worked toward was finally upon her, she felt it had arrived far too soon, before she was completely ready for so monumental a step. Quite honestly, she was scared silly.

"Victoria, do stop frowning. It completely ruins the appearance of your gown," her mother admonished, standing off to the side, her hands positioned on the wide hips that had served her well when she'd borne her two daughters, her feet spread apart like those of a ship captain who thought none would disobey him. "Your father paid a princely sum for your attire. Your gown and veil look very much like the ones Queen Victoria wore the day she married her dear Albert."

Her mother's adoration of the queen was irritating at times. Honestly, one would think

Britain had never had a female monarch before. And everyone's husband was a dear except for her own mother's.

"Everything is lovely, Mother, and I do appreciate that Father went to such expense to make this day memorable. It's only . . ." She let her voice trail off. It was too late.

"Spit it out, girl."

Torie attempted to inhale a deep breath but the whalebone corset prevented even the smallest of breaths. She released two tiny ones before confessing, "I'm having second thoughts concerning the wedding."

"But you selected the loveliest of flowers and ribbons," her seventeen-year-old sister said, standing off to the side.

"Diana, I'm not talking about the details of the trimmings. I'm talking about the actual wedding, the exchange of vows, the becoming a wife."

Her mother snorted in a most unladylike manner that more closely resembled her common roots than her present station in life. "Bit late for that, my girl."

Torie had hoped for advice a tad more enlightening. After all, her mother had far more experience with men, marriage, and . . . duty to one's husband.

"Mother, I've been so busy preparing for the wedding that I really haven't had time to prepare for the marriage. Unfortunately, now it occurs to me that I'm not quite certain I love him." That admission sounded awful, so she quickly amended it. "Or at least not as deeply as I should."

Brushing her maid aside, her mother moved up to stand beside Torie and began tugging on the gown here and there as though she thought if it were fluffed out a bit more, she could rearrange the worry lines on her daughter's face as well.

"Love is highly overrated," her mother said. "The best a woman can hope for is a man who is kind, generous with a spending allowance, and quick when it comes to taking care of his husbandly duties in bed."

In the mirror, Torie caught a glimpse of Diana dropping her mouth open in astonishment at the unexpected vulgarity spoken. Like Diana, Torie knew that one simply didn't mention what passed between a man and woman beneath the sheets. Well, at least not loud enough for anyone to hear.

Torie quickly clamped her own mouth shut. She licked her lips and dared to say what she and her friends had once whispered among themselves. "I thought the marriage act took all night."

"Dear heavens, no. If a lady is fortunate, her husband will be finished in fewer than ten minutes."

"And if she isn't fortunate?"

"Then it becomes a matter of endurance. However, your young duke appears to be a most virile man. I'm certain he'll require no time at all to get the job done, so I see no point in worrying over a situation which is unlikely to occur." Her mother began waving her hands in front of her face, as though she'd suddenly become heated and needed cooling off. "Oh, I shouldn't be speaking of such personal matters."

"But you should." Torie spun around and faced her mother. "I have no earthly idea what to expect. I have a vague notion, but I'm not entirely certain exactly what transpires between a man and a woman after they're married and the lamps are dimmed."

Her mother began waving her hands more frantically. "It's too private to speak of."

"Lovely. Now I'm terrified with the prospect of experiencing something that a mother can't even speak to her daughter about."

Her mother stilled her hands, her brow

pleating as she studied her firstborn for what seemed an eternity. Finally she reached out to cradle Torie's cheek. Her smile was almost sad. "You'll learn soon enough what it's all about, but I assure you that you have no reason to be frightened. The act is merely an inconvenience that prevents you from going to sleep as soon as you might like."

"Does it hurt?"

"Only a bit and only the first time or two as a woman's body learns to accommodate a man's."

"Perhaps there should be a school for such things," Diana piped up.

Torie's mother heaved a sigh. "Diana—"

"Well, honestly, Mother, if a body must *learn*, the best place is at school, is it not? What if a woman's body can't learn to accommodate a man's? And what is there to accommodate?"

Torie fought not to smile at her sister's teasing, while her mother's cheeks turned a bright red. "I'm really not comfortable discussing this subject. After all, it is your father with whom I do it, and it is a very private matter. I'm sure the duke will make everything most pleasant."

"But does he love me?" Torie asked, returning to the serious side of her concerns.

"I believe he cares a great deal about you."

"But caring isn't love."

"Try having love without caring, my girl. You'll find that it doesn't work so well."

Torie had no doubt that the duke cared, but she often worried that he cared more about the money and land that marriage to her would bring him. Her father was a landed gentleman who owned four thousand acres that provided him with a very comfortable income, comfortable enough that her dowry made her quite the catch and allowed Torie to wander in circles closed to her family until recently. Her mother had been quick to make certain that the aristocracy realized that her elder daughter brought a large fortune to a marriage.

Torie had always wanted a suitable marriage, but now she feared she'd set her goals too low. Suitable. It sounded so boring.

She couldn't deny that comfort existed in her relationship with the duke, but not an ounce of passion. No true excitement, no wonderment. She'd experienced more joy in selecting her gown than in accepting his proposal of marriage. The past few months had been a whirlwind of meetings with dressmakers and stationers and cooks and florists. She'd hardly had time to take a breath, much less to realize that the anticipation she felt as each decision was made wasn't experienced when she thought of spending the remainder of her life with the duke. And what if it was a long life?

"Do you love Papa?" she asked.

"I'm quite fond of your father. He has treated me well all these years, and as I've stated, that's the most any woman can hope for."

"It doesn't seem enough. Now that I'm standing at the threshold of marriage, it quite simply doesn't seem enough."

Until that moment, Torie hadn't realized that fondness wasn't love. But then what was love? An elusive feeling she had yet to experience. Oh, she loved her parents, loved her sister, but she couldn't say that she'd ever loved a man to whom she didn't share a familial bond. Didn't love require time to develop, to come to fruition? Shouldn't one wonder how one might survive if the object of her affection were no longer there?

Her mother heaved a deep sigh as though she were lifting a trunk filled with nothing but troubles. "I daresay you've been reading too much Jane Austen of late. You're confusing the romantic love found in her silly novels with the reality of love in a marriage. It would be best if young ladies were not allowed to read books that created an unrealistic view of courtship."

"I must say that I absolutely *adore* Mr. Darcy," Diana said, pressing her fist to her heart, a dreamy look coming over her face. "Such a tormented soul."

"He was a man with too much pride," her mother said. "Which was the whole point of the story."

"I disagree. The whole point was for Elizabeth to fall madly in love with him and for him to fall madly in love with her."

"Nonsense. A woman does not seek love. She seeks an advantageous marriage, which your sister has accomplished far beyond my expectations. I'd hoped for a viscount, and here your sister has snagged a duke. If you were wise, girl, you'd follow her example."

"I'm never getting married," Diana announced with resolute certainty as she plopped into a chair.

An expression of unbridled horror crossed

her mother's face. "Don't speak such rubbish. Of course you'll marry."

"No, I won't. Why settle for one man? How can you ever be certain which one is the *one* man with whom you should spend the remainder of your life? Each man is so very different from the others. Today I might want a man who is filled with gaiety, and tomorrow I might be in the mood for one who is a bit more pensive."

"I think you should concern yourself with finding a man who is content with a woman who doesn't know her own mind."

Torie bit back her laughter as Diana worked to lighten the somber mood that Torie had inflicted upon them. Her sister had such an uncanny gay outlook on life, and she so loved goading their mother, who was always so easily provoked.

"Come now, Mama," Diana said. "Having one man in your life is very much like having the same dish served at every meal. It becomes boring after a time, no matter that you began requesting it because it was your favorite. You grow weary of it."

"Good heavens! Whatever has gotten into you to speak of such ludicrous things?"

"I just don't know how a lady can determine today what she'll be in the mood for tomorrow."

"You're talking nonsense!"

Torie, on the other hand, was beginning to fear that her sister had touched on the heart of the matter. She wanted something different from what she was being served, but the meal had already been prepared. She could hardly send the dish back to the kitchen without offending the cook.

"What if after she's married," her sister began, "Torie meets a man she likes far better than she does her duke? What is she to do then?"

"It is a chance one takes when one accepts an offer of marriage, which is the very reason one shouldn't be hasty in accepting."

"But what is she to do?"

"She forgets about the other man, the one to whom she is not married."

"Did you ever meet someone and wish you'd married him instead of Papa?" Diana asked.

Her mother briefly closed her eyes. "You girls will be the death of me." She opened her eyes and pinned each daughter with a hard-edged glare. "We will dispense with this nonsense immediately. Victoria is marrying a very likable fellow."

Torie didn't miss the fact that her mother had failed to answer the question her sister had posed. Had someone else come along later? What would Torie do under a similar circumstance? If she wasn't in love with the duke, then it seemed likely that she could meet someone else . . . and she would absolutely hate it because she wouldn't be untrue to her vows or her husband, which meant she would be untrue to her heart. Neither choice seemed quite fair.

"Likable because he's a duke," Diana chided.

"You're beginning to vex me, Diana."

"Would you be so keen on her marrying him if he wasn't?"

"I don't understand why we're discussing this today, rather than six months ago when the duke asked for her hand in marriage."

"Because now Torie has doubts where she didn't before."

"Every bride has doubts on her wedding day. I daresay every groom has doubts. The reality of the moment is unsettling, because it is an enormous step to be taken." Her mother looked at Torie and held her gaze. "Do you care for him?"

Did she? She liked him well enough. She enjoyed his company, although there were times . . .

"Sometimes he leaves me," she admitted.

"Well, of course he does, dear girl. He doesn't live in our house. After today his departures will occur with less frequency."

"No, I'm not talking about his not being in a room with me. I'm referring to times when he is sitting right beside me, but he seems to have . . . gone away."

"You're talking in taxing riddles. He can't *not* be there if he's there."

"I'm unable to explain myself adequately, Mother. But his leaving has been happening more and more often of late, and I find it quite troublesome. It's as though he's thinking such deep introspective thoughts that they carry him far away from me. Then he will turn to me, and a look will come over his face as though he's almost surprised to find me beside him."

"It sounds as though you are saying he's merely distracted."

"Distracted is as good a description as any, I suppose, although I'm not certain it's quite that simple."

"He's a duke, Victoria. With four estates to see after, and only God knows how many servants, tenants, worries . . . It's quite understandable that the responsibilities weigh on his mind, and when they do, it appears he's giving less thought to you. Your father often pays me no attention. It's nothing to worry over."

"I suppose not, but still—"

"Victoria, you're wearing on my nerves. Your father and I have worked incredibly hard so that you might have a better life than the one we've had. My dreams have been realized beyond expectation. Be happy."

But what of her dreams, Torie wanted to ask. Except she feared she'd waited too late to give them much credence. It had all seemed so romantic when the duke had swept her off her feet, but now . . .

"You'll be presented to the queen," her mother said, changing the subject, as she moved the veil a quarter of an inch to the right and a quarter of an inch to the left where it flowed past Torie's shoulders. "It won't escape her notice that you carry her name, and when you become close friends, as I'm sure you must, I shall be invited to the palace."

"Mother, I'm a commoner."

"After today, you'll be a duchess, dear. She'll want to meet you. I'm sure of it."

Another of her mother's dreams. That her daughters should have the distinction of being presented to the queen. Torie was beginning to feel that her life was about fulfilling her mother's dreams rather than her own.

She looked back in the mirror and began to wonder who this lady was standing before her. Had she ever truly seen her before? Did she truly know herself?

Or had she always simply been a reflection of her mother's desires?

Chapter 3

Only your wedding, Your Grace.

His valet's words had hit Robert in the chest with the force of a battering ram. Of the numerous things he'd considered as he'd plot-ted his escape and retribution, his brother being married—or getting married—had never once crossed his mind.

But from the moment those fateful words had been uttered, Robert had carried on an internal debate with himself while his valet had prepared him for this most monumental of occasions.

A wedding. *His* wedding.

No, his brother's wedding.

Not really, not any longer.

But should it be? Should it be John's wedding?

Or was it merely the wedding of the Duke of Killingsworth?

The distinction was small, but incredibly important, and had weighed heavily on his mind, influencing his assessment of the situation. In the end, he'd decided that he had no choice except to follow through on the plans already made.

Robert now stood at the front of the church, reconciling himself with the decision he'd made to go forth with the blasted ceremony. He'd reasoned that most marriages among the aristocracy were based on many factors, none of which involved love. Political gain, monetary gain, a father desperate to rid himself of a daughter, a man in need of an heir. He had little doubt that the lady, whoever she might be, had consented to marry the Duke of Killingsworth because of his title, his position, not because of the man himself. In other words, she'd consented to marry the duke, not John, and therefore she would acquire exactly what she, or her father, had bargained for.

She would marry the Duke of Killingsworth.

The fact that a different man would stand before her as the duke today than had yesterday was merely a minor inconvenience that should cause her no distress. It was inconceivable to him that she could actually hold any affection for John, and while Robert didn't dare hope that she might come to care for him, he also recognized that from the time he was old enough to understand his duties as the heir apparent, he'd known that marriage was expected, required, and that he would base his selection of a wife on the suitability of the woman to become the Duchess of Killingsworth, not on any romantic notions of love as spouted by poets.

Marriage was a duty. Finding a lady who complemented his status among the peerage was imperative. That John had undertaken the task in his stead saved Robert the trouble of doing so himself. Of course, it also left him in the precarious position of knowing nothing at all about the young lady—he assumed she'd be young—and wondering what she might know about John. Presumably very little, since she'd consented to marry him.

So tonight he would have a wife, and as his body had yet to be sated, he was filled with expectation, relief, and anticipation. He would welcome his new role as husband—and he would see to it that his wife welcomed him.

Beside Robert stood a tall, dark-haired man near his own age whom he was fairly certain was the Marquess of Lynmore. Since the man had assumed Robert was who he thought he was—and the man was serving as his best man—he'd seen no need to introduce himself.

And Robert couldn't very well nudge him, wink, and whisper, "I say, old chap, you look rather familiar. Who are you again?"

The uncertainty was but a small disadvantage to be endured and overcome.

The advantage to this day was that John had set everything in motion, and all knew their respective roles and his. Robert hadn't been forced to give a single command. His valet had known exactly what he was to wear for the occasion—a wine-colored frock coat, the trousers several shades lighter—and had helped him get dressed after giving his hair a proper trimming. The driver of the coach bearing the ducal crest had known precisely when and where to deliver him and, upon their arrival, had pointed to the open carriage parked nearby and explained that it would be used following the ceremony to carry the duke and his new duchess away. A man had met him on the church steps and escorted him to where he needed to be. All in all, this day might be incredibly easy to pull off.

While waiting for his bride's arrival, he surveyed the crowd bunched up within the church and experienced a moment of dizziness. So many faces, so many people. Sitting on open pews without walls separating them from one another. Staring at him. A few leaning over to whisper to the person sitting beside them. It was a sight he'd seen numerous times in his youth, but suddenly it seemed strange, disorienting.

What were they saying? What were they thinking?

He had to remind himself that all was normal around him, that people were supposed to sit in the open, not be blocked off from viewing each other. People were meant to have the freedom to whisper to each other. They weren't to be denied the pleasure of another's company.

Many of the people looking at him were elderly. Some he thought he recognized as friends of his father's and grandfather's. Men like them, who had approved the building of Pentonville in 1842, who had agreed about and advocated for the separate system of confinement. Men who considered themselves modern-day thinkers.

The irony of their beliefs and how they'd affected him didn't escape him. These men would never experience what they had wrought on others. Robert had, and once he no longer needed to worry over proving who he was and could safely take his place in the House of Lords, he was going to become an advocate for those imprisoned during this enlightened age—which, in his humble opinion, was anything but enlightened.

The isolation didn't reform men as argued. It drove them insane. Unfortunately he often felt that it had carried him right up to the precipice of madness. He didn't think he'd crossed over, but he experienced moments when he wondered, when he had doubts, when he wasn't certain how he'd managed to hold on to his sanity in that madhouse of desperation.

Suddenly the organ music rose in crescendo, the unexpectedness of it taking the very breath from Robert's body. A Gray's organ had provided the music in the chapel at Pentonville, and for a heartbeat, he was transported back to the horror of isolation and loneliness . . .

He found himself breaking out in a cold sweat, unexplainably feeling exposed and vulnerable. He hadn't realized how accustomed he'd become to hiding his identity, to people not knowing who he was, to people not seeing his face, to looking at the world through peepholes that until that moment he'd not realized provided a certain amount of security. Everything with which he'd become familiar during the past eight years was no longer surrounding him. He'd thought he'd welcome shedding the vestments of captivity. Instead he found himself longing for the comfort of the familiar.

It wasn't that he wanted to return to Pentonville. He was simply completely unprepared for the moment. He'd expected his first ventures out after his escape to involve small crowds, only a few people he'd selected to surround him. Not a church packed to the rafters with near strangers.

He wanted to run, to escape, but this time he couldn't. He'd not worked loose the flooring beneath his feet. No hole was going to open up for him to squeeze through. He had to stand firm and make the best of this situation. At its very worst, it would be better than what he'd endured the day before.

It was time. Time to follow through on the masquerade that his brother had begun.

He focused on a young girl walking down the aisle, tossing petals from a basket dangling on her arm. Two young ladies soon followed. Lovely ladies. Smiling, graceful. Unfamiliar to him. He wondered if he should know their names, if he would be forced to speak to them. Good God, he hoped not. He was terribly out of practice when it came to politely and charmingly speaking with ladies, when it came to talking to anyone. As they neared, he did nothing more than acknowledge them with a curt nod.

He returned his attention to the aisle where a lady and gentleman—a man he assumed to be her father—now made their way toward him. His bride, no doubt. Her gown was white satin and lace, the satin train trimmed with flowers. A lacy veil flowed down to her shoulders.

Should he recognize them? Was she someone he might have known in his youth? Was her father titled?

"I daresay, Killingsworth, you are one fortunate man, one fortunate man indeed," Lynmore murmured.

As the woman came to stand before him, her father beside her, Robert acknowledged the truth of his best man's words.

She was lovely beyond measure. The lacy veil provided an ethereal quality that couldn't quite hide her features. Her hair was dark, pinned in place, giving him no hint as to its length or thickness, although it appeared a few strands curled about her face. Her dark eyes were focused on him, and he wondered if they were brown or black. It was difficult to tell. She was small, her head barely reaching his shoulder. She looked to be so incredibly young.

Or was it only that he felt so incredibly old?

Either way, he could well imagine come nightfall that John would throw his body against the door, would pound the walls and floor, would be desperate to escape as he was filled with the knowledge of what Robert might be doing with the bride John had planned to marry. That was the true horror of Pentonville.

The unbearable imaginings that isolation could bring forth in a man's mind when it was continually tortured by silence and loneliness.

It took determination, control, and concentration to hold the nightmares at bay. And sometimes, no matter how much he wanted to, Robert couldn't latch on to any of the skills needed to be free of the nightmares. He would be too weary, too beaten, too tired. The emotional strain . . . yes, his brother would suffer tonight.

The archbishop was asking something, her father answered, and Robert realized that he couldn't continue to drift off into reminiscences of the hell he'd endured, but that he had to remain focused on this precise moment. If anyone suspected that he'd swapped places with his brother, he could very well find himself trying to justify his own scheming before he was ready, and it would place him at a huge disadvantage.

He had to remain cautious and alert until he could determine the best course of action.

No one around him was speaking, everyone seemed to be waiting, and he feared he might have reached the portion of the day when he was supposed to know precisely what to do without assistance from anyone.

"If you'll extend your arm to your bride, Your Grace," the archbishop whispered.

Of course. Her father was giving her into

Robert's keeping. He was familiar with this part of the ceremony, having attended a few weddings as a guest. It was simple enough to perform. So he held out his arm.

Then she smiled, an incredibly sweet, joyous smile, her eyes shining with such happiness that the veil couldn't disguise the hope, faith, and affection that she was showering on him.

Oh, dear God. He'd made a ghastly mistake, vastly misjudged the situation. It wasn't the duke she was here to marry, it was *John*. As unlikely as it seemed, she cared for John. If the warmth reflected by her expression was any indication, she might actually love his brother.

It was an aspect to the marriage that he'd not even considered. The ramification of what he was about to do almost brought him to his knees.

During all his scheming, his carefully thought out plans, the many hours he'd lain on the hammock that stretched between the walls of his cell and stared at the unadorned high ceiling, pondering his strategy, his escape, his retribution, he'd not once considered that he might shatter a young woman's heart, that he might betray an innocent.

He should simply stride out of the church while murmuring his apologies and regrets. Better to embarrass the lady now than mortify her later. He could say that he'd had a change of heart, which was the truth. The duke's heart was different, because the duke was a different man. Convoluted reasoning to be sure, but the truth nonetheless.

But if he marched out, he'd find himself in a worse situation than he was already in. Because people would want to know exactly why he wasn't willing to go through with the ceremony.

Besides, crying off generally carried grave consequences, and he had no idea what those might entail. All he knew was that he wasn't in a position to deal with them while righting all the other misbegotten affairs of his life. He cursed his brother, cursed his own lack of planning, and cursed his wife-to-be for good measure. Even though she was innocent, she was going to sticky up an already dreadfully sticky situation.

He saw no other recourse except to go through with the ceremony. But not the marriage. He would find an excuse to distance himself from the woman—to allow her to remain chaste. And once he'd determined how to prove he was the true duke—then what would he do?

He would release his brother from captivity, undo the ridiculous marriage, and magnanimously return his brother's love to him, not so much out of kindness to his brother but rather his concern for fairness to the woman. It wasn't honorable for her to have to marry a man other than the one she'd intended, especially when she looked upon him with such adoration.

Yes, his plans could all still work. Not as smoothly as he'd originally hoped, but it could come about. He would set himself to the task—as diligently as possible—to prove his claims. Then they would all be free from his brother's troublesome—not to mention illegal—meddling.

He forced himself to give her what he hoped was a reassuring smile.

She placed her hand on his arm, and they both stepped forward, giving their attention to the archbishop, whose voice began to ring out to the rafters with the words that would soon seal both their fates.

Robert surreptitiously slid his gaze over to the woman who was to have been John's bride and was now his. She was much more interesting to study than the aging archbishop. Her eyes were her dominant feature: large and almond-shaped. They were almost exotic. He wondered what details the curtain of lace held secret. Were her lashes as long as they appeared, or was that merely an illusion of the lace? Did she have blemishes or delicate lines that had been etched by laughter? Did she smile often, or did she save her smiles for the most special of occasions, such as when greeting the man whom she was to marry?

He knew about women from a distance, as mothers, governesses, servants. But he had no intimate knowledge of them, of how they reacted, of what they expected.

He found himself wondering the silliest of things: what colors did she favor, what foods did she relish, what entertainments might she enjoy?

And he found himself speculating about the most important of all questions. What had brought her to this moment? What had she seen in his brother? What had caused her to want to marry the blighter?

Was there goodness in John? He'd once thought there was, but John's actions had stripped him of any favor he might have found in Robert's eyes. Still, should Robert have been less bent on revenge and given his brother a chance to apologize, to explain, to make amends?

For surely an angel such as she appeared to be wouldn't dare dance with a devil.

She turned her head slightly and peered over at him. Her mouth curled up, her gaze grew warm. His heart tightened, and he wished her adoration was truly for him, not his brother.

Yet Robert couldn't help but consider that John had taken everything from him. Would it be poetic justice if Robert now took his brother's lady? Not only her body, but her soul and her heart? To hold them all as though they rightfully belonged to him—as his brother had held his titles, his inheritance, his position in family and society?

It was something to ponder, to debate within himself. A possibility that would no doubt keep him awake at night, when he'd so been looking forward to sleeping without care.

Again he bestowed on her a semblance of a smile that he hoped concealed his misgivings and his perilously treacherous thoughts.

Forcing his attention away from her, he

concentrated on the rituals of the ceremony, kneeling when he was supposed to kneel, repeating words that meant nothing to him as though they meant everything. And in the process, he did at least learn something of great importance: her name was Victoria Alexandria Lambert. Such a large, important-sounding name for such a petite and delicate woman.

The archbishop made mention of a ring. Robert turned to his best man, then stared at the delicate circle of silver that he'd placed on his gloved palm. He should have known, should have prepared himself. His mother's ring. He closed his fingers over it and battled for the strength to finish what he'd begun.

He distanced himself from everyone and everything around him until the vows were exchanged, only then acknowledging that they were both well and truly locked on to this matrimonial path.

Then the archbishop announced that Robert could kiss the bride. Kiss Victoria Alexandria Hawthorne, the new Duchess of Killingsworth.

Drawing on his memories of a distant cousin's wedding, Robert slowly lifted the veil. Dear Lord, but she was lovelier without the mist of lace to blur her features. Her lashes were indeed as long as they looked. Her eyes a deep brown, outlined in gold. He'd never seen eyes such as hers. She had no blemishes, no freckles, no lines formed by worry. Her lips were plump and moist-looking, and he wondered how many times his brother might have kissed them. Would she notice a difference in the shape of his mouth, the feel of his lips against hers, the taste of his kiss?

He raised his gaze to hers, surprised to find tears shimmering within the dark depths of her eyes. Then he chastised himself because her tears of joy made a mockery of what he'd just done. She thought he'd reaffirmed his love for her, that she'd exchanged vows with the man who had asked for her hand in marriage. She was crying because she was happy, overjoyed at the prospect of being his wife until death parted them. She was crying because she wanted this moment—when he sealed their vows with a kiss—more than anything else in the world.

"I'm sorry," he heard himself whispering hoarsely right before he placed a light kiss near the corner of her terribly tempting mouth.

She seemed as surprised as he by his words and his actions, her eyes blinking, the tears disappearing, her brow furrowing. And he realized that he might have made a grave error in judgment, might have revealed himself to be not who she thought he was.

But then the archbishop, in his booming voice, was presenting to the gathered assemblage the Duke and Duchess of Killingsworth, and Robert was left with no recourse except to escort his wife from the church.

Chapter 4

Torie sat in the open carriage, striving not to take offense that her husband was fairly hugging his side of the conveyance, his gaze averted, as though he wished to be as far away from her as possible.

Within the vestry of the church they'd signed their documents before heading out to the carriage. Because an aristocrat's wedding tended to draw a crowd of strangers, they'd had to weave their way through the gathering, she clinging to his arm while he tried to keep his top hat from flying off. They'd both waved at the people milling about as they'd been driven away from the church, but she'd sensed that he held little enthusiasm for the ritual. It was ceremony only, something to be tolerated, and now that they were beyond the crowds, he seemed to have forgotten that she sat beside him.

She fought to hold on to her happiness and push back the ominous sense she had that something was dreadfully wrong. That she'd somehow disappointed him beyond measure, perhaps in the choice of her gown or the style of her hair. When she'd joined him at the altar, he'd stared at her as though he couldn't quite determine who she was.

Or worse yet, perhaps he'd sensed her misgivings. She was so terribly unskilled at hiding her true feelings. Although she'd been wearing a veil, he might have been able to see through the lace to the doubts reflected in her eyes.

But they would have been apparent for only a moment. Because she'd seen the same qualms swirling within his, and she'd wanted to quickly reassure him that all would be well. One of them needed to believe that if their marriage was to have any success at all. And so she'd smiled as lovingly as she could, with all the hope for a blissful future that she could bring forth. Her overture seemed to have given him the confidence to offer her his arm.

Once they'd taken their places before the archbishop, she'd found herself returning her attention to Robert, unable to believe that she was about to truly become his wife.

He was so amazingly handsome, now and in the church. The deep wine color of his frock coat enhanced his dark features, brought out the incredibly rich hue of his eyes. Sunset always reminded her of him, just before the sky gave way to night, when it was at its most vibrant blue. The light gray of his cravat gave him an air of nobility.

But now they were no longer in the church, no longer in need of concentrating on ceremony. They were free to give their undivided attention to each other. Yet here he was, glancing around as they traversed through the crowded streets as though he'd never before visited London.

After his courtship, and the time they'd spent together while she planned their wedding, she knew she should be accustomed to his penchant for staring off into space, but it always managed to unsettle her.

"Is it John?" she asked softly.

He jerked his head around, his brow deeply furrowed, something akin to fear in his eyes—which made absolutely no sense.

"What about John?" he asked, his voice hoarse as though he'd dredged the words up from the bottom of a deep well.

She smiled warmly, sensing his tenseness, unable to fathom the reason behind it, but desperately wanting to put him at ease. "You seem so melancholy, I thought perhaps you were thinking of your brother. I know how very disappointed you were when his missive arrived stating that he'd be unable to come to the wedding, but I'd like to think he's with us in thought if not person."

Relief washed over his features, removing the harshness of the lines around his eyes that she'd never before noticed. Was it the brightness of the sun that deepened them? That made no sense as they'd often ridden in an open carriage on sunny days.

"Yes," he finally said quietly. "I'm fairly certain he is with us in thought."

Reaching out, she squeezed his hand. "Perhaps we can go visit him in America."

"America," he repeated as though he'd never heard of the country.

She'd always thought only brides were

nervous on their wedding day, but it seemed that her mother had been correct in her earlier assessment: grooms harbored the same doubts and anxieties.

She'd have never thought it of Robert. He always seemed so sure of himself and his place in the world. Now he seemed so . . . lost.

"I'd like to stroll over his plantation in Virginia. I so enjoy when you read me his letters," she added. "He describes his surroundings with such fondness."

"Virginia . . ."

She laughed lightly. "Why do you repeat everything I say?"

She could almost feel the touch of his intense gaze as it roamed over her face. She tried to decipher what she read in his expression. His eyes somehow seemed different. They were the same blue that they'd been the last time she looked into them, but they weren't quite the same. He seemed almost wary, as though he feared making a misstep, as though he hardly knew what to expect of her.

"I'm a bit unsettled, I suppose," he said. "The enormity of what has just transpired . . .

I don't know why the reality of it didn't strike me sooner."

She released a slight laugh. "It struck me this morning as I was dressing. The doubts, the worry. Mother assures me that it's only natural. I suppose we've just changed the course of our lives."

"In ways I doubt we can even begin to imagine."

"I, for one, will be grateful when our obligations are behind us."

"What obligations would those be?"

"The most immediate one is the breakfast that Mother has prepared."

"I ate before leaving for the church."

She laughed a bit longer this time. "You're such a tease. You know perfectly well that I'm talking about our wedding breakfast, the reception for—as my mother refers to them—those who matter most."

"Ah, yes, I'd forgotten."

"I *wish* we could forget it."

"Do you think we would be missed if we didn't go?"

"Most assuredly. Besides, my mother would be mortified. She is quite pleased that I'm moving up in society."

"Then I suppose it wouldn't do to embarrass her."

"No, it wouldn't. Besides, you don't want to fall out of favor with her when you've done such a splendid job at charming her when she is not easily charmed. But perhaps we can get by with only staying a short while. It's a stand-up breakfast, after all."

His eyes glazed over as though he were striving to decipher something of monumental importance.

"I'm sorry, but I'm not familiar with that sort of affair."

"How can you say such a thing when we talked about it endlessly?"

"Remind me."

She rolled her eyes. "So typical of a man. My mother warned me that men rarely truly listen to what a woman says."

"Your mother is most wise, and I apologize for my previous lack of interest. Would it be a bother to repeat what you've obviously told me before? A stand-up breakfast sounds rather unappealing."

"But it is so in vogue. Everyone is doing it in that manner these days. All the food is placed on a large table in the library. Gentlemen prepare a plate for the ladies, then we all stand around while dining. The trick is to prepare foods that are easy to eat while not sitting."

"Perhaps it is good that I ate before leaving the house."

He appeared so deadly serious. She smiled at him. "I would beg of you to put only the sparest of helpings on my plate. My stomach is still in knots from standing in front of everyone at the church, having so much attention directed at me."

"I would have thought a woman as beautiful as you would be accustomed to attention."

Pleasure spiraled through her. He'd never told her that she was beautiful. Had never actually complimented her at all, now that she thought on it. "Is that the reason you married me? My beauty?"

"My reasons are numerous, impossible to explain."

"You might try."

"Are my compliments such a rarity that you must seek more?"

His gentle rebuff caused her to blush. "Of course not. It just seems that after a wedding, the bride and groom should shower each other with attention."

"I've paid little notice to the rituals of weddings. I fear I shall cause you embarrassment throughout the day."

"Oh, Robert, it is I who has the greater chance of embarrassing you. You were born to this life; I have only just married into it."

"You would never be an embarrassment to anyone."

The heartfelt delivery of his words caused the heat to rise in her cheeks.

"I've managed to accomplish exactly what I feared," he said. "I've embarrassed you."

"I'm not sure I've ever heard you deliver flattery so sincerely."

"I apologize if my words were inappropriate. I've not yet adjusted to my new role as husband. I'm not quite sure how to behave."

"Just be yourself, Robert. It's you that I care for so desperately."

"How desperately?"

She squeezed his hand again. "Incredibly desperately. Today I'm the happiest woman in all of London."

"Are you?"

"Whatever is wrong with you? You sound so doubtful, so unsure when you never have before. Has something happened, something I need to know about?"

He looked to be on the verge of announcing that the world as they knew it was about to come to some dreadful end.

"What is it, Robert?"

He shifted his gaze to where her hand was atop his. "It's of no importance."

"But I can see that you're troubled."

"I have a great deal on my mind, that's all."

"They say if you share your troubles it divides them in half."

He peered over at her, the corner of his mouth lifted in a wry smile. "I don't think that'll happen in this case."

"I do wish you'd tell me."

"Perhaps later."

Although she dreaded hearing the answer, she had to ask, "Does it have any bearing on the reason you apologized to me right before you kissed me?"

He gave a barely perceptible nod. "I fear a day will come when you'll regret that I married you."

"Don't be ridiculous. I'll never regret the day that I married a man I care for so deeply."

He turned his head away as though looking at her had suddenly become unbearably painful.

This wasn't at all how she'd planned for

her marriage to begin. It was to be a joyous occasion.

She'd caught his attention last Season when her mother had called upon a cousin and asked her to introduce her daughter into society. Torie had been all of twenty, well past her prime, and her mother was beside herself with worry that her daughter would never find a match. But she had. At her first ball, she'd danced with the Duke of Killingsworth, and his gentlemanly manners and kindness had fairly stolen her breath away on the spot.

His courtship had been satisfying to her, caused envy among others. An occasional walk in Hyde Park. An opera. A dinner. A carriage ride. Nothing earth-shattering. Always with a proper chaperone.

Still, he'd seemed as content with her as she was with him. She thought they were well suited. But now she was no longer certain. Why was he suddenly aloof, not as easy to converse with?

She'd not grown up in the circles he frequented, and she worried that in spite of everything, she wouldn't make a proper duchess. He was hardly expressing the enthusiasm she'd expected him to once they were married. Was she somehow to blame?

"Do you worry there will come a day when *you'll* regret marrying *me*?" she dared to ask.

Or perhaps she hadn't dared to voice the question aloud. Perhaps she'd only asked the question in her mind. Because he neither acknowledged it nor answered, but simply continued to give his attention to everything around him except her.

Chapter 5

Robert had an uneasy feeling he'd find himself burning in hell for the actions he'd taken today. And rightly so.

He'd been convinced the woman was marrying the *Duke* of Killingsworth, cared only about the title, the prestige, the political gain, but the manner in which she gazed at him, the manner in which she spoke to him, the manner in which, even now, she frequently lovingly touched his arm as they stood in the drawing room greeting the guests who arrived at her parents' home proved his assumptions false. Without question. Without doubt.

He was a fool. She cared for him. *Incredibly desperately.*

No, she cared nothing for *him*, he chastised himself harshly. She cared for *John*, John who had called himself Robert all these years. His brother who'd told the world that John had gone off to America to seek his fortune. A plantation in Virginia, of all places. And he was writing himself letters to tell of his imagined exploits. Diabolical.

At least now Robert had an inkling regarding the manner in which his absence had been explained, although he still wasn't quite certain how John had managed initially to meet with such success. His parents must have questioned why one of their sons hadn't returned from a night of merriment. The servants must have wondered. Friends, acquaintances . . . any number of people must have suspected something was amiss.

Surely Weddington, of all people, would have harbored suspicions—

"Don't you think so, darling?"

He glanced down into the eyes of the woman looking up at him so painfully adoringly. "I'm sorry. I was distracted for a moment."

Worry flashed in her eyes, before she

smiled more brightly and lifted her chin ever so slightly. "Lady Catherine was just saying how much her parents regret not being able to attend today's ceremony. I was assuring her that we would plan to visit them as soon as possible. I was simply asking if you concurred with my suggestion."

Who the deuce were Lady Catherine's parents? She looked vaguely familiar, but the only Catherine he remembered was a distant cousin his father had once talked of Robert possibly marrying. But then the girl had bloodied John's nose and the discussions had, thank goodness, come to a halt. The girl preferred trees and frogs to tea and frills. Of course, she was also all of twelve . . .

"Lady Catherine," he murmured.

She smiled becomingly. She was certainly no longer twelve.

"You must tell your brother that he need not stay away on my account. I hold him no ill will. And I would so love to see him again. Perhaps now I'd give him the kiss he fancied rather than a bloody nose."

"I shall tell him. And we shall see to visiting your parents, although it might be a while. My wife and I shall be rather busy for a time."

Her smile increased. "Of course you will, and well you should be."

While she walked off, his wife squeezed his arm and whispered, "You'll have to share that story sometime. I regret never having met your brother."

Before he could comment or reflect on not only the irony but the inaccuracy of her statement, a gentleman was standing before him, demanding his attention, and Robert once again found himself drifting back to thoughts of Weddington.

The memories bombarded him. Why hadn't he thought of Weddington sooner, questioned his absence on such an auspicious occasion?

Weddington had been his closest friend. How could Robert have forgotten? Perhaps because it had been so terribly long since he'd thought of anything other than escape and retribution.

But now that he had a moment to reflect, he realized that Weddington should have been there. Yet he hadn't stood with Robert at the church. Of course, he wouldn't have if he were married. Only an unmarried man could serve as best man. But still, regardless of his marital state, he would have been in attendance to witness the ceremony; he would have been at this inconvenient breakfast to wish Robert and his new wife well. Why wasn't he? *Was* he indeed married? Or was he dead? Ill? Abroad?

Who could Robert ask regarding the status of his friend? No one, for surely it was a question to which he should know the answer. But he didn't. He didn't know the details of his best friend's life. Didn't know the details of his wife's life, for that matter.

Or the details of the lives of the people surrounding him. Or the details of the nation. What had transpired since he'd been in Pentonville? What wars had been fought? Did England continue to reign supreme? He assumed Victoria was still queen, but then he was coming to realize that he couldn't rely on his assumptions to get him through this nightmare.

He'd thought he would have time to adjust to being back in society, and instead he found himself in the unconscionable position of trying to appear normal when he no longer had any idea what normal might entail.

He felt as though he were suffocating: his throat was closing off, his chest was tightening. For years he'd been isolated, alone.

He'd fantasized about his freedom, about having others near, about being touched, talked to . . . but now he found that close proximity to anyone caused his heart to race, his palms to sweat, his skin to itch. He could think of nothing to mutter other than thank you, good to see you, appreciate your coming. How did one carry on a casual conversation when all he wanted to murmur was "Talk to me, about anything, everything. Just let me enjoy the sound of your voice."

Especially his wife's voice. He enjoyed its musical lilt, wished people would speak to her only so that he could concentrate on the soft sounds. Her voice reflected such caring, such devotion, as though for that moment in time when someone stood before her, only that person mattered and nothing else. What a gift she possessed. So gracious, so charming. He could clearly see why John had chosen her.

Robert would be content to look at her, to inhale her sweet fragrance, to hear her voice, to touch her hair—a rich mahogany sheen—and know its silkiness, to gaze into her dark eyes and have her gaze into his. Instead he would have to distance himself from her, because he yearned for all the things a woman could give a man . . . and he had no right to take them from her. She was bound to him by vows and documents—but not her heart.

He'd expected her heart to be unfettered, unbound—something he might come to possess in time, but she'd already given it away, at least in part, if not in whole. And she'd given it to a man he'd come to despise.

She complicated matters. He would have to do what he could, as quickly as he could, to ensure that the title remained with him. How to prove his claims, though, remained the crux of the problem. There were no physical characteristics to distinguish him from his brother. It would be one's word against the other's.

And he had little doubt that John in the outside world all these years was more capable of mounting a defense than Robert, who had eight years of talking to no one. Deprived of company, men had gone insane within those prison walls. Perhaps he had as well, to entertain the notion that he could so easily recapture what was his by birth.

As people filed past, offering congratulations, he thought he recognized a few of them, but he couldn't put a name to a face. Men he'd gone to school with, men with whom he'd been friends, were noticeably absent, and he was left to wonder if John had purposely alienated them.

It would make sense that he wouldn't want Robert's intimates to be too close. After all, there might be the danger that John would reveal his true self. And Robert was now faced with the same dilemma. How would he give the appearance that he knew these men, that he knew the status of their lives, that he had visited with them at the club during the last week—and that they knew him—without revealing who he really was?

He was grateful that men were acknowledging his distraction with a knowing smile, a conspiratorial wink as though they knew the cause, the cause being his charming and lovely wife.

And she *was* a distraction. He could hardly take his eyes off her, while she was giving her undivided attention to each guest. What an exquisite hostess she was, what a gracious duchess she would make. Yet how would she feel when she learned a duchess she was not to be? Not if her heart belonged to John. Not if this mockery of a marriage was to be undone.

He wondered if there was someone here

in whom he could confide, someone whose opinion he could seek out. And once anyone learned how he'd disposed of John, then what? He would be brought to task for his actions, as he should be. He knew his solution had not been the best, but eight years of isolation could make it difficult for a man to think clearly.

But then so could a lovely wife. She had a most delicate profile, and when she smiled, even slightly, a small dimple appeared in her cheek. It fascinated him, as much as anything else about her. He could well understand why John had taken to her. He wondered what their courtship had entailed, and if there were promises John had made that she'd expect Robert to carry out tonight.

He could well imagine the promises he himself would have made. To love, honor, and cherish seemed paltry by comparison. To love deeply, passionately, unendingly. To honor and cherish in the same manner. She would have his devotion. He knew he was assessing her on nothing of any consequence or significance, and after so long without the company of others, he no doubt lacked the ability to judge accurately or with any precision. Yet something about her went beyond the most fundamental of appearances. He could hardly explain it. But he sensed in her an incredible strength, determination, and gracefulness.

Perhaps it was the lack of hesitation in her voice when she spoke. The manner in which she sounded truly glad to greet guests, grateful for their time and attention. Perhaps it was the way she put them at ease.

Perhaps it was the direct contrast between her and her mother, who was standing on the other side of them with her father, speaking loudly, excitedly, as though their company's presence somehow reflected on her, while Victoria Alexandria Hawthorne gave the impression that she was humbled by their attendance.

She wasn't arrogant, showy, boastful, or proud. She quite simply fascinated him.

"Robert?"

He'd been staring at her, and although she'd been speaking, not a single word had registered in his mind, so lost in his thoughts had he become. Her cheeks reddening with embarrassment, she tilted her head slightly toward the man standing in front of him.

"Lord Ravenleigh wished to know if you'd heard from John."

Lord Ravenleigh. He recognized him now. Of course, the Earl of Ravenleigh. And beside him were his two sons. Twins. What were their names? He couldn't remember. They were a dozen years younger than he was. He wondered if he should warn them of the treachery one might someday inflict on the other.

"My brother sent his regards," Robert forced out.

"I daresay I find his adventures interesting reading. Do hope you'll bring his next letter by the club and enthrall us all."

Robert cleared his throat. "Of course. I shall be delighted to share his letters should I receive any more." But since John wasn't free to write them, Robert doubted he would receive any.

His wife touched his arm, a little differently than she had before, as though she were trying to impart some knowledge to him.

"I hope you'll forgive my husband if he's not at the club for a while. We're leaving immediately after the breakfast to go to Hawthorne House."

He supposed he would have discovered that bit of information eventually, but he was grateful to know it now. It removed a good deal of his tension. The breakfast was merely an inconvenience, to be endured a short while. Once finished, they would be on their way. Thank goodness they had no plans to stay in London. He needed to get away and contemplate his options.

"Of course, of course," Ravenleigh said. He winked at Robert. "When you're back in London then."

The earl leaned toward Victoria, whispered something Robert couldn't hear, but the flush in her cheeks deepened.

Ravenleigh walked away, then his sons were offering their congratulations. Robert noted the burn scar beneath one of the young men's chins. He remembered hearing that their father had marked the younger son when he was born so he'd forever be able to tell his twin sons apart. Robert found himself wishing his father had done the same thing. He wouldn't have minded if his father had marked him as the elder—to have a few moments of pain he couldn't remember in order to have been spared years of agony he'd never forget.

The twins were the last to arrive, the last to walk away.

Victoria's mother approached, her face glowing as though she'd just been told she'd ascend to the throne. "You and Victoria shall lead our assemblage into the library where we're serving breakfast."

The library. He had no earthly idea where it might be or if he should even know where it was located. "I would be honored to follow you."

She blinked. "But that's not the way it's done. The bride and groom lead the entourage."

"And if I'm distracted by your daughter's beauty and lose my way . . ."

"Victoria will see that you arrive safely."

So much for his awkward attempt to cover his ignorance regarding the layout of the house. Mrs. Lambert left him there, going off to issue orders to others as to how they should follow. He looked at Victoria, offered her his left arm. "Shall we?"

"Do you really fear that you might lose your way?"

"I must confess to being overwhelmed today. It's a wonder I remember my name."

"But the difficult part is behind us."

No, my darling, I fear it still faces us, when you learn the truth. How can I spare you from the scandal that will erupt?

"I am quite ready to be on our way to Hawthorne House," he murmured.

She blushed yet again, and he realized she might have mistaken the lowering of his voice because he'd not wanted to offend others as a sign he wished to have her alone, to be with her the way a husband longed to be with his wife. He couldn't very well disabuse her of that notion. But when she placed her hand on his arm and whispered, "Simply stay in step with me," he could do little more than be grateful and determined to worry about what he would do later.

She guided him down a hallway, into the library. A table laden with food and adorned with flowers occupied the center of the room, and smaller tables were set along the far wall. Sunlight streamed in through floor-to-ceiling windows. He thought he would forever appreciate the sight of glass in place of stone or wood.

"I have to confess that my stomach is still too knotted to eat."

He peered at her. "You promised the worst was over."

"A true gentleman wouldn't toss a lady's words back at her."

She had a mischievous expression, and he couldn't help but wonder if she was flirting with him, if he'd perhaps inadvertently started it. He'd once been skilled at charming the ladies, but then he'd been skilled at a good many things. Lack of practice left him floundering, unable to render a suitable reply until finally . . .

"Perhaps I am no gentleman." The words spoken aloud didn't come across nearly as witty as they had while rambling through his mind. He wished he'd left them there and not released them to dangle between them like dirty laundry.

It took her a moment to react, but when she did, her words were hardly what he expected.

"You are the truest gentleman I've ever known. I think it was that aspect about you that caught and held my attention. Your gentlemanly mannerisms. I was besotted the first moment we met."

Lovely. So John had become quite the charmer, had he? Not surprising. Before his captivity, Robert had exhibited an abundance of charm himself. Unfortunately, it appeared it hadn't escaped from Pentonville with him, but had been left behind to languish.

"I was equally besotted the instant I saw you," he finally dared to reveal. Her gaiety was intoxicating, and he thought moments spent with her would ease a man's worries far better than indulging in liquor.

People were milling about the room, stopping briefly at the central table. Gentlemen placed food on platters, then handed the platters to their respective ladies. It all seemed incredibly civilized. As well as intimidating. It had been a long while since he'd engaged in the social graces. He spotted the decanters on the table. "Shall we have some champagne then?"

She nodded, and he signaled to a servant, who brought over two glasses.

"I suppose it would be improper to begin before a toast is made," he said. "Let's move to the side a bit."

To the side a bit when he would have preferred to wedge himself in a corner or slip out through the French doors at the other end of the room. More people filtered in, and Robert observed them, trying to learn what he'd forgotten. All the manners, customs, etiquette. "Your mother seems quite pleased," he murmured.

"Of course. Today she acquired what she's always wanted."

"Which is?"

"Prestige."

"And what have you always wanted?"

She stared at him as though he'd asked her to remove her clothing, and he realized it was a question he should have known the answer to. He'd no doubt asked her before, and she'd responded. He was supposed to have courted her, for goodness' sakes. He should know a good many details of her life.

She touched his arm, her surprise shifting into worry. "Not prestige. I'm not my mother. Your being a duke isn't the reason I married you. I married you because—"

"You hold affection for me."

She nodded. "I know you must find the feelings I hold toward you odd when we've spent so little time together—"

How little?

"—and we know so little about each other—"

How little!

"—but we seemed so well suited. You must feel the same or you wouldn't have asked me to marry you. Surely it was more than my dowry that attracted you to me."

He had no idea what her dowry entailed. Was it substantial? Property? Money? Whatever it was, he knew one truth that he could speak with absolute certainty.

"I assure you that even if you had no dowry, I would find myself attracted to you."

Her pleasure at his words was instantaneous, causing her cheeks to flush, and he wished he had kept his thoughts to himself. The conversation was only serving to worsen the situation.

A tapping on glass drew their attention. An older, robust man was standing with wineglass lifted. Robert was rather sure it was the Duke of Kimburton. If he was making the toast, then he was the gentleman of highest rank.

"A toast to the health and happiness of the Duke and Duchess of Killingsworth," he said.

As glasses were raised, Robert wondered if this nightmare would ever end. He took a sip of the champagne, savoring the taste. Today, tonight he'd wanted to experience all the things he'd been denied. Liquor was but one of many indulgences, but what he wanted most . . .

He couldn't have, because he had a wife, a wife he couldn't touch. And in the not touching he was once again being denied.

How could one brother take everything away from another for eight long years? Would John have ever given it back?

Robert knew the answer before he'd finished asking the question. His brother had taken his place, and he'd intended it to be for eternity. John had no doubt covered his tracks well, but Robert would find the weakness; he would find a way to reclaim all that was his without keeping his brother locked away.

Perhaps the woman was the key. Perhaps his brother would be grateful enough that Robert returned her to him untouched that he would accept that he was not the true duke. Perhaps Robert could send them to America, with a bit of money, so that they might find their happiness there. To Virginia, a plantation in Virginia. It seemed only fitting.

Whatever he planned, he couldn't allow an innocent to suffer. This battle was between him and his brother. They alone had to fight it.

He realized with startling clarity that she was waiting for something from him, then it dawned on him what he needed to do. He tapped his glass against hers. "To your happiness, Victoria."

She smiled with such fondness that he wanted to charge out of the room, leave the charade behind, only he wasn't the charade. His brother had been.

He watched as she sipped the champagne, so delicately, her tongue darting out to capture the sparkling drops that lingered on her lips. He thought of gathering those drops himself, his lips pressed to hers, his tongue . . .

Clearing his throat, he took a healthy swallow of his own champagne. He couldn't afford to get lost in her beauty, her innocence, her femininity.

"Now that we're married, you're not going to be formal with me, are you?" she asked.

"Formal?"

She laughed lightly and rolled her eyes. "Victoria?"

Ah, dear Lord. His brother didn't call her Victoria. What pet name would John have had for her?

Victoria . . . Vickie? No, she didn't look at all like a Vickie, however he thought a Vickie might look. Vic? Brown eyes? Sweetheart? My love? Beautiful?

It could be any number of things. How could he work the question into a conversation without seeming like a dunce? He couldn't, so he simply forced himself to smile. "Of course not, but I thought a toast to your happiness required a bit of formality."

Worry lines appeared between her brows. "You seem different today."

"As I explained earlier, it's only the unfamiliarity with being a husband."

"Simply be yourself."

"I'm trying . . . desperately."

She smiled. "Don't try so hard."

Aware of movement off to the side, he turned to watch as a young lady approached. He remembered her as one of the ladies who'd stood beside Victoria at the altar. He was more aware of a resemblance between them now and deduced that she must be a relation, a sister possibly. Another fact that he should know.

She stopped before them and smiled a smile very similar to his wife's. A sister. He was sure of it. But how many did she have? And did she have any brothers? Surely they would have approached by now.

"Do I have to call Torie 'Your Grace' now, Your Grace?" she asked, a bit of mischief in her expression, as though she were daring him.

But deciphering her game was of no interest to him. Rather a mystery had been solved.

Torie? Victoria. His wife's preferred name. It suited her, and he wondered why he hadn't realized it sooner, hadn't figured it out on his own.

"A bit more informality exists among family members," he assured her sister, finally returning his attention to her inquiry.

"May I call you Robert, then?"

"I think you're being a bit too informal here, Diana," Victoria—Torie—said.

"Only if the duke thinks so." Diana looked at him, challenging him.

What was John's relationship with the sister; what would she expect of the duke standing before her now? "Perhaps when we return from our wedding trip we can discuss informalities," he offered, delaying the decision.

"Oh, all right. I say, I do wish John had been able to come. I would so like to meet him. His stories fascinate me. Being captured by Indians, then becoming best friends with the tribal chief. Most younger brothers would be content with an allowance and laziness, but yours has made something of himself. He's quite remarkable."

"Indeed he is," Robert murmured. What fanciful tales John had woven to cover the truth of what he'd done.

"Actually, Mama sent me over to see if you're ready to change into your traveling clothes," Diana said to Torie.

Torie darted a glance at him before looking at her sister. "Yes, I'm most anxious to leave."

"That's the beauty of a stand-up breakfast. Only one toast and you need not wait until all the courses have been served—since they're served all at once," Diana said.

"If you'll excuse me," Torie said, touching his arm lightly, gazing into his eyes. "I won't be long."

"Take whatever time you need."

He watched the sisters walk away, wondering what Torie saw when she looked at him as intensely as she did. An impostor? No, the true impostor was the man to whom she'd been betrothed. He wondered how she'd react to the news, if he could confess to her . . .

Just as suddenly he acknowledged that he could confess to no one, not until he discerned whom he could trust and whom he couldn't. He was now in the world, surrounded by people—yet still as alone as he'd been in prison.

Chapter 6

"I see what you mean."

"What are you talking about?" Torie asked as she stood before the mirror, waiting patiently while her maid buttoned the last of the buttons on her traveling suit.

"Your duke. The way that he stares. I'd never noticed before. But he begins to get this look on his face as though he's popped over to France or somewhere equally boring."

"I thought you liked France."

"I like the way Frenchmen kiss."

"When did you ever kiss a Frenchman?"

"Wouldn't you like to know?"

Torie captured her sister's challenging gaze reflected in the mirror.

"If you've kissed a Frenchman then I'm not a virgin."

"Won't your husband be surprised when he discovers that?"

Her maid, Charity, cleared her throat.

"You're teasing me," Torie stated.

"Am I?"

"If you've truly kissed a Frenchman then tell me what I don't know about kisses."

"Why must you always call my bluff?"

"Because you always bluff," Torie said, again looking in the mirror, watching as Charity worked to arrange her hair so her hat would sit perfectly at an angle. "I think he's missing his brother."

"Who?"

Torie rolled her eyes. "The duke. That's who we were talking about. Honestly, sometimes I think there's something amiss with you, the way you speed through conversations."

"I'm just always so frightfully bored. I want to get onto the next thing. So you think he misses his brother?"

Diana also had a habit of jumping back and forth between conversations. Torie had to stay on her toes sometimes to keep up with her.

"Yes, I think that's the reason he seems not quite himself today. We were discussing his brother on the drive over. A special bond exists between twins. I think that makes it all the harder when they're separated. Don't you think?"

"I think I shall miss you desperately when you're no longer here. And we're not twins."

"Thank God. You have a funny nose," Torie said, striving to keep the mood light when she knew it was in danger of becoming filled with the sadness of parting. She'd never been away from home without her family before.

"Better a funny nose than a hole in my cheek," Diana retorted.

"It's called a dimple."

"The duke stares at it as though he's never seen one."

"You spent an awful lot of time watching my duke."

"Oh, so now he's *your* duke." Diana crossed her arms over her chest. "The doubts seemed to have left you."

No, they were still there, but it was far too late for them. As Charity moved aside, Torie turned and spread her arms wide. "I shall miss you desperately as well."

Diana moved into her embrace and hugged her tightly. "Send for me when you can."

"As soon as we've settled into marriage." Torie stepped back, took her sister's hands, and squeezed. "Be kind to Mother while I'm gone."

"You want to take away all my fun."

Leaning forward, she kissed her sister's cheek. "And watch out for Frenchmen. I hear they use their tongues when they kiss."

Diana gave her an impish smile. "Indeed, they do."

"I'm so looking forward to going to your ancestral home," Torie said as the coach traveled through London. "You've spoken of Hawthorne House so often that I feel as though I know every hallway, every chamber."

"I look forward to sharing it with you," Robert said, his response paltry, hardly significant. Knowing that she knew little about him didn't help his situation at all, because in some ways it increased his likelihood of making a misstep. The fewer details she knew, the more likely she was to have a clearer memory of them.

She seemed disappointed in his answer, and he could hardly blame her. She was so vibrant, so alive that he felt very much like a corpse sitting on the seat opposite hers.

Her traveling clothes were dark green. Perched jauntily on her head was a little hat with a feather slanting off to the side. Her hair was piled up beneath it. He wanted to reach out and touch her hair, touch her cheek, touch her. But he feared one touch wouldn't be enough, would never be enough.

"I would like to invite Diana to join us, once we've settled into marriage."

"Of course."

"Do you think she and John would get along?"

"I hardly think so."

"Really? Why?"

Because he would have chosen her from the start if he had an interest in her.

"Living in America, he no doubt has come to appreciate a lady with a more uncivilized nature."

"Trust me. Diana can be most uncivilized when she sets her mind to it. Just this morning she was goading Mother with nonsense about never marrying."

"Why do you consider her never wanting to marry as nonsense?"

"Because it is a woman's purpose in life—to seek out a favorable marriage."

"So by marrying me, you've achieved your purpose."

She looked up at the coach's ceiling. "I don't believe I've ever poked my foot into my mouth as much as I have today." She lowered her gaze to him. "No, marrying you wasn't my *purpose* in life. My purpose"—She furrowed her brow. "I'm not really sure exactly what my purpose is. Perhaps to be a good wife, an exemplary mother, a charming duchess."

"Then I have no doubt you shall achieve your goals with tremendous success."

"I never realized you had such faith in me."

"I wouldn't have taken you to wife otherwise."

He was beginning to lose sight of which thoughts were his and which were attempts to utter sentiments he thought his brother might. He didn't want to be a reflection of John.

"After we sit for our official portrait, we shall have to have a smaller copy made for John," she said.

"Our official portrait?"

She smiled indulgently at him. "Yes. You'd told me that shortly after their marriage every duke and duchess has a portrait painted to hang in the family gallery."

"Ah, yes."

"And you want us to have ours done very soon, since we're now the Duke and Duchess of Killingsworth."

"Very soon," he murmured, "but not immediately. I've never enjoyed standing for portraits."

Besides, no sense in having her portrait done when it would not long hang in the gallery. He couldn't promise that she would remain the duchess. As a matter of fact, she probably wouldn't. The vows she'd spoken today had been for another man, and Robert wouldn't hold her to them.

"It is a rather boring endeavor, isn't it?" she asked. "And I know you detest being bored."

A trait he and his brother shared. And there was nothing except boredom within Pentonville.

"I fear even Witherspoon finds it a challenge to assist me with my morning routine, as I'm not one to stand idle for long," he said, rather pleased with himself because he'd managed to learn the name of his valet.

He'd had a stroke of brilliance after they'd arrived at his London home so they could transfer from the carriage to the coach. He'd called out all the servants and insisted that each be introduced to the duchess, while he simply walked along beside her, making note of the names as the butler introduced each one. His valet was Witherspoon—a good thing to know since Witherspoon was accompanying him to the estate, traveling in the coach behind this one, and Robert couldn't very well *never* call him by name.

Torie had also brought along her lady's maid, a woman named Charity who seemed rather young, but capable, and very fond of her mistress.

"As I understand it, it's quite a long journey," she said.

"Yes."

"Shall we play one of our word games to pass the time?"

Dash it all! They had little games that they played.

"It'll make the time pass more quickly," she continued. "We'll play Alphabetical Geography. Give me a letter."

"A letter?"

"Of the alphabet. You remember. You say, 'W,' and I say, 'I'm going to Windsor for water and waltzing.' Then I'll give you a letter. I know you enjoy it more when several people are around to play, but we can make it work with only the two of us."

"I don't mean to disappoint you, but it's been a long morning and I'm weary," he said, rather than confess that he didn't know anything about the word games she'd played with his brother, and while this one seemed fairly easy, it wasn't of interest to him. The games he longed to play involved her mouth, pressed up against his. The games played by men and women, not those favored by children.

"Of course. How silly of me. It's been a long morning for us both. Will you try to sleep, then?"

"Possibly."

She gazed out the window, her smile withering, and he feared he might have hurt her tender feelings. She was so incredibly lovely and smelled so enticingly sweet, like a flower that kept all its petals tucked neatly away only to blossom at dawn and release the fragrance that made it special, like no other.

Her rose and lily scent filled the coach and wafted around him. He took one deep breath after another, holding each and savoring the sweetness, allowing it to wash away years of stench filling his nostrils. Sitting with her in the coach was achieving what his bath that morning had failed to accomplish: granting him the feeling of normalcy.

In retrospect, he probably should have sought an excuse to leave her in London, but what would the gossips say about a man who abandoned his wife as soon as vows were spoken? They would no doubt question his virility. While he himself would question his sanity, for no sane man would willingly distance himself from her, not for a day, certainly not for a night.

Yet there he was: inches from her instead of nestled up against her, whispering sweet love words into her ear while plying her neck with his kisses. To get to that neck, he'd have to release a few buttons, because she was done up as tightly as a drum. Although they were married, he was no doubt expected to follow tradition and be the pursuer.

Did women even know precisely what happened during the wedding night? It wasn't as if they could visit a brothel and learn all the particulars. Although he had visited one the night he'd turned eighteen, his enjoyment of the offerings had been cut short when he was drugged and carted away. Over the years he'd had many a lonely night of imagining exactly what he might do with a woman. He might lack experience, but he damned well didn't lack imagination, and he was having a difficult time reining it in now. It was taking liberties that he couldn't, and even as he cursed it, he welcomed it.

She was a temptation in which he couldn't indulge. Yet he found himself blessedly content to simply be within the coach with her. To not be alone. Even if the silence stretched between them, he was not alone.

Then a horrible thought occurred to him. Was he giving himself away by *not* speaking to her?

She'd begun every conversation, if the few sentences passing between them could be considered conversation. He realized she didn't appear to be enjoying the view beyond the window. Rather she seemed sad, as lonely as he.

He was going to have to do something, come up with some safe topic of conversation, perhaps even agree to play a silly game. He looked out his own window, hoping inspiration would strike, when something caught his eye.

"Stop!" he yelled. "Stop the coach!"

"What is it, Robert? What's wrong?" she asked, suddenly straightening, ever alert.

He couldn't explain it. He merely shook his head. The coach rocked to a stop.

"I'll be only a moment," he said, not waiting for a footman, but flinging the door open and stepping out. He walked only a few feet away from the coach so he'd have an unobstructed view.

The building was as ominous from the outside as it was from the inside. Foreboding as well as forbidding. He broke out in a light sweat. He swore he heard the clanging of doors, the shuffling of feet as prisoners were escorted to the exercise yard or the chapel, the absence of voices—

"What is it about Pentonville that fascinates you so?"

Robert nearly leaped out of his skin at the unexpected question, her unanticipated nearness. He'd not heard her clamber out of the coach, not heard her approach, and yet she was beside him, studying him. He wasn't certain what she might see, what his face might reveal, so he tore his gaze from her, striving to keep any sort of emotion out of his voice.

"What makes you think it fascinates me?"

She released what she probably hoped would be a laugh, but sounded more like she was choking. "Because twice before when we've been out on a drive, you've done this very thing: had the driver stop so you could stand in that exact spot and stare at that horrid prison."

So twice before when his brother was with her he'd stared at the prison. Fancy that. Robert wondered how many times John might have come to look at it when he wasn't with her. If he ever stood nearby with guilt raining down on him, guilt for all he'd acquired and all it had cost his brother, the true heir.

Had John considered confessing his sins to her, or had he simply been taking a moment to revel in his unbridled success at replacing his brother? What had he thought when he'd stood there? And what could Robert now say to his wife to explain his actions?

"I'm not certain why it fascinates me. It's a morbid sort of fascination, to be sure." Like gazing at one's home in hopes of remembering pleasant memories where none existed.

"I've seen a drawing of the prisoners taking their exercise. They're tied together—"

"They're not tied together," he interrupted. "They're merely forced to hold a rope, knotted at five-yard intervals, to keep them from getting too close to each other. The distance prevents them from carrying on a conversation with another man."

"In the drawing I saw, they wore hoods—"

"Yes," he interrupted, not wanting to hear any more of the details with which he was so horrifyingly familiar. "It's a bit of frippery called a scotch cap."

"Why do you call it frippery? It saves the prisoners the embarrassment of having their faces seen."

"By whom?" he asked, unable to keep the anger from surfacing. "By other prisoners? Other guilty men? Imagine living your life day in and day out at a masked costume ball . . . only everyone wore the same mask. You could easily go insane when everyone looks exactly alike. Watching the men come out is like bees swarming from the hive. You can't tell them apart. The sameness of it.

Everything always the same. The same thirteen-by-seven-foot cell. The same clothing, the same hood, the same—" He broke off. He'd not meant to go on so, but the misery of that existence was buried deeply inside him, struggling to escape with tenacity equal to his own.

"I thought this new prison system was considered far superior to what we had before. It is clean, modern. And while the hoods may be a bit of a nuisance, if I were within those walls, I wouldn't want anyone to know it was me. I believe I would welcome the anonymity while waiting to be transported to Australia."

"Yet you would lose that anonymity the morning you were marched to the transportation ships. Hoods are not worn then. Faces are revealed, so why bother to hide them at all?"

She furrowed her delicate brow. "Oh, I see your point. I suppose it does seem a rather unnecessary practice, but I'm certain the decision wasn't based on a whim. Surely there is a good reason that we've simply failed to consider."

"None that I can think of."

"Which isn't proof that a good reason

doesn't exist. Only that we can't fathom it. I'm sure all the decisions were made with a great deal of wisdom and forethought. Why does this place fascinate you so?"

She moved in front of him so he was forced to either look into her eyes or peer over her head. He chose her eyes and quickly wished he hadn't. They reflected a pleading that he didn't quite understand. His gaze drifted lower, to her lips, and he realized that he was making a thousand mistakes today, because looking at them reminded him of how close he'd come to kissing them earlier in the church.

Her tongue darted out and moistened her lower lip. His body tightened in response. He jerked his gaze up to look over her, toward the prison, the model prison, the pride of England. It wasn't fair that he'd spent eight years in that place; it wasn't fair that John would spend only a few nights. It wasn't fair that this woman cared for his brother.

She cradled his cheek, forcing him to look at her once again.

"Don't leave me," she said softly, pleadingly. "I don't know where you go when you look at that horrid building, but somehow it takes you away. Even though you're standing right here, you're no longer with me. Please, let's go now."

He placed his hand over hers, so small, soft, and warm. Even through the gloves, he felt the warmth. Turning his head slightly, he nodded as he pressed a kiss to the center of her palm and caught a stronger whiff of her perfume. She must have placed a drop on her wrist, and he wondered where else she might have placed droplets. Along her throat, between her breasts, behind a knee. Places he would dearly love to kiss, with or without the scent of her perfume to tantalize him.

He turned away, fearful she would read the desire harboring within him. For eight years he'd not known the touch of a woman, the sound of a woman's voice, the gentleness a woman brought into the world. But his brother had possessed all those things. Would he be as appreciative toward her as Robert found himself, or would he take everything for granted?

He offered her his arm and led her back toward the coach. Once they were settled in and on their way, he soon found himself gazing at his wife, his brother's love. And knowing a fury at the unfairness that continued to be visited upon him—a fury far greater than any he'd experienced before.

Once they returned to the coach, Torie lost her inclination to try to start a conversation. She was as weary as he claimed to be, having gotten up before dawn to begin the preparations for her wedding. And while she was undeniably disappointed in Robert's lack of enthusiasm for any topic she broached, she had to admit that perhaps her inability to engage him in any meaningful discussion was the result of his experiencing the same weariness, and not because he was suddenly finding fault with her, when he never had before.

He'd always maintained a quiet reserve when they'd been together in public, but then they'd *always* either been in public or had a chaperone nearby fairly breathing down their necks. They'd never been totally and completely alone.

It was the private man that she'd thought marriage would introduce her to. She'd not expected him to be more reserved. She'd thought that finally, alone, they'd come to know each other better, to stir within each other the passion that was lacking before.

They had always been politely comfortable with each other, but even that seemed to have vanished.

"It's strange, isn't it?" she finally ventured to ask.

His gaze came to rest on her. "What's that?"

"This is the first time that we've been completely alone. I expected it to be somehow different."

"In what way?"

She nibbled on her lip, wondering if she should dare to confess—

"I thought you might ravish me as soon as possible."

It was impossible to confirm from this distance, but she thought her husband might be blushing.

"Surely you've no desire to be taken in a coach," he stated, his voice rough as though he were struggling against images of the ravishment she'd suggested.

"I suppose it would be rather awkward." Although she wasn't entirely sure. Could he ravish her while sitting? Or would they need to be lying down? As well sprung as his coach was, it was still a bumpy ride.

"Decidedly so," he commented laconically.

"Have you ever . . . in a coach?" she asked.

He gazed out the window. "No. And even if I had, I don't believe I'd tell a lady of my exploits."

"So you might be lying now to protect my sensibilities."

He jerked his head around. "I'm not lying."

"Even if you had no plans to ravish me, you could sit by me, now that we're married. It's perfectly acceptable."

"If I sat beside you, I'm not certain that I could resist ravishing you."

Now she thought she might be the one blushing.

"We could test your restraint."

"I would rather not."

"So it is a matter of temptation that has you sitting there rather than here?"

He gave a brusque nod before turning his attention back to the window and the scenery beyond. She took what satisfaction she could from his confession. At least she was desired.

His insistence on not testing his restraint became abundantly clear when the coach pulled to a stop in front of an inn, and she and Robert were immediately taken to a private room. Her heart had fluttered with the thought that he'd decided he could wait no longer to make her his wife. But the room was prepared for dining, not bedding. She didn't think a table would be any more comfortable than a coach.

Robert had crossed the room and stood staring out the window while servants brought in food and arranged everything nicely upon the table. Apparently the proprietor was accustomed to the duke stopping here on his way to Hawthorne House, because as he was leaving the room he assured the duke that fresh horses would be available.

Now she sat across from her husband at the small table. She wanted to eat with the same enthusiasm that he did, but her stomach and throat were a tangle of knots as she wondered when he might seek to truly make her his wife. She feared eating would only serve to embarrass her when she would be unable to swallow what she'd chewed.

"How long will we stay here?" she finally asked.

He looked up from his plate—bewilderment in his eyes—as though he'd forgotten that she was there. Slowly he chewed, almost as if he were searching for the answer while he did so. At last he swallowed and spoke.

"Only until they've swapped out the horses."

"They seem to know you here."

For the merest second, it seemed an expression of fear crossed his features, but it was gone so quickly, hidden behind the reserved mask he usually wore, that she suspected she'd only imagined it.

"Long ago, my grandfather made arrangements with several innkeepers to have a few of our horses boarded so they would be available and we could travel quickly from London to our various estates. I now benefit from his strategy."

"Where will we stop for the night?"

"If you have the stamina for the journey, I'd rather not stop. I'm anxious to get to Hawthorne House."

She wished he was as anxious to be alone with her. But perhaps he would be more comfortable at his home, perhaps things would return to what she knew and expected. "I've no problem in traveling through the night."

"Splendid."

He returned his attention to his meal, carefully cutting into the ham, placing the piece into his mouth, closing his eyes as though he'd never tasted anything quite so delicious.

She sliced off a sampling for herself. She detected nothing special: no spicy glaze, no enticing seasoning. She was surprised that he seemed to relish the offerings, when she knew he was a man of singular tastes, who preferred the unusual over the sublime. She was beginning to realize that his courtship of her had revealed very little about him.

She could hear the birds chirping outside the window, the scratching of silver over china, and her tension began to increase. It was annoying, frightening not to know exactly what to expect. Would this be her life? To be ignored? To never know what he thought, felt, dreamed?

"Do you remember the night we met?" she decided to ask.

He finished chewing, swallowed, and took a sip of water. "I shall always remember the moment I first gazed upon you."

She flushed with his words. They were more along the lines of his flirtatious style, more of what she'd expected.

He took another sip—

"You frightened me."

He jerked, brought a fist to his mouth, and coughed several times, his eyes watering.

He cleared this throat. “Pardon me. I seem to have swallowed improperly.” He cleared his throat again, dabbed at his mouth with his linen napkin, and dropped his gaze to his plate as though trying to determine when it might be safe to continue eating. Then he peered up at her. “Why?”

“Because you were so confident, so sure of your place.”

“Yes, well, maybe I shouldn’t have been . . . so sure of my place, that is.”

“But that’s one of the things I admire about you. You never doubt a single decision, a single action.”

“Trust me, Torie. I have a good many doubts.”

Leaning back in his chair, he studied her as though she held the answer to whatever it was he sought. “I have concerns that, in time, your feelings toward me will change.”

She laughed lightly. “Of course, they’ll change. They’ll deepen as we spend more time together, as we come to know each other better.” She reached across the table and placed her hand over his where it rested on the table. “I *want* to know you better.”

"I'm afraid that's not possible."

Her heart leaped into her throat as he snatched his hand away from hers and came to his feet.

"You must forgive me, but I am not in the habit of sharing myself, my feelings, my thoughts," he said quietly, combing his fingers through his hair, a look of bewilderment flashing over his face as though he was surprised by what his hand encountered. "Therefore getting to know me better will not be an option. I need to attend to other matters at this precise moment. I suggest you see to your own comfort before joining me at the coach. I wish for us to be away as quickly as possible." He gave a brisk nod. "If you will excuse me?"

Swallowing hard, she nodded.

"I would greatly appreciate it if you wouldn't tarry."

And with that, he left the room, leaving her confused and trembling. Whatever had she done to earn his displeasure?

As for not sharing, well, he certainly had up until this morning. His comment made no sense. How could an exchange of vows so drastically change a man?

Chapter 7

Robert couldn't seem to bring himself to look away from his wife, even as he wished he could erase the memory of her stunned expression, her disappointment in his response. Her thinking that she would come to know him *better* assumed that she knew him at all—which she didn't. She knew John, and she would soon know John better. Perhaps he should tell her the truth of the situation. But to her he would be an impostor. He wanted to talk to her, desperately, but he feared discovery of his deception—he was the rightful duke but not the man she thought she was marrying.

It had been easier for John to imitate Robert because he'd been around to see how Robert acted, to whom Robert spoke, how he addressed people and they addressed him. Robert was lost, drowning in a sea of unknowns.

Even the most innocent statement, uttered without complete thought, could betray him.

They'd not spoken once since she'd joined him and the coach had sprung forward to continue the journey. Her gaze was locked constantly on the scenery beyond the window. Even as darkness fell, she'd provided him with only glimpses of her profile as the evening shadows began to work their way into the coach. Eventually she'd removed her hat and set it aside.

Upsetting her seemed to have had the effect of silencing her. Now she seemed like a wounded creature, nursing its injuries. He desperately wanted to apologize, but this way was better, and in the end, she would be grateful that he had sought to distance himself.

Her profile was lovely, but what did he expect when her face was that of an angel? An angel who had married the very devil himself.

A part of him thought he should despise

her on that fact alone. Yet he couldn't quite bring himself to feel anything except . . . enchanted by her loveliness.

Her scent should have faded away by now, but it still lingered. The moonlight limned her perfect profile. He watched as she lowered her head slightly, then jerked it upright. Falling asleep, trying to stay awake.

He contemplated telling her to give in to the weariness, but he feared she might say something about other journeys they'd made together, and how would he respond then? He didn't remember the night he met her because he hadn't met her at night, hadn't met her at a ball, and he certainly hadn't been confident when he *had* met her.

Once they were at Hawthorne House, they would be situated in different wings—he would no doubt have to come up with an explanation for that circumstance. He could pretend to be ill, but what if she wished to nurse him back to health?

Damnation! She was a complication he didn't need.

And how to explain his unwillingness to bed her? Only it wasn't an unwillingness. He was most willing indeed.

His body ached for the surcease a

woman's body could offer. He found himself drawn to this woman, even though he had no wish to be.

She finally dropped her head to the side and allowed it to stay there. He'd spent many a night sleeping in an uncomfortable position, and he knew, come morning, she would suffer because of the odd angle at which she now slept.

It was none of his concern. She was none of his concern. An inconvenience only.

Still, he found himself moving her hat from her bench to his. He eased across the space separating them, until he was sitting beside her. He closed his eyes and remembered the many journeys he'd made with his parents, the times his father had placed his arm around his mother and drawn her near until she was resting comfortably against his side. It had seemed such a natural thing for his father to do, but he had loved his wife, and it often seemed that they communicated without speaking.

Robert barely knew this woman, had no earthly idea how she would fit against him, but he did know that it was his haste to get home that was responsible for the awkward position of her body now. It was hardly fair that she should suffer for his inconsideration. He should have allowed them to stop at an inn for the night.

As gently as he could, he placed one arm around her while using his other hand to gently hold her head steady as he tipped her toward him until her face was nestled within the crook of his shoulder. Perfectly. As though it belonged there.

He held his breath as she released a hushed murmur and burrowed more closely against him. She was warm, so incredibly warm, and so dainty. She must weigh no more than a feather. With his hand still resting against her cheek, he couldn't resist the temptation to stroke her skin. Soft and silky. Flawless.

The oddest thing. His eyes began to sting. He blinked several times until the sensation went away. He'd not even contemplate that he might have been on the verge of weeping at the comfort such an innocent touch could bring.

"Robert?"

He stiffened at the sound of her voice, as soft as a caress in the dark.

"I'm sorry if I've done something to displease you," she said, her voice so low that he barely heard it.

Slamming his eyes closed, he laid his cheek against the top of her head, once again feeling that unaccustomed stinging behind his eyes. "You haven't displeased me, Torie."

"You seem so different."

Tell her; tell her the truth. The perfect opportunity had been laid in his lap, so to speak. Her. Here. Yet as soon as he revealed everything—that he was not the man who'd asked for her hand in marriage—she would move away, completely and forever. What would it hurt to savor just a few more moments with her in his arms?

"May I make a confession?" she whispered.

A confession? One as innocent as she? What could she possibly confess? That she only pretended to eat her vegetables?

"Of course," he murmured.

"I was thinking this morning that our wedding had arrived too soon, before I was ready. I thought you read in my eyes the doubts I was harboring at the church."

"I saw no doubt."

"It's simply that I realized this morning that

we've had no time to get to know each other without the company of others. You've never even kissed me properly."

"Have I not?"

She didn't look at him as she said, her voice lower, "No."

"Should I remedy that situation, do you think?"

The words escaped before he had a chance to think them through. He felt her barely perceptible nod in the nook of his shoulder.

Then she was turning her face up to his. She was little more than shadows, captured by an occasional beam of moonlight dancing in through the window. He couldn't read her expression, and perhaps that was for the best, because neither could she read his.

He cradled her cheek and skimmed his thumb over her mouth. "It's been a while since I've kissed a lady," he rasped, "but I believe I remember the basics."

"I've never kissed a man."

Groaning low at her admission, he was acutely aware of her lips parting slightly, her tongue grazing his thumb, and he knew he was on the verge of making a dreadful mistake, but he seemed unable to stop himself.

He lowered his mouth to hers.

He'd never known such softness as her lips shaped themselves to match his. Or warmth as she opened her mouth, allowing him entry. The blinding heat shot through him, as he explored her offering with his tongue, darting, thrusting, relishing the velvety textures as much as the rougher ones.

He angled his head to get a more comfortable fit and was immediately greeted by a waft of her perfume—from behind her ear, and he envisioned her delicately placing the droplet there. He thought about kissing the spot but didn't want to leave her mouth unattended, a mouth that had teased him all day with hints of smiles and bits of conversation. A mouth that could create a dimple upon command. He thought about kissing the dimple as well, thought about kissing every inch of her, and even as he thought it, he knew it could never be.

He was taking liberties to which he had no right, but she had invited him to kiss her, and he'd gone too long without invitations to turn one away when it was delivered by such a lovely lady and presented with such enticement. And so he took what she offered and fought back the guilt. It was only a kiss, after all.

Only a kiss.

The thought made it seem insignificant, when it was anything but. It washed over him and through him, and filled the empty vastness of his heart that had been alone for far too long. It drew him away from the darkness of despair with a bold sweep of her tongue. She wasn't shy. She gave far more than she took, boldly setting a path that he thought would lead directly to her heart.

A heart she'd reserved for his brother.

He deepened his exploration, relishing her warmth, tasting her sweetness. At this moment she was his—his wife, his duchess, his seducer.

He pulled back slightly, pressing a kiss to one corner of her mouth, then the other. He nestled her face back into the crook of her shoulder, listened to her rapid breathing, and the thundering of his blood between his ears.

Ah, yes, he'd made another ghastly mistake.

"That was quite simply . . . marvelous," she said when her breathing had quieted. "I don't understand why society frowns on kissing."

Because it was much easier for a man to deny himself the pleasure of a lady he'd never tasted. But to know the reality of his mouth fastened to hers and to still deny oneself—Robert didn't know if he had the strength.

"You should try to sleep now," he said, his voice sounding like sand blown over rocks.

"Did you find the kiss pleasing?" she asked.

"Remarkably so."

"It's a wonder people don't spend all their time kissing."

"The danger in a kiss is that it can lead to other more intimate pleasures, and not all men have the strength to resist the temptation to explore those other pleasures."

"Marriage removes the need to resist."

"Yes."

"Will we arrive at Hawthorne House tomorrow?"

"In all likelihood, yes. You would do well to sleep now."

He didn't want to discuss what she thought would happen once they arrived at his family estate, because what she hinted she wanted, could not occur. Not if he was to return her to John.

He relished the feel of her body relaxing

against his, her hand curled against his chest. Such an innocent display of trust.

He wanted to stretch out full-length and have her lying beside him, completely, with no space separating them. It didn't matter that they were both fully clothed. It mattered only that her weight pressed against him, and it was the most incredible sensation. After so long, he was no longer alone.

And although he knew it was but a physical impression creating an emotional deception, he still welcomed the joy that it brought, to once again be out in the world where he could travel in a coach at his leisure simply because he wished to, where he could hold a woman beside him and welcome the possibilities . . .

He moved his hand up, gingerly skimming his fingers over her hair. More silk. Or perhaps satin. He was incredibly tempted to remove the pins holding everything in place so the strands could fill his hands. The moonlight glinted off her dark hair, her pale skin, giving her an ethereal quality.

She sighed, and he wondered what visions filled her dreams. Did she dream of the man she cared for incredibly desperately? Or did she dream of the man who had kissed her?

He had no plans to give in to sleep tonight, because the waking dream was more wonderful than anything his imagination would conjure.

She tempted him to truly make her his wife. The law gave him the right, which was more than his brother had ever given him. She was his wife; her body belonged to him. But her heart . . . apparently it belonged to his brother.

He had no intention of making her suffer for his brother's sins, yet even as the thought took hold, he realized he was doing exactly that. By taking her as his wife, by not revealing the truth of the situation.

As he held her, he couldn't help but wish that she was truly his.

Chapter 8

Sitting on the floor in the corner of a darkened room, Prisoner D3, 10 stared into the gray darkness. He'd awoken to find himself there, in solitary confinement, no windows, no light, the damned hood covering his face. He had yet to remove it.

What if someone opened the door? What if someone saw this face that he hated? This face that looked exactly like his brother's?

He wondered at the time. What was his brother doing now?

Surely he'd not carried through with the wedding ceremony. Of course he had. His brother had always wanted everything—

everything to which he wasn't entitled. He'd want the future duchess of Killingsworth as well.

With a growl, Prisoner D3, 10 smashed his fist against the floor.

He can't have her! She belongs to me. Everything belongs to me!

He got to his feet and began to pace. The voices of his ancestors were calling to him. He'd failed them.

He had to escape. He had to reclaim that which belonged to him.

Sunlight danced across her eyelids, only Torie didn't want to awaken. She wanted to stay where she was. It was so comforting there. She felt safe, secure. And above all, cherished.

As she worked her way through the fog of sleep to wakefulness, she became increasingly aware that she *was* protected, nestled within a cocoon—the plush softness of the coach seat on one side of her, the firm warmth of a man on the other.

Her husband.

Holding her breath so as not to disturb him, she carefully twisted her head until she could see his face. He was asleep, just as she'd been only moments ago.

His head was tilted at an odd angle that she was certain would cause him to have a stiff neck for a good part of the day. His hair was no longer styled, but locks had fallen across his brow. One of his arms was beneath her, the other draped innocently over her side, not holding, but simply resting.

She studied his face, features she'd thought she knew, but in sleep he seemed more like a stranger. His lips were slightly parted. Long, thick eyelashes rested on his cheeks. She'd never realized before how many lines fanned out from the corners of his eyes and mouth. And how deep they were. As though they'd been carved by hardship and suffering, rather than joy or merriment.

Reaching up, she touched his unshaven chin. She'd never before seen him so unkempt, and yet she found herself attracted to the disorder. It made him seem incredibly approachable, not quite so noble.

She realized she would see him like this every morning for the remainder of her life.

She turned her hand and feathered the back of it against his dark, rough stubble.

Before she'd barely begun, his eyes fluttered open, and she found herself gazing into a blue as deep as the night. And yet there was sadness, like someone on Christmas Eve staring into a shop window at his heart's desire, yet knowing he would never possess it.

With a tender touch, he skimmed his thumb over her cheek. "You have the softest skin."

His voice was raspy from sleep, but his eyes contained an intimacy born from having her within his arms, and it would take little now for those arms to close around her, for that mouth to play over hers . . .

"Cucumber."

His brow furrowed. "Pardon?"

She felt the heat rush to the very spot he was touching. "I apply a special cream that is made with cucumber."

"I've always fancied cucumber—but to eat, not to put on my face." He gave his head a subtle shake. "Women are such odd creatures."

"I'm not certain I appreciate that assessment." She ran her finger up to his temple. "You don't look as though you slept well."

He shook his head slightly. "I watched you sleep for a good part of the night."

"You must have been bored to tears."

"I was fascinated. The moonlight on your face . . . I have never seen anything that brought me such pleasure." He looked suddenly uncomfortable. "We need to untangle ourselves."

Only she didn't want to untangle herself. "Let's begin the morning with another proper kiss," she rasped.

His gaze drifted down to her lips, his fingers tightened on her wrist. Sometime during the night, he'd loosened his cravat and unbuttoned the first two buttons of his shirt. Now she watched the movement of his throat as he swallowed.

"Please," she whispered, hating that she sounded as though she were begging, hating that she had to suggest it again rather than have him take the initiative. He was a man, and it was a man's nature to want a woman, and it was a woman's nature to hold him at bay—until they were legally wed. Then the barriers could come down and the passion could rush in.

She watched his eyes close, his lashes rest along the curve of his cheek, as he lowered his head slightly, bringing his mouth slightly above hers. She felt the whisper of his breath wafting over her lips, warming them, just before he settled his mouth firmly over hers.

It was a cautious kiss, not much different from the one he'd delivered at the church, only this time his mouth was centered over hers, rather than to the side, but it was fraught with . . . insecurities. As though he feared she'd not welcome his advances.

She wasn't certain why she knew that. Only that she did. He didn't come after her with amorous intentions or passion. He seemed to be simply testing the waters of her desire, and she wondered if desire was stirring through him at all.

Last night his kiss had contained more passion. Was it because he'd delivered it through a veil of darkness? Did the sunlight make him self-conscious—even of a simple meeting of the lips?

As his mouth played lightly over hers, she wanted him to lose control, to want her, to need her . . .

"Robert," she began, the word forming the opportunity for him to slip his tongue into her mouth.

At that moment, everything changed. The nature of the kiss deepened, heated. She heard him groan, felt the rumble of his chest against hers, the almost painful tightening of his fingers on her wrist. His tongue swept through her mouth, igniting her passion as easily as a match to kindling.

She heard a whimper, a sigh, surprised to discover they were coming from her. She angled her head slightly to give him easier access—

Then he was gone, pulling away from her, the look in his eyes that of a man horrified by his behavior.

"Forgive me," he said hoarsely, his breathing coming in short pants.

"What is there to forgive?"

"I will not take you in the coach, like a barbarian."

She knew she should have felt insulted; instead she was elated. He wanted her. He truly did. Did he think lovemaking required gentlemanly behavior? How boring. At this moment she thought she might prefer a barbarian.

"I wouldn't mind," she stated truthfully.

"Wouldn't mind?" he asked as though he'd forgotten his earlier comment.

"Being taken in a coach. The intimacy—it's all I've been able to think about of late—what it's truly like between a man and a woman. I know it's scandalous—but surely you've thought of it as well."

His eyes darkened with intensity, his gaze seemed to turn inward as though he could see those very thoughts. "Every moment since I met you."

She released a self-conscious laugh. "But you were always so proper. I had no idea. You never even hinted—"

"It's easier to hold at bay that which has never experienced freedom."

"I don't understand."

"To give voice to my desires would make them more difficult to control. It is the nature of the beast, to be aroused by a scent, a touch"—he skimmed his finger along her cheek—"a promise."

"I've never known you to be so poetic."

"Perhaps it would be easier if you pretended that you only just met me yesterday."

She smiled. "But then we'd have no history, no memories of times spent together. I can't erase twelve months of knowing you as though they didn't exist. Without them, I might never have found myself beside you at the altar yesterday."

"Of course."

Strange, but she thought she heard disappointment in his voice.

"It's because you mean so much to me that I don't want to cast those memories aside," she said, trying to persuade him of her sincerity.

"If not the memories, then you must at least cast me aside. My body grows numb."

"I'm sorry, I didn't even think—"

Without creating further intimacy or being too personal, he tried to extricate himself from the intimate position of having her lying atop him. He lost his precarious balance on the edge of the seat, his arms flailing as he sought to keep himself from falling off the bench while she scrambled to move away from him, so he could move more freely. He succeeded in righting himself and lurching to the opposite side of the coach.

"Damnation!" he bellowed, jerking upright, hitting his head on the coach ceiling. His hand had gone to his backside and he was twisted around, looking back, and she realized with startling clarity that he'd sat on her hat pin.

She pressed a hand to her mouth to stop herself from laughing at the comical expression of confusion on his face. The coach began to slow, and he tumbled back onto the seat. She swallowed back her laughter.

The coach stopped, the door opened, a footman peered inside. "Is everything all right, Your Grace?"

"Everything is fine. Do have us stop at the next inn as I'm quite famished."

"Yes, Your Grace."

The footman closed the door. She heard him talking to the driver, then they were once again off.

"Your hat, Duchess."

She took it from him. He'd not only sat upon a pin, but the feather as well, because it was broken, hanging limply to the side.

"And your pin," he said gruffly.

She took the bent object from him. A bubble of laughter escaped. "I'm sorry."

"As well you should be, laughing at another's misfortune."

The second bubble of laughter stopped abruptly, because she couldn't quite identify his tone. It wasn't anger. It sounded quite a bit like amusement, an attitude more along the lines of what she'd expected.

"I believe you shall have to purchase me a new hat."

"I would rather you wear your hair unadorned, preferably without pins."

"Without pins, it would be"—she touched the nape of her neck and realized she must look a fright—"rather untidy."

Something flashed over his face that she couldn't decipher: desire, anticipation. And she couldn't help but wonder if he had visions of mussing up her hair while ravishing her with more kisses.

He looked out the window, gazed behind him. "We're nearing a town. We should be stopping soon."

"Good," she said. "I think I need to put myself back to rights."

He gave her a sly look. "No need to do so on my account."

She averted her gaze. He seemed more at ease this morning. But then so was she. Marriage required adjustment, and she was beginning to think they were moving along splendidly.

Robert wanted to tiptoe his fingers rapidly up and down her sides, poke her stomach, tickle her, make her laugh. Her short burst of laughter in the coach had left him yearning to hear more. Her laughter was a bright, jovial sound, like sunlight piercing a dark forest, offering hope that something brighter waited just beyond the shadows.

Damnation, he thought he might spend his life willingly dropping on hat pins just to hear her laugh.

As he sat across from his wife at the table in the inn, he wondered how often she'd laughed for John. If she was truly Robert's, he would seek to make her laugh all the time, to smile, to have her eyes sparkling. He would strive to bring joy to her because so doing would bring joy to him.

He wished he knew how to amuse her now, short of making a fool of himself.

Her appetite seemed to be with her as she finished off the last of the eggs on her plate. She'd left him for a while. He was fairly certain she'd scrubbed her face because her cheeks were pink. And she'd straightened her hair because the few errant strands that had worked their way free during the night were now in place again.

A pity, that.

He hated to see anything deprived its freedom—even a strand of hair, but especially hers. He would so like to see all of it free, cascading around her.

"How long is your hair?" he asked.

She looked up from her plate, her brow knitted, and he feared for a heartbeat that it was a question to which he should have known the answer.

"It stops just past my hips," she finally said quietly. "Perhaps you'd care to brush it sometime."

He thought of gliding not a brush or a comb through the strands, but his fingers. Over and over until they became entangled in the dark curtain of her hair. It reminded him of polished mahogany, a sheen so rich that just the thought of it cascading around her was enough to stir his desire.

"Would you brush mine?" he asked, meaning to tease.

But the warmth he saw in her eyes only served to ignite his passions further.

"Could I use my fingers?" she asked.

His voice became lost to him, and he could do no more than nod.

Her lips parted, her tongue slipped out slightly, slipped back in. "Then, yes, I should like very much to brush your hair sometime."

He held her challenging gaze for what seemed a lifetime. Were women no longer the shy creatures he'd known in his youth? Dear Lord, but she was a danger he could ill afford.

Clearing his throat, he came to his feet with less force than he had during their last meal together. "I must check on the preparations for our departure. Excuse me."

If it were at all possible, he needed the driver to deliver them to Hawthorne House before nightfall, before he once again had the opportunity to hold her within his arms, because he wasn't certain he'd be able to restrain himself from doing more.

Torie found the journey today to be more pleasant, a bit more as she'd expected. She regaled him with tidbits from her youth, about which he'd never before expressed an interest. While he relied heavily on her to carry the conversation, he seemed enthralled by anything she told him, as though he was as enamored of her voice as of the details of her stories.

Originally she'd wanted to pass the time with a word game, but he'd merely shaken his head.

"What is your earliest memory?" he'd

asked. "Begin there and travel forward. Tell me everything."

"It will take me all day."

He'd given her a smile. "We have all day."

"Will you return the favor?"

"Perhaps, but let's begin with you."

So she'd begun with her earliest memory—sitting atop her father's shoulders watching a parade. She told him of all the pursuits her mother had insisted she follow: riding which she loved, piano which she tolerated, embroidery which she abhorred, painting which her mother had labeled atrocious.

When she would ask a question of him, he would merely shake his head and say, "We're not finished with you yet."

She'd never been with anyone who was so interested in every aspect of her life. The men she'd flirted with on occasion were more interested in talking about themselves than asking about her. Even Robert, before they were married, had seldom inquired into her history. She was rather flattered that he was suddenly taking an interest.

"You and Diana are close," he murmured at one point.

"Very much so. She is more than my sister. She is my friend, but she is such a tease. She drives Mother to distraction. She was teasing me yesterday as well, telling me she'd kissed a Frenchman."

Which Torie realized now she must have done to know that kisses involved tongues.

"Whyever would she do that?" he asked.

"I don't know. Especially when there are plenty of Englishmen to kiss."

He chuckled low. "And you should know as you have kissed so many."

She turned up her nose. "I have kissed one, the only one who matters."

He favored her with a smile, seemingly pleased by her assessment.

But as they neared their destination, he began to grow introspective, all curiosity and interest cast aside, his gaze turning inward as she'd seen it do countless times, and she'd eventually stopped talking because she'd realized he was no longer listening.

It was well into night when they arrived at Hawthorne House, and yet Torie could see her husband's face clearly. Torches lined the drive, lined the steps leading up to the massive manor that had seemed to rise up from the earth as they'd traveled nearer. Looking at it made her feel small, insignificant, but then looking at her husband usually did as well, because he was tall and well formed and held himself with such authority.

He stood beside the coach, staring at the manor house with a sort of unnerving awe, as though he'd not seen it in ages. When he finally did walk forward, he got only as far as one of the huge stone lions that guarded the stone steps that led to the entrance. He ran his hand up one of the carved legs. "When I was a child, I would sit on this massive beast and pretend I was exploring the jungles of Africa."

His voice held a wistfulness as though the long-ago memory was as painful as it was comforting. He started up the steps, and she quickly followed. His behavior seemed rather odd in light of the fact that she knew he'd visited his ancestral home within the last month.

An elderly man came rushing out of the manor. "Your Grace, we've been expecting you." The man stopped, bowed slightly.

"Whitney, it's good to see you again."

The duke's almost strangled greeting held a measure of doubt mingled with relief that Torie couldn't understand.

"Is this lovely lady the new duchess you

informed us would be returning with you?" Whitney asked.

Robert turned, looking somewhat surprised to find her standing beside him, as if only just remembering that he'd brought her along.

"Duchess, allow me to present Whitney. He has overseen this household for as long as I can remember."

"Whitney," she said softly.

He bowed. "Your Grace, welcome to Hawthorne House."

"How long have you been here, Whitney?" she asked.

"Thirty-eight years if one were counting, which I assure you I'm not. I shall see to it that your belongings are moved immediately into the family wing—"

"No."

Both she and Whitney turned their attention to the duke, who had spoken the single word with unbending resolution and conviction, as though the butler had suggested something unheard of. Her husband appeared extremely uncomfortable, his gaze darting between the two of them as though he wasn't certain where he should place it.

"I need a bit of time alone," he said quietly. "My darling, if you don't mind, I think you'll find the accommodations in the east wing quite satisfactory for the present time."

Not mind? Not mind being banished to the other side of the manor? Not mind being banished for all the household to know? Not mind? Was he mad? Of course she minded. Whatever was wrong with him? Why was he treating her with such blatant disregard after all the interest he'd shown her today?

Before she could get over her shock enough to form a coherent reply, he'd returned his attention to Whitney. "See to the duchess's needs. I'm going to the family wing, and I don't wish to be disturbed."

"Yes, Your Grace," Whitney said solemnly.

The duke marched up the steps like a soldier going into battle, leaving his wife and servants behind him. With no more than a flick of his hand, Whitney began issuing orders to the various footmen who had quietly appeared shortly after the coach arrived.

Whitney then turned to her, sympathy in his green, kind eyes. "It is the duke's habit to seek solitude shortly after arriving."

"Is it truly?"

"Yes, Your Grace. After his brother left for America and he lost his parents to influenza, he's never been quite the same."

"In what way?"

Whitney shook his head. "It is not my place to explain the duke or his actions, but I simply wanted to reassure you that it is not unusual for him to want time alone."

Normally she would agree, but immediately following his wedding? When his new bride stood at the threshold?

"How often has he brought a wife home?" she asked testily. "And left her on the steps like so much discarded baggage?"

"He is a complex man, Your Grace."

"He is likely to find his wife is equally complex."

"May I show you to your quarters?" Whitney asked.

She took a deep breath. She had no business turning her anger on Whitney when she wanted to lash out at her husband. It made no sense for him to abandon her.

She couldn't help but believe that something was terribly, terribly wrong.

Robert sat in a plush, ornate burgundy chair facing the bed where his mother had once slept. Just as he had disappointingly discovered in the town house in London, he could find little evidence of her here now: her scent no longer lingered, her laughter no longer echoed, the soft lullabies she'd once sung to him were silent. No clothes remained for him to touch. It was as though she'd never been, yet memories of her had sustained him during his years of isolation.

He had well and truly belonged more to her than to his father. She'd been the one who guided him, counseled him, advised him. His father's influence had been there as well, but it was his mother he had always strived to please. His mother who had smiled at the wildflowers he'd picked and given her—smiled as though they'd come from the most elaborate of gardens. It was his mother for whom he'd drawn pictures. His mother whose approval he had always sought and found.

How could he now move another woman into this room? How could he himself take up residence in his father's bedchamber? To do so would truly acknowledge that they were no longer alive.

For eight years he'd prayed he was but living in a nightmare, that he would escape from it and discover his parents were still living. But the nightmare merely continued beyond the walls of Pentonville.

He had little doubt that John had already made their father's bedchamber his own. Perhaps Robert would find comfort and strength by sleeping in the bed where his father and grandfather and great-grandfather and all who had come before him had once slept. There was tradition there. Good, strong men who had served king, queen, and country. Men of destiny. Men of duty. Men of loyalty.

He had been raised within their shadows, while John apparently had been raised beyond their influence.

With a sigh, Robert dropped his head back, closed his eyes. He was exhausted, pretending to be his brother's version of himself. It was insane.

He should go to the Lord High Chancellor, declare his right to the dukedom—but how to prove that he was in fact Robert? It would be one brother's word against another.

It was a worry for tomorrow, when he was refreshed.

His wife was safely ensconced in another wing of the manor, and he could find all sorts of reasons to avoid her, and he must do so at all costs. She enchanted him with her stories and her smiles and her wretched innocence that he could so easily destroy with the truth. He had to avoid the one person who might know John well enough to reveal Robert's charade—which wasn't really a charade.

In truth, he was Robert Hawthorne, Duke of Killingsworth. But to her, he would be an impostor, because he was not the man she loved, the man she'd promised to marry.

And that, too, was a worry for tomorrow.

For tonight he wanted nothing more than to sleep again in a comfortable bed, surrounded by warmth and familiarity.

Tonight the true Duke of Killingsworth was home.

Chapter 9

Torie stood before the window, the heavy velvet drapes drawn aside so she could gaze out on the night while servants puttered about putting away her things. It was a lovely room, a bit musty from lack of use, but still lovely.

The burgundy wallpaper was decorated with tiny white flowers. Burgundy seemed to be the preferred color in the manor, along with a dark hunter's green. And gold and silver and white. The ceilings she'd viewed on the journey to her bedchamber very nearly took her breath away. Each was a series of squares. In the wide hallway leading to the bedchambers, each square had held a carved ivory cameo. In this room, angels surrounded by various flowers or relaxing in gardens were painted on each square.

A thick burgundy velvet comforter covered the bed, and the velvet canopy had been pulled aside. With chairs, tables, and a fainting couch, this bedchamber was designed to make a female guest feel welcome.

Unfortunately the fire lit in the marble fireplace did nothing to diminish the chill surrounding Torie's heart. Had Robert simply been toying with her all day, appeasing her by asking for stories of her youth? What maniacal game was he playing? To kiss her with such wild abandon, only to relinquish her beyond his sight once they arrived?

What had she done wrong? Why was he casting her aside?

"We're finished, Your Grace," Charity said quietly. "Would you like me to help prepare you for bed?"

Trying to hold on to her pride, she faced her maid of only a few years. The girl's eyes contained sadness. Pity, even. How mortifying that all would know that her husband didn't want her.

"Not yet," she said kindly, smiling warmly,

pretending she wasn't mystified by her husband's actions.

Charity furrowed her brow more deeply. "Shall I fetch you something to eat?"

"No, thank you. I think I'm going to take a stroll."

"But it's dark."

"I'll ask Whitney to locate a lantern I can use."

"I thought I heard thunder earlier."

"I'll be fine, Charity. And like my husband, I need a bit of time alone."

Robert felt like a ghost, ambling through the family wing, opening a door, going inside a room, inhaling sharply the familiar scents, touching an heirloom, a statuette, a bauble, searching, searching for what he'd possessed before. His brother had taken far more from him than he'd realized. Not just the years that could never be recaptured, but the memories, moments spent in this house with his family.

Of course, he'd not had an opportunity to attend his parents' funeral. Tomorrow he would visit the family mausoleum. Offer his respects. It would be a moment of self-indulgence, taking the time to grieve. He wasn't certain that he'd truly accepted that his parents were gone. When he was in London, it had seemed that they were merely at Hawthorne House. Now it seemed as though they were merely in London.

Perhaps that was the reason he'd felt the need to hurry home. He'd thought to find them. But they weren't here. He could chase all over the world, and he'd never again see them.

He brought his journey to an end at the bedchamber that had once belonged to him. He wasn't quite ready to move into his father's bedchamber, but if John had already moved into that room, how would Robert explain his sleeping in his old room?

For nostalgia's sake. Simple enough. Whitney wouldn't question him. No servant would question him. After all, he was lord of the manor. Their positions were dependent on their ability to keep their master's behavior private.

He had his hand on the doorknob when he heard the light patter of feet on the stairs. The steps echoed with a cadence that brought back memories, and he knew whom he would see emerge at the landing.

Whitney appeared, just as Robert had

known he would. A bit slower, a little breathless, but his feet still carried the quick, determined step as always.

"Your Grace, I'm sorry to disturb you, but I thought you should know that the duchess has yet to return."

Robert combed his fingers through his hair, still surprised to find it so much shorter. Then he angled his head slightly as though he thought the action might help him decipher Whitney's statement. "I'm sorry, Whitney. I don't understand. Return from where?"

"The duchess went out over an hour ago. She said she wished to take a walk around the grounds."

"At night?" He looked at the large windows that allowed sunlight and moonlight to spill into the end of the hallway. Lightning flashed, and he knew thunder would soon rumble. "It's raining," he said, somewhat mystified.

"Yes, Your Grace. It wasn't when the duchess departed, but I fear she might have become lost. She seemed distraught, distracted. She took a lantern, but little else."

"A lantern? But if she was walking the grounds, there are lights . . ." He let his voice trail off. He shouldn't be discussing or revealing his doubts regarding his wife's actions with a servant. Even one as trusted as Whitney.

"Rouse the servants. Gather some more lanterns. Have some horses readied. We'll need to go in search of her."

"Yes, Your Grace."

Robert walked to the end of the hallway and looked out the window into the night. Was he responsible for his wife's wandering off? Was his avoiding her, delegating her to a bedchamber in the other wing responsible?

Of course. She had to be devastated by his inattention. What wife wanted to be told that she wasn't welcome in the family wing?

She'd married him in good faith, and he'd been so concerned with his own needs that he'd failed to consider hers. He could be the duke she deserved even if he couldn't be the husband. He could be a friend, if not a lover.

He hurried down the wide, sweeping, marble-inlaid stairs. "Whitney!"

The butler appeared almost immediately after Robert reached the foyer. He was holding a coat and helped Robert put it on.

"Have my wife's things moved into the duchess's bedchamber."

"Into your mother's chamber?"

"My mother is gone, Whitney. We have a new Duchess of Killingsworth."

"Yes, Your Grace. I'll see to having her things moved immediately. I assume you'll be sleeping in your father's bedchamber . . . as usual."

He studied Whitney, trying to determine if the man was questioning him or offering him a hint as to what was normal for this household. Did he suspect that Robert didn't know?

He couldn't suspect. He was simply . . .

Robert was tired, weary. He didn't want to try to guess others' actions or put more weight behind the words than they deserved.

"Yes, Whitney. The Duke and Duchess of Killingsworth will sleep in their respective bedchambers."

"Very good, Your Grace. Those who will help in the search are awaiting your arrival at the stables."

"Thank you, Whitney." He turned toward the door.

"It's good to have you home, sir."

He stopped and without looking back, because he feared the butler would see the truth of the situation in his eyes, he said quietly, "It's good to be home."

Then he rushed out into the storm.

* * *

There was no hope for it. Torie was completely lost.

She'd become so absorbed in her thoughts that she'd paid little attention to the road she was traveling—or the road she wasn't traveling, more like it. That was the crux of the problem. She'd left the paved path, wandered into a forest, and now with dark clouds blocking the moon, she was hopelessly lost. To make matters worse, an unexpected storm had arrived, and she was soaked to the bone, the damp chill adding to her misery.

She was surrounded by trees, and her lantern shed so little light that she could see only a short distance in front of her. She pressed her back to a tree and slid to the ground, unable to hold back the tears. She'd never felt so uncared for, so unwanted, so miserable.

Whatever had become of the man who had laughed gaily with her? She'd apparently not known Killingsworth well, but she certainly felt as though she'd known him better before the wedding ceremony than after. Why had he banished her to a distant corner of the house? His actions made absolutely no sense.

This was to be their wedding trip, a time when they grew closer, consummated their marriage vows. Yet she instigated every conversation, every *kiss*, for that matter. She rambled on about her life, her dreams, her favorite color while he did nothing more than sit and watch her, as though she were a specimen in a jar.

All the doubts she'd experienced yesterday morning were once again with her, doubling, tripling. How could she fall in love with him if she wasn't spending time with him? How was she to know him better if he did nothing but ask her questions and provide no answers? And how the devil could he be a proper husband if he was never around her?

Was she to meekly accept his treatment of her or rail against it?

His behavior was baffling. Not at all what she expected of a man who had sought her out. Not that it mattered. She'd probably expire there on the spot from cold and chills. Never knowing what it was to lie with a man for whom she felt great affection.

She wanted to live and be loved. And while she'd heard that the reality of marriage to a peer was more often than not disappointing, she'd held out hope that hers would be one of the few to be envied. She didn't want to settle for complacent. She wanted excitement, emotion, passion.

She heard a distant sound like horse's hooves splashing in the deepening puddles over the ground, and she saw lights bobbing in the night.

"Victoria!"

She recognized the voice. It belonged to her husband. She didn't know why she was incredibly surprised that he'd come searching for her, but she was. And relieved. Maybe she meant something to him after all. Maybe he'd spoken true. He simply needed to be alone for a bit. But what odd timing. Immediately after your wedding. Those should be the moments when you didn't want to be alone.

"Victoria!"

Whatever his reasons for his earlier behavior, he'd come after her now, and she was grateful for it. She struggled to her feet and raised the lantern high. "Here! I'm here!"

Then the rain stopped as suddenly as it had begun, the clouds moved beyond the moon, and she saw the outline of the riders. She had no trouble at all distinguishing her husband from the others. It was simply the way he carried himself. A regal air. No one would ever mistake him for a peasant.

He dismounted quickly and strode up to her, removing his heavy coat as he approached. "Are you all right?"

"Yes, I . . . I went for a walk and it started to rain and I got lost."

He tossed his coat around her shoulders before he wrapped his arms around her, drawing her up against him where the warmth lingering in his coat and the warmth of his body began to chase away the chill in hers. He felt incredibly good, sturdy, and strong.

"I was so worried," he said, his head bent, his lips near her ear. "You gave me such a fright."

Although that hadn't been her intention, she was a bit ashamed to realize that she was glad that she had. If he was worried, then he had to care.

"I'm sorry. I simply had to get away, to think. Robert, what have I done wrong? Why do you no longer want me?"

She felt his arms tighten around her, almost crushing her in the process.

"I do want you," he rasped. "But if I'm not careful, I'll hurt you."

"I'm not so delicate that I can't be touched."

She heard a low growl, but she didn't think it was a beast of the forest, rather she thought it was her husband.

He pulled back. "We need to get you home, get you warm."

He lifted her into his arms, walked over to his horse, and with the help of another man placed her on the saddle and mounted behind her. His arms came around her as he reached for the reins. The horse began walking, and she found herself leaning in to her husband.

"I've had your things moved to the family wing," he said solemnly, "to the bedchamber next to mine."

"But you don't want me there."

"You belong there. I was wrong to think otherwise."

"I know you don't love me, Robert, but I always thought you at least liked me, that you were interested in more than my dowry."

"We'll talk when we reach the manor and your teeth are no longer clattering."

His voice contained a bit of anger and chastisement, and she found herself grateful for that as well. As long as he exhibited some sort of emotion, all was not lost.

* * *

It was a gorgeous bedchamber. The one that belonged to the mistress of the manor. A fire was burning on the hearth. Behind a silk screen, in a copper tub, a heated bath had been prepared.

Her husband had carried her up the sweeping staircase as though she weighed nothing in his arms, in spite of her weak protests that she could walk. The truth was, nestled against him, she'd rather enjoyed being carried into this room.

He'd set her on the bed, their damp clothing serving as a magnet between them, each soaking up the other's warmth. Leaving behind the scent of rain, he'd exited through the door on the opposite side of the room, a door that no doubt led into the changing room and from there into his bedchamber. She'd heard him call for Witherspoon right before the door shut securely behind him.

While her maid was preparing her, his valet was preparing him. Perhaps in a very short time, she would discover if her mother had judged the duke's virility accurately—she would learn if he was quick or slow. And while her mother claimed that quickly was best, Torie couldn't help but believe that going slowly might be more enjoyable. It might allow for a savoring much like her bath.

While her body had luxuriated in the hot water, she'd thought about how lovely it had been that morning to awaken in his arms. She wondered if he might stay with her after they made love, if she might fall asleep in those very arms.

She might have remained in the warm water all night—it felt incredible after the chilly dampness of being caught in the rain—but she knew her husband would soon join her and she wanted to be prepared for him. She sat at the dresser where her silver brush, comb, and hand mirror had already been set out. Charity brushed the tangles from her hair and used a soft towel to dry it. Then she helped Torie worm her way into a rose-colored nightgown that left little to the imagination as it outlined her curves. Torie climbed into bed and brought the covers up to her chin, thought better of it, and eased them down to her chest. She didn't wish to be too wanton, but neither did she want her husband to think she was dreading his visit.

When a knock sounded on the door, all Torie could think was that the moment she'd been both anticipating and dreading had finally arrived. And again, it seemed too soon. Before she was completely ready.

She kept her gaze focused on her clenched hands while Charity opened the door. She heard Charity murmur something before stepping out of the room, the door shutting, her husband's footsteps—so much louder than the servants'—as he approached.

"How are you feeling?" he asked, in the same apologetic tone he'd used in the woods.

She glanced up, surprised to find him fully clothed, not in a silk dressing gown as she'd expected him to be, but in trousers and shirt. Standing there, holding a . . .

Teacup.

A teacup on a saucer.

Not wine or champagne with which to celebrate this impending union or to help her relax.

But a teacup.

"I brought you some warm cocoa," he said, and she was certain his cheeks turned red with the pronouncement. "I thought it might help you sleep."

"Oh." Carefully she scooted into a sitting position, trying to keep the blankets covering her. When she stopped squirming, he handed her the cup on the saucer, then tilted his head toward a chair.

"May I?"

She nodded and took a sip of the cocoa. It was heavenly and was quite clever on his part, because she realized it relaxed her more than wine or champagne ever would.

He dragged the chair over, sat in it, and leaned forward, his elbows on his thighs, his hands clasped, his eyes downcast.

"I must apologize for earlier," he said, lifting his gaze from his hands to her face. "For sending you to the other wing. I realize now that my actions may have made you feel . . . unwanted . . . and may have had some influence on your foray into the woods."

"I was distracted, thinking about one thing then another, not really paying much attention where my feet were going," she said quickly, wanting to reassure him.

A corner of his mouth lifted. "Yes, I know, but if I'd ensured that you considered yourself welcome here, you might not have felt the need to travel quite so far."

She set the saucer on her lap, studying it, trying to determine if she should ask him why he'd not tried to make her feel more welcome, why he was fully clothed, why cocoa and not wine?

"This was my mother's bedchamber," he said solemnly. "I wasn't quite ready for it to belong to someone else—"

"Six months. Robert, I don't mean to come across as a shrew, but you've had six months to prepare."

"I was very close to my mother, and when the moment came—"

"I'm not trying to take her place."

"I didn't mean to imply that I thought you were. I was merely trying to explain my strange reaction upon our arrival."

"I can move to another room. We passed at least half a dozen doors on the way to this chamber, and I really don't mind—"

"No." He held up his hand to silence her, then pressed his finger against his lips, his brow furrowing as though he were giving great weight to the words he wished to speak next. "When I took you as my wife, you became the Duchess of Killingsworth, and this bedchamber belongs to the duchess, more than it belonged to my mother. What I mean to say is that every duchess slept here. It was my mother's room because she was the duchess, not because she was my mother. I was remiss in not welcoming you into it. And for that I apologize."

"I believe you've apologized to me more since we exchanged vows than you did in all the time we were together before yesterday."

He smiled softly. "I'm sure I have. The past two days have been . . . extraordinary. As a result, I'm unaccountably weary. Too weary to be an especially attentive husband this evening."

"Oh." She ran her finger along the rim of the cup. "I see. So I shall sleep alone."

"Yes, I don't think the joining of a husband and wife should be rushed."

She peered over at him. This time she had no doubt. He *was* blushing.

Abruptly he came to his feet. "Good night, Duchess."

"Robert?"

In his haste to get away from her, he'd already taken several steps before he slowly turned to face her. "Yes?"

"Do you love me?"

Slowly he closed his eyes and released a sigh. "I care for you. I would never wish you harm."

"If I'd not had a substantial dowry, would you have married me?"

He opened his eyes, took a step toward the bed, and wrapped his hand around the square post. "I believe I would have married you if you'd come with no dowry at all."

"What do you like best about me?"

Furrowing his brow, he cocked his head to the side. "You wish for me to choose only one thing?"

She nodded. "I'm hesitant to admit it, but I feel a bit insecure regarding my place in your life. You always seem to be in such a hurry to escape me, even when we're getting along, and I—"

"Your smile," he interrupted before she could finish her ranting.

Her smile? She shook her head in astonishment. "But a smile is so inconsequential—"

"I disagree. Yours especially is a pleasure to behold. The tiniest dimple forms in your right cheek. It somehow makes you appear impish and mysterious at the same time. Alluring. And kind. Your smile is like an overturned rainbow; your eyes the pots of gold on either end."

"I've never known you to be quite so poetic."

"Those prisoners at Pentonville that we discussed yesterday, they never see a smile."

"Wearing those hoods, I doubt they ever see a frown, either."

She'd expected him to laugh at her carefree comment, but apparently he saw no humor in it because he remained deadly serious.

"A smile is made of magic, Torie. It lightens the heart. Even a smile in passing can create joy. Imagine if you never had anyone smile at you. I've only recently begun to appreciate its power—since having yours bestowed upon me."

She was overwhelmed by his praise. "I hardly know what to say. I always thought of my smile as quite ordinary."

"No smile is ordinary, but yours is exceptional. I know that we are discouraged from smiling when we have a portrait made, but I should very much like for you to break with tradition, for you to be the first Duchess of Killingsworth to smile while her portrait is painted. And I should like a miniature of it to carry with me always."

"It takes such a long time to have a portrait done that I have little doubt my jaws will begin to ache, but I shall endure it for you."

"That smile right there. That is the one I want to carry with me."

She hadn't even realized that she was smiling. "And will you smile for me?"

"I have little practice at it, but I shall see what I can do. Sleep well."

It was a kinder dismissal than he'd given her earlier, and so she let him go. She snuggled down beneath the covers, sipping her lukewarm cocoa. There were facets to her husband that she'd never known existed. Who would have thought he would have placed so much importance on a smile?

And to still care so much about those unfortunate prisoners.

Who was this man she'd married?

She is the Duchess of Killingsworth. You are the Duke of Killingsworth. She is your wife.

But I am not the man who courted her. Who wooed her. Who asked for her hand in marriage!

I have no right to yearn for her as I do. No right at all!

But she is your duchess. *Your* duchess!

Through no fault of her own.

In bare feet, his brother's ostentatious silk dressing gown wrapped tightly around him, Robert paced over the thick carpet in his bedchamber, back and forth, in a circle, his hands over his ears, but nothing stopped the voices in his head from arguing his case.

As much as he was loath to admit it, he'd carried on numerous conversations with himself while in Pentonville, lending different voices to his thoughts, and while he knew, he *knew*, all the thoughts were his and he was in control of them, it was during times like this when he felt as though he was truly going insane.

Because he couldn't stop the voices, couldn't stop them from bantering back and forth, couldn't stop them from trying to give him the freedom to do exactly what he wanted to do. Make Torie his wife in every way possible.

Even before Whitney had alerted him to her disappearance, Robert had come to the conclusion that she deserved the honor of sleeping in the family wing. Whether she was to remain was another question entirely, but she had, in all good faith, taken as her husband the Duke of Killingsworth, and that fact allowed her to sleep in the duchess's bedchamber.

He would have had her things moved in tomorrow, rather than tonight, but he'd seen nothing to gain in delaying once he realized she'd not yet retired for the night.

How could something as simple as an evening stroll go completely awry? How could she become lost? His fear was that she'd thought to turn the walk into an escape. He could hardly blame her. Marriage to him most certainly was not turning out to be anything as she'd envisioned it would be.

He hardly spoke to her, and he didn't know what to say when he did. Amazing what eight years of talking to oneself could do to a man. While he'd been a witty conversationalist before, and while he'd occasionally entertained himself at Pentonville to the extent of actually making himself laugh, he now found himself totally inept at carrying on the most inconsequential of conversations.

The weather. They could discuss the weather. As a matter of fact, she might not have gone out at all if he'd simply said, as they neared Hawthorne House, "I smell rain on the air. We'll have a storm before midnight."

Because he had smelled it and he'd relished the scent, but he'd kept his observations to himself. So out she'd walked with no thought to the consequences of a storm.

He'd gone after her with no thought to the outcome of what that might mean when he'd found her. He'd not even thought to have a horse saddled for her, and that little lack of planning had resulted in heaven and hell combining to torture him as she'd sat nestled between his thighs, her back rubbing against his chest with each step the horse took, her warmth seeping into him until her scent had permeated his clothes.

It was a miracle that they'd found her, a miracle which had allowed him to wrap his arms around her when he'd first found her, draw her near, so near that he'd been acutely aware of her nipples, hardened by the chill of the night, pressing against his chest as her breasts flattened against him. He had been as wet, as cold, and yet he would have been content to stand there through the night, until dawn peeked over the horizon, simply holding her pressed up against him, with her sweet scent still filling his nostrils. Not even the rain had the power to wash it away.

He supposed that when he revealed the truth and had the marriage undone, he would be able go into the bedchamber beside his and still smell her presence there.

Because she was lying there now, separated from him by merely a door. A heavy, ornate door, to be sure, everything in this house was heavy and ornate. All he would have to do was open it and reveal that he'd lied to her about a good many things.

Too weary to be attentive?

Good God. He'd been more than attentive. He'd had to clasp his hands until they ached to stop himself from reaching out for her, from running his hands through her unbound hair, from tracing his finger over her plump lower lip where a drop of cocoa had lingered until she'd lapped it up with her tongue.

That small action had very nearly been his undoing. His body had hardened so quickly that he'd gotten dizzy.

Too weary?

He thought he could be on his deathbed and still find the energy and stamina to make love to her.

He'd been enamored watching her struggle to keep her modesty, fighting to keep the covers in place as she'd sat up. But they'd slipped down slightly when she'd reached for the cocoa, revealing the curve of one perfect breast molded against the cotton of her nightgown. He didn't have to see it to know he'd find it perfect. He didn't have to cup it in his palm or stroke it to know its perfection.

He had but to see the shape that it gave to her nightgown to know that he would find everything about her pleasing.

He dropped down on the settee before the fireplace, the fire burning on the hearth almost cool when compared with the heat radiating through his body with thoughts of his wife. What he needed was another cold bath, the last thing he'd ever expected to force himself to endure. A bath in frigid water that had set his teeth to chattering.

But he'd needed something to tamp down his ardor because he couldn't seek release in a manner that his body would find satisfactory.

He couldn't bed his wife because he wasn't the man to whom she'd granted the honor. He couldn't bed another woman because he possessed a wife. And while he had no plans to make her his wife in truth, she had exchanged vows believing she was speaking to the man who had asked for her hand in marriage.

So he would remain faithful to the vows until he could have them undone.

He needed to go to bed, follow the advice that he'd given to her and sleep well, so he'd be rested in the morning and could begin going over the books, the records, searching for anything that might enlighten him as to how he could hold on to that which his brother had once taken.

But when he finally retired more than two hours later, after doing little more than staring at the fire and thinking of the woman in the next room, he didn't dream about holding on to his dukedom.

He dreamed about holding on to his wife.

Chapter 10

The next morning, Torie awoke surprisingly well rested. Last night after she'd finished the warm cocoa, she'd lain in bed, listening to creaking floorboards, the result of her husband pacing late into the night. From the moment she'd come to stand beside him at the altar, she'd sensed that he was troubled, not quite himself. The journey yesterday had been pleasant enough that she'd thought they were well on their way to a comfortable marriage, but their arrival had certainly proven that assumption false.

He was troubled. He'd even admitted it. She wished he'd share the burden with her.

Why did men always think they had to be strong enough to carry their worries alone?

With a sigh, she threw back the covers and clambered out of bed. She crossed the room, slipped her hands between the draperies, and peered out. The sun was shining, little evidence remained of the storm from the night before—only an occasional puddle. It was going to be a glorious day. Her first as mistress of the manor.

She marched back to the bed, leaned over, and yanked on the bellpull to summon her maid.

She could barely sit still as Charity prepared her to face the day. She wondered where Robert was now. Was he seeing to business, awaiting her in the breakfast room?

They'd not bothered to discuss their plans for the day, so she had no idea what to expect. Still, she was certain that her day would very much reflect her mother's: greeting her husband, going over the items to be dealt with, deciding what should be prepared for dinner.

After she was dressed in a gown of pale green, she took a leisurely stroll through the manor in search of the breakfast room, several times stopping to ask servants for directions. The house was monstrously huge, and she wondered if she'd ever learn her way among the maze of corridors. She'd expected enticing aromas to guide her closer to the breakfast room, and as she entered, she discovered the reason that they hadn't.

The room was bare of food.

She'd not overslept, nor had she risen unreasonably early. It was the proper time for breakfast to be served. Obviously she had things to put to rights here, and she wanted it done before her husband was ready to be served.

She looked at the footman standing at attention beside the sideboard as though he actually had something of importance to guard.

"Where is the kitchen?" she asked.

"Through that door, Your Grace," he said with a tilt of his head. "Down the corridor, to the left. You can't miss it."

He then proceeded to cross the room and open the appropriate door for her. She strolled through and continued on down the hallway. As she neared the bricked arched portal that clearly led to the kitchen, she understood immediately why breakfast had yet to be served. She could hear full-throated laughter and a deeply resonating one wafting out of the kitchen along with the enticing aromas of pork, beef, and pastries that caused her mouth to begin watering. She'd not realized how hungry she was until that moment.

And if the cook wasn't too busy flirting with one of the other servants, Torie would have been appeasing her stomach's pangs already. And what of her husband? Surely he was starving and would expect food to be waiting for him. She had to take the matter in hand, immediately. She was the duchess, and pleasing her husband was of paramount importance. That she had yet to be introduced to the cook was of no consequence. She would make her presence known and see to it that food was made ready so when Robert—

She arrived at the open doorway and paused, unable to believe what she was seeing, or hearing, for that matter.

Indeed it was the cook laughing, but not with another servant. No, indeed. The man with whom she was having such a jolly good time was none other than the duke himself. They were sitting across from each other at a table where Torie was certain the servants took their meals.

She'd never seen him look so joyous, so at ease, as though he was exactly where he was supposed to be. An odd notion when she'd always thought he *was* right where he belonged, and yet it was the only way she could describe what she was observing. He was at home, completely at home with his surroundings.

His laughter stopped as he shoved something into his mouth, closed his eyes, chewed madly, and dropped his head back. He appeared to be in rapture, and the cook—a short, white-haired woman who obviously believed in sampling the food she prepared—was gazing at him as though he were her favorite child.

Torie was mesmerized, watching the way his throat muscles worked as he swallowed. He wasn't dressed properly, but wore only trousers, boots, and a loosely fitting white shirt with two buttons undone, leaving the material parted to reveal only the smallest portion of his neck, the top of his chest.

Opening his eyes, he gave the cook a smile of pure pleasure. "Ah, Mrs. Cuddleworthy, no one cooks a raspberry tart like you do."

"It's a wonder I still remember how. You've not asked for one in years."

"I want one every morning from now on. At afternoon tea as well. Might as well have them at dinner." He held up a finger as though he'd suddenly thought of something incredibly important. "And lunch."

"After saying you never wanted one prepared again. They were always your favorite. I didn't know why you ordered me not to make them any longer."

"Clearly I was not myself that day."

He came partway out of his chair, leaned over, and kissed the elderly woman's cheek, causing her to giggle like an infatuated schoolgirl and her round cheeks to redden until they resembled apples.

"It's been years since you've been so attentive, Your Grace."

"An oversight I shall seek to rectify." His eyes twinkling, he reached for another tart, suddenly stopping, his hand frozen over the plate. He must have become aware of Torie's presence, because he jerked his head around, his gaze falling on her. He shoved himself to his feet, the chair's legs clattering over the stone floor.

She felt like an intruder standing in the doorway, watching this friendly exchange between the master of the house and his servant. More, she was having a difficult time reconciling the fact that the man standing in the kitchen was the same man who had asked for her hand in marriage.

Oh, on occasion she'd heard him laugh, encouraged a smile from him, but neither had been delivered with such absolute joy. She'd never heard him laugh with such carefree abandon, never seen him smile with such pure warmth. Certainly she'd never seen him peck a kiss on a servant's cheek. Come to think of it, he'd always treated servants as though they didn't exist.

Was it possible that there was a London lord and a Hawthorne House lord? One man whose personality altered depending on where he lived? Or was it simply marriage that had changed him? He'd been acting differently since the ceremony. No, not since it. During it, as well. Gazing at her as though he didn't know her, apologizing . . .

She became acutely aware of tension beginning to radiate through the room, chasing away the relaxed atmosphere that had been there only moments before. He tilted his head slightly. "Good morning, Duchess."

"Good morning. I apologize for intruding, but there's no food in the breakfast room—"

"My apologies to you, Your Grace," the cook interrupted. "The duke wanted to eat his breakfast in the kitchen here like he did when he was just a lad. I'd assumed you'd want a tray brought up. I'll get busy right away on seeing that food is laid out on the sideboard."

"No, no, that's not necessary. A plate will do me fine."

"I'll see right to it then."

Her gaze still locked on Killingsworth, Torie paid little attention as the cook began bustling around the kitchen, placing various tidbits of food on a large platter. Robert seemed most uncomfortable with his wife's presence.

"You seem more at ease here than in London," she finally ventured, even though his comfort with her had yet to surface.

"I've always considered Hawthorne House to be my home. London is simply a place I visit, because I must on occasion do so."

"Here you are, Your Grace," the cook said. "Let me carry this to the breakfast room for you—"

"No need," Torie interrupted. "I can eat in here."

"Of course, Your Grace," the cook said.

Torie gave her attention to the woman. "Mrs. Cuddleworthy, is it?"

"Yes, ma'am." The cook curtsied.

Torie decided the name fit. She could imagine a child sitting on the woman's lap, his head pressed to her pillowy bosom, while he munched on raspberry tarts, his mouth and hands stained, as well as her apron where he sat against her. The woman would no doubt be as comfortable as a soft bed.

Looking back at her husband, Torie said, "If you don't mind?"

"Of course not. You are the lady of the manor, free to do as you wish."

Not exactly the answer she was hoping for, because in spite of his words, it didn't appear that he truly wanted her there. He pulled out a chair. She walked to the table and sat. Mrs. Cuddleworthy placed the platter in front of her.

Robert bent down, pressed a kiss to her temple, and said, "If you'll excuse me, my darling, I have some urgent business to which I must attend."

And just like that, he took his leave, making her wonder once again why he was so anxious not be around her. What in the world was going on?

Mrs. Cuddleworthy seemed as surprised by his abrupt departure as Torie did. Looking at her plate, Torie wished she'd decided to have her meal in the breakfast room after all. At least that room was brighter, more open. It lent itself to cheer more than this room did. And right this moment, she needed some cheer.

"Shall I prepare you a cuppa tea?"

Torie lifted her gaze to the cook and smiled. "Yes, please."

She moved the food around on her plate, her appetite having deserted her. She didn't understand her husband's reserve, his endearment, his quick kiss. It was as though he were performing, doing what was expected rather than what he desired.

She jumped when the tea was suddenly placed before her. "Thank you."

"Do you not like what I've prepared?" Mrs. Cuddleworthy asked.

"It's lovely," Torie said, forcing herself to take a bite.

"I have to admit that I take pride in my raspberry tarts."

"The duke seems to favor them," Torie admitted.

"He does. He always did. As a young lad, Lord Robert was always pleading with me to make some for him, which is the reason I never understood his forbidding me to prepare them."

Torie had just lifted her cup to take a sip of tea. She sat there, cup aloft, trying to make sense of the cook's words. "He forbade you to prepare something he so enjoyed?"

She nodded. "Until this morning. He was in here before the sun, wanting my tarts. Strangest thing."

Strange indeed, considering the enjoyment he'd obviously taken in eating one. "I wonder why," Torie mused, not really seeking an answer.

"Haven't a clue," the cook responded anyway. "It was right after he became duke. Sometimes it goes to a young man's head—the power of the position. He changed quite a bit after that, he did. The ordering about of the tart making being only the start. Perhaps he thought his love of tarts was something only a boy should have, not a man with the burden of responsibilities he was carrying on his young shoulders."

"I would have thought if they were his favorite, he'd have ordered you to cook them three times a day. I'm always comforted when I eat something I enjoy."

"You'd have thought," the cook muttered as she turned her attention to the oven.

Another of his idiosyncrasies to file away, Torie thought.

Robert had always thought that if he were free of Pentonville Prison, the veil of despair would lift, and it had briefly, but as he studied the ledgers and documents before him, it returned with a resounding clank, like the prison doors being shut on him.

The ledgers seemed to indicate that his brother had somehow managed to take the estate to the brink of ruin. Robert had to have misread something or John hadn't been good at marking income, because surely this couldn't have happened.

Their family had resources, mining ventures, horses, investments . . .

He leaned back in the chair, stared up at the frescoed ceiling, and wondered why he was surprised to discover that his brother had put himself above the estate and titles. John had always preferred play to work, had always skipped out on his lessons, had been lazy whenever possible, had flirted with the young female servants, had been tossed out of one school after another.

He wondered if his brother had planned to change his ways after he married, or if falling in love with Victoria had perhaps changed him. For surely he'd fallen in love with her. How could any man not?

Robert closed his eyes, and with no effort at all, he could see her so clearly. The rich luster of her hair, the deep brown of her eyes, the small dimple that appeared in her right cheek, but not in her left, when she laughed. Why one side and not the other? What other inconsistencies might her body reveal? He thought he might be the luckiest of men if given the opportunity to explore, to trace her face, dip his finger—no, his tongue—into that tiny dent that only appeared when she was exceedingly happy. He would like to trail his fingers over her throat, take his kisses as far down her body as she would allow. And if she allowed no liberties on his part, still he would be content to do nothing more than gaze at her for hours at a time.

The door opened, and Robert jerked his head up to find his wife walking hesitantly into the room. No doubt wondering why her new husband was not giving her attention. He was going to have to come up with a reason to explain his distance. Some sort of pox, perhaps.

He shuddered at the thought of that rumor spreading. Then no woman would want him, and he desperately wanted a woman. He hoped he was having more luck masking the yearning in his eyes than he was the desire exhibiting itself below his waist. To get his body under control, he glanced down at the depressing numbers in the ledgers before very slowly bringing himself to his feet.

But her eyes were not on him. Rather they were focused on something behind him. The painting. Of course. The one of his lovely mother with her two sons, one nestled against each side.

"Oh, my goodness. Is that you and John with your mother?" she asked.

"Yes."

"You look exactly the same."

"Of course. We're twins."

She shook her head, the tiny dimple appearing as she lifted a corner of her mouth. "I've always known you were twins, but I've never seen a portrait of the two of you. I thought something would distinguish you from each other. A blemish perhaps, a slightly different chin."

"There's nothing—which makes it impossible for anyone to tell us apart."

"How old are you in the portrait?" she asked.

"I believe we were nearly eight."

"Was it strange?"

"Strange?"

"Having a twin. I can't imagine how odd it would seem to look at someone who looks exactly as you do."

"I didn't consider it strange. When I looked at John, I saw John. That he looked as I did was simply . . . the way he looked."

Her dimple deepened as her smile grew. "Did you ever try to trick people, pretend to be each other?"

How was he to answer that question? With the truth? It was the perfect opportunity to explain the situation, to tell her of John's deception. But he couldn't quite bring himself to do it. To lose her completely. So he simply said, "On occasion."

"Were you ever found out?"

"No," he answered quietly. "No one ever knew what we did."

She moved toward the desk, interest reflected in her eyes. "Tell me about one of the times. Tell me what you did, how you managed to pull it off."

"It wasn't that difficult. As you say, we looked exactly alike, our mannerisms were very similar. I daresay the only one who could truly tell us apart was our mother. We could never fool her."

"But you tried?"

"On occasion."

"So reveal to me a time when you successfully pretended to be John."

He shook his head as a memory came upon him, one from years ago, one he'd locked away and not thought of in a good long while. "It's not a moment I'm proud of."

"I won't tell anyone."

"You will think less of me."

"Impossible."

He ran his finger along the edge of the desk, studying the fine grain of the wood. He'd never told a soul. Even John had held his secret when he'd had no reason to. "You owe me, brother," he'd said afterward.

Surely that incident hadn't led to John hiding him away in Pentonville.

"Robert?"

He glanced up, having almost forgotten that she was there.

She shook her head. "Where do you go?"

"Pardon?"

"You get a faraway look in your eyes. I've seen it happen countless times, and I'm left alone even though you are beside me."

"I stole an apple," he said hastily, deciding it was better to reveal the story than to explain where his mind drifted off to. "From a grocer in the village. John very much liked the grocer's daughter, and I'd been flirting with her, pretending to be him, because she favored him with kisses."

"So you stole her kisses."

"Yes, and an apple. The grocer saw me take the apple, not the kisses, and he reported the theft to my father. Only since I'd told his daughter I was John, he told my father it was John who took the apple. So John was punished."

"Punished? For stealing an apple?"

"My father had a strict moral code. You did not take that which did not belong to you. We were fourteen, John and I. But my father made him hold out a hand—the hand that supposedly took the apple—and struck it three times with a cane. Then he made John pay for the apple."

He realized that he'd tightened his hand into a fist. The blows had been delivered to John, but Robert had felt the sting of each one of them, because he'd been made to watch his brother being made an example of.

"I should have confessed, spared John the punishment, but I didn't wish to disappoint my father. Or perhaps I was simply weak. A coward. John had no proof other than his word that it was me and not him."

And now Robert found himself in the same predicament.

Reaching across the desk, she took his balled hand in hers and slowly unfurled his fingers.

She kissed the center of his palm as though it was he who had been struck. He curled his fingers slightly so they would touch her cheek. "It was a harmless prank. I'm sure there were times when John pretended to be you," she said.

"I'm sure you're right. In retrospect, however, perhaps my father did know the truth of it. Punishing me by forcing me to witness his punishing John. If that was his thinking, it was very clever on his part. I never pretended to be John again."

He worked his hand free of her hold before he did something dangerous like wrap his hand around the nape of her neck and draw her near for a kiss.

"I've asked the groomsman to saddle a horse for me so that I might go riding," he announced, for no other reason than to change the subject and to alert her to the fact that she'd best be on her way because he was soon to be on his.

"May I go with you?" she asked.

"I have the pox." The words came out, barely audible even to his own ears.

She tilted her head. "Pardon?"

"I said . . . I have a fox."

"Are you going hunting then?"

"No, just looking."

She gave him a smile that almost brought him to his knees, and in that moment he thought he might truly hate his brother for having a claim to this woman.

"I would like to take a look as well."

She was tempting him beyond all reason, and his resistance was weakening.

"Actually another time might be better. I

plan to visit the family mausoleum. Not exactly a jolly place."

"I'd like to pay my respects to your family."

What could he say to that heartfelt declaration?

"I'll have another horse readied then."

"Thank you. I'll change into my riding dress and meet you at the stables."

She unsettled him, confused him, threatened his plans. But he couldn't bring himself to do anything more than nod and say, "I look forward to your company."

Chapter 11

In the end they walked, leading their horses behind them, because the family mausoleum was not that far from the manor. They reached it by strolling through elaborate, well-maintained gardens. Torie was left with the impression that the gardens had been designed to bring tranquillity to anyone traveling through them so that when they reached their final destination, they would arrive with a sense of peace.

Like everything else Torie had seen at Hawthorne House, the mausoleum was magnificent. It sat in a clearing, its stone spires competing with the surrounding trees for height. Stained-glass windows adorned and brought muted and colored sunlight into the cold building.

Torie thought it was probably the marble tombs inside that held the warmth at bay. Several lined the walls, each providing a place where an intricate carving of a man lay next to that of a woman—both exhibited in their prime even if death had not arrived until long past that moment. A kindness to those housed within and to those who would visit their ancestors—who were always displayed at their best.

In the center of the building were the resting places of the fifth Duke and Duchess of Killingsworth, who'd been taken from this earth much too soon. Robert's parents.

He stood there now, his hands resting on his mother's marble form, his head bent, his eyes closed in solemn reflection. Although eight years had passed since he'd lost them, it was evident he still mourned their passing. It was another side to him that she'd never before witnessed: a man who cared so deeply.

Her heart tightened at the grief he so clearly still felt. Quietly she moved up and placed her hand on his firm back, to provide him with a small measure of solace.

"I wasn't with them when they died," he rasped.

She placed her other hand on his arm, squeezing gently, offering what comfort she could, although she knew nothing would be enough. "Few children are."

"I should have been."

His voice contained a tinge of anger. Not that she could blame him. His parents weren't so very old when they'd died.

"I've never known anyone who has mourned so deeply for so long. You must have loved them a great deal." And she couldn't help but hope that a day would come when he'd love her as much.

"Indeed I have held on to my grief. This is the first time—" He cleared his throat. "I've never visited them here before today. I . . . couldn't . . . bring myself to come, but seeing their peaceful images carved in white marble serves to make their deaths all too real."

"They wouldn't want you to continue to mourn."

"I'm sure they wouldn't. Would you mind allowing me a few moments alone?"

Although she wished he would welcome her nearness, she understood the process of grief, having been close to her grandparents and losing them when she was young. She squeezed his arm again before walking quietly from the building into the sunshine, grateful for its warmth chasing away the chill.

It was several moments before Robert joined her, his eyes reddened slightly, and she thought perhaps he'd wept. She'd never before considered that he was a man of sentiment, of deep emotion. His courtship of her had only allowed the surface of the man to be seen, and she thought it unfair that society didn't allow unmarried couples to spend moments alone so they might come to know each other better before they were expected to know each other intimately.

Glancing around, he took a deep breath, tugging on his gloves. He finally brought his gaze to rest on hers. Yes, she was certain now that he had wept.

"I believe we should attempt to find something a bit more pleasant to do."

"Search for your fox perhaps?"

He appeared momentarily flummoxed, then grinned. "Yes, let's see if we can find my fox."

The last thing Torie had ever expected was to be intrigued by her husband. He was a contradiction, a mystery, a complete . . . stranger.

That was the best way to describe him. As though she was only just being introduced to him.

Perhaps that was the way of marriage. Certainly courtship provided little opportunity to get to know the object of one's affection intimately, which begged the question: what prompted fondness?

She was only now beginning to realize that until she'd actually married Killingsworth, her feelings toward him had all been based on superficial circumstances: the way he danced, the way he carried on a conversation, the color of his hair, the shape of his brow, the knife-edged cut of his nose, his firm chin, his dazzling eyes.

Her assessment of him had been based on nothing of substance, nothing of import. Was it any wonder that so many couples seemed to be unhappy with their choices?

But now at long last, she was coming to know him a bit better, and she realized that he was a man composed of fascinating layers. The way he'd held her in the coach. The way he'd sought to welcome her last night—with warm cocoa. The way he teased the cook. The way he mourned his parents still.

Somewhere she'd once heard that still waters ran deep, and only now was she beginning to understand the complexities of the expression and the complexities of her husband. His public persona was quite different from his private one, and she was discovering that the man riding beside her touched a place deep within her heart that she'd doubted he'd ever be able to reach.

She adored the way he looked at everything as though it was all wondrous, as though he appreciated the simple beauty of the countryside that surrounded them as they rode their horses across a field toward a forest. It was as though he was grateful to be out and about, with the sun warming his face and the song of birds filling the air.

He'd not spoken a single word since they'd left the mausoleum. Occasionally he'd glance over at her, give her an almost shy smile, then look away. She wondered if he was embarrassed because he'd been unable to hide from her the depth of his love for his parents. She thought of explaining that she cared for him that much more because of what she'd witnessed, but she feared it would only serve to distance him, to make him feel more self-conscious. So she sought instead to bring him back to her with a reminder of their present business.

"What will you do with the fox when you find it?" she asked.

His eyes widening, he released a short laugh. "Oh, no, I . . . no, I'm not searching for a fox. I've not ridden in a while—"

"You rode last night when you came in search of me."

"Well, yes, but that hardly counts. My mind was centered on you, not enjoying the feel of a beast beneath me."

"We rode together last week," she reminded him.

He creased his brow. "Yes, but that was in London."

His statement sounded almost like a question, as though he were guessing.

"In Hyde Park," she affirmed.

"It's much different to ride in the country." He brought his horse to a halt near a stand of trees. "I believe I'd like to walk now."

He swung his leg back and dismounted before glancing up at her. "The brush grows thick in there, you might find it easier to walk."

"All right."

He looked up at her, not moving.

She waited. He waited.

Finally she said, "I'll need assistance dismounting."

He jerked slightly as though suddenly awakened from a long nap. "Yes, of course."

He came around and wiped his hands on his trousers before placing them on her waist with such care, as though he thought she was made of glass and easily broken. He'd never touched her with such gentleness, such awareness. Not even when they'd danced.

She unwound her leg from the horn of the sidesaddle and placed her hands on his shoulders, surprised to find them so firm, so sturdy. He seemed slightly broader than she remembered. Perhaps it was simply that she'd only ever placed one hand on one of his shoulders—while dancing.

He lifted her up, held her aloft for a heartbeat, before slowly lowering her to the ground, his eyes locked on hers. For a moment she felt as though she was gazing into those eyes for the first time, as though she'd never before seen them.

They held warmth, wonder; they looked as if he was seeing her as differently as she was seeing him. Perhaps their not rushing into lovemaking was a good thing, because it gave them an opportunity to build the emotional bond between them before they created the physical one.

When her feet touched the ground, she swayed toward him slightly, while his hands remained on her waist. She felt his fingers flex, jerk, while his smoldering eyes dipped down to her lips. She was certain he was going to kiss her, so she couldn't have been more surprised when he suddenly released his hold on her and stepped quickly away.

"I'll just tether the horses so we don't find them gone when we're finished with our exploration of the woods," he said.

She watched as he immersed himself in tying both horses to a low-lying bush. How remarkable that his nature contained a shyness that revealed itself at the oddest of moments.

He turned to her and smiled uncertainly. She didn't know why she found it so endearing, and yet she did.

"Shall we go then?" he asked, nodding his head toward the forest.

"You changed your side whiskers," she

said, wondering why she'd not noticed sooner, wondering if they were the reason that he seemed so different.

Before they had covered a good portion of his cheek, coming down to leave only the strong square of his chin visible. Now he rubbed that chin, those cheeks, his fingers grazing along the thinner side whiskers that went no farther down than his earlobe.

"Yes, this morning. I decided they were a bit bothersome. A tad showy."

She pulled her hands into tight fists to stop herself from doing what she suddenly had an irrational urge to do: brush her fingers over them. "I like the way they look."

He released his self-conscious laugh, dipped his gaze to the ground, then looked back up at her. "Do you?"

"Yes, they're more friendly." She rolled her eyes. "I'm not explaining it well. But they suit you better."

"I shall give your compliments to my valet."

"Please do."

They stood there as though this were an awkward first meeting, unsure what to say, yet feeling the need to say something.

"Follow me," he announced, breaking the spell before heading for the trees.

She hurried to catch up with him, intrigued by this man who was so completely different from the man she'd known in London. If she didn't realize that it was absolutely impossible, she'd think he was someone else entirely.

Robert had only trekked a few feet when the forest thickened, and he decided he'd best stop to wait for his wife. She moved carefully, cautiously, elegantly. He didn't know if he'd ever seen anyone as graceful as she was as she picked her way over the forest floor.

As she neared him, she lifted her gaze, smiled, and with her attention no longer on the ground, she tripped, squeaked—

He quickly reached out, caught her hand, her waist, and it was as though the world receded and time stood still. Although they both wore leather riding gloves, in the coolness of the forest he could feel the heat of her skin mingling with his. He wanted to draw her nearer, press the length of her body against his, until her warmth completely saturated him. At the same time, he wanted to hold her away so he could gaze into her wondrous brown eyes. He'd never seen eyes so large, so lovely, and when she smiled or laughed, they danced like a thousand stars in the night sky.

He could clearly see why his brother had chosen her.

His brother.

And she had chosen John.

The reality of that choice hit him hard in the gut.

"Steady now?" he asked, hoping she didn't detect that he sounded as though he was strangling.

She nodded.

"Good." He let go of her and stepped back. "We should go a bit more slowly, to prevent any mishaps."

"Did you play in this forest when you were a boy?"

He began the journey again, going at a leisurely rate until she fell into step beside him, then increasing his pace only a bit. Her strides weren't as long as his, so he adjusted his to accommodate hers.

He thought for her that he could make many such adjustments. Perhaps his brother had felt the same. Not to the extent that he might have released Robert from his hell, though. To do so would reveal John for the fraud that he was, and a woman who had thought she'd become a duchess would have discovered that she wasn't. Her disappointment might well have made for a miserable marriage.

"Yes," he finally answered, remembering a time when he'd thought he was happy, when he'd loved his brother and thought his brother loved him. He wondered if Abel had possessed the same misconceptions regarding his brother Cain's feelings toward him. At least John hadn't killed Robert. Although there were many moments when Robert had wished he had. Only now he was grateful that he hadn't, grateful for the woman walking beside him, her sweet fragrance wafting over him from time to time to mingle with the pungent earthy smells of the forest that surrounded them.

"What did you play?" she asked.

"The Napoleonic Wars. John liked to be Napoleon."

"And you were Wellington?"

"Of course."

"I always thought it would be great fun to have a twin. Tell me about one of the times when John pretended to be you."

She'd given him the perfect opportunity to

reveal the truth of the situation. *While he was courting you. When he asked for your hand in marriage.*

But he couldn't quite bring himself to do it. He convinced himself that the forest wasn't the proper place for such a revelation, but he suspected his real reason for delaying was the knowledge that with the truth he would lose her completely. And he wasn't quite ready not to have her near.

She'd provided comfort at the mausoleum, and her smiles brought sunshine into his soul. So he would borrow her for a time. John had borrowed a good deal more.

"There were far too many to recall." When they were lads, he'd only found it mildly irritating when he'd discovered that John had been masquerading as him, stealing the first kiss from a girl Robert had favored, convincing Mrs. Cuddleworthy that Robert's favorite dishes were those he abhorred, challenging their father—in the guise of Robert—as Robert never would have, but when the punishment fell, John was suddenly John again, and Robert took the brunt of his father's lectures and firm hand. Even as a lad he'd been unable to prove that John was playing the pranks, that John was pretending to be Robert.

If his own father hadn't believed him, how could he expect the rest of England to see the truth?

Of course, Robert had been equally mischievous when pretending to be John. Torie was correct in her assessment. It had been quite fun to fool people—but John had taken their games too far. They were men now, and it was time for them to behave as such and to put away their childish pranks.

"Bad memories?"

He twisted his head to look at her. The depth with which she studied him astounded him. He'd expected his brother to marry a woman with little sense and a voluptuous body . . . not that he found fault with Victoria's body. She was trim, but not overly so. He could well imagine that a man would find great satisfaction in gliding his hands over her—

She stopped walking and whispered, "Robert, you're going away again."

Going away? Drifting into thoughts that he couldn't invite her to share. He stopped as well. "My apologies. You asked about the memories."

"Yes, you were scowling."

"I was simply remembering all the times that John pretended to be me and got me into trouble."

"As you did him."

"Yes."

"I always thought it was the role of brothers and sisters to get the other into trouble."

"Yes, but John would take it to the extreme. And I bore the brunt of his pranks—which I think was the real purpose behind the pranks. Not pretending to be me to see if he could get away with it, but pretending to be me so he could get me into trouble."

"And if he got you into trouble, then he succeeded at the pretense, which must have been a victory as well."

"I suppose you're right."

"Why do you think—" she began, but he heard a slight brushing noise nearby and placed a finger against her lips, trying to ignore the warmth of her breath traveling over his glove, more than ready to turn the direction of the conversation away from his memories of John. "Come," he whispered.

Taking her hand, he carefully threaded his way through the brush until the clearing and the small pond he remembered became visible. Just as he suspected . . .

He pulled her in front of him, taking delight at her soft intake of breath as she looked at the doe and the fawn sipping from the pond.

She twisted around to look at him, and the beauty of her smile, the dimple in her cheek, the joy in her eyes was his undoing. He removed his glove and touched the strands of her hair that had escaped the pins holding them in place. So soft. Then he touched her cheek. Silk beneath his fingertips.

"You are so lovely." In spite of his best intentions, he lowered his mouth to hers, drawing the taste of her into his own, relishing the heat therein, the moistness of her lips, the rasp of her tongue over his.

He didn't remember reaching for her, pulling her against him, but suddenly she was there, her curves flattened against his chest, her hands resting on his shoulders. Like a man drowning, searching for salvation, he deepened the kiss, sweeping his tongue through her mouth, wanting more, so much more, his body aching with needs unfulfilled, needs that were not hers to satisfy . . .

In spite of papers that stated otherwise, she belonged to John.

In spite of the fact that John had strived to take everything from him, Robert would not take from his brother that to which he had no right.

He broke off the kiss, stumbled back, breathing heavily. She was staring at him, her own breathing labored, her lips swollen, her cheeks flushed, the dimple gone as though it had never been.

"My apologies," he stammered. "I had no right."

"You're my husband. You have every right."

"Not in the forest."

She laid her hand on his chest, just above his heart, and he wondered if she could feel the steady, hard pounding that he thought might be in danger of cracking his ribs.

Her dimple appeared. "And not in a coach."

He shook his head, swallowed hard. "No, not in a coach."

"And not when you're weary."

"Not when I'm weary."

She angled her head thoughtfully. "If you didn't look at me as though you might devour me on the spot, like you are some primal beast that might reside in these very woods, I might think that you have no interest in me whatsoever."

He lifted his gaze to the canopy of branches above him. Perhaps if he counted the number of leaves, the evidence of his desire for her would dwindle. "Trust me, Torie, I have a good deal of interest in you."

"Then why do you work so hard not to express that interest?"

He looked down to find the dimple gone and concern mirrored in her eyes. How to adequately explain his behavior without revealing the truth or increasing suspicion?

"As you've said, we've had little time alone. I thought it would be best to ease into the intimacy."

She slid her hand up his chest, his neck, until she cradled his jaw. "I'm not frightened. I know you won't hurt me, so don't take too long . . . easing into . . . anything."

Before he could react, she spun around, leaving him to wonder if there were double meanings to her words, if she were aware of them, embarrassed by them.

Dear God, but she tempted him to lay her down now, here, on the forest floor. Take her, so there would be no returning her to John. Hold her, because he had no desire to let her go.

He cleared his throat. "I think we should return to the manor." *Before I do something we'll both regret.*

She glanced over her shoulder at him, giving him a teasing smile, something in her eyes telling him that she knew the battles he waged and that she would see to it that he gained no victory, and in losing he would win.

But would she feel that she had lost?

Abruptly she averted her attention and began trudging along the path they'd taken to arrive at this spot, and he fell into step behind her.

It was imperative that he set himself to the task of proving himself as soon as possible, more important than undoing the damage to the estates that his brother had managed. He could take care of everything later, set it all to rights.

For now, he must rid himself of this woman before she brought him to the edge of insanity that he'd managed to avoid while in Pentonville.

Chapter 12

He didn't say another word until they arrived at Hawthorne House. And even then, it was merely "I'll see you at dinner" after he'd walked her back to the manor and seen her safely inside.

Then he went back outside. She crossed over to a window and looked out. He was strolling up the wide cobbled path that led to the manor, his hands clasped behind his back, his head bent. Dejected. He appeared to be utterly dejected and so incredibly alone.

Why was he not seeking her company to ease his loneliness? It made no sense. He drew her near only to push her away.

During the late afternoon, she spent an inordinate amount of time preparing for dinner. She chose a lilac gown trimmed in Brussels lace. A string of pearls adorned her throat. Simple yet elegant. She wore her hair pinned into a stylish coiffure.

Based on her husband's reaction when she joined him in the library, she'd met with success at presenting herself in an alluring fashion. He stood by the fireplace, a white-knuckled hand gripping the mantel as though it was the only thing preventing him from rushing forward to take her in his arms. It was an incredible thrill to see such blatant desire smoldering in his eyes.

While he'd always provided her with attention, in the past two days the intensity of it was sharpening. She understood it completely, because she was feeling the same way. A tightening in her midsection that caused her breasts to tingle and her lower regions to shimmer. A need to touch him and to be stroked by him.

The heat was building, and she considered that when they did finally come together, they might ignite a conflagration that would set the bed afire.

"Would you like some wine before dinner?" he asked, his voice raw, the words sounding as though they'd been pushed up from the soles of his feet.

"Yes, please."

He released his death grip on the mantel and walked over to a small table where several decanters rested. Although his back was to her, she could hear the clatter of glasses hitting each other, like someone unable to control trembling hands. She watched as he grew momentarily still, the clattering absent when he continued with his task.

He turned back to her, and she discovered, much to her disappointment, that he'd successfully banked his desires. She took the glass he offered.

He tapped his glass against hers. "To your happiness."

"To yours," she replied, studying him over the rim as she sipped the dark red wine.

He took a gulp, then backed away, moving closer to the fire. Normally in summer a fire wasn't necessary, but this manor was ancient and drafty, and a chill lingered. She was tempted to step nearer to him to see if he'd take another step away. She thought she might be able to march him around the room with such a ploy. Instead she ran a finger around the edge of the glass.

"You look particularly handsome this evening," she offered. "But then, like most ladies, I've always found you incredibly attractive."

He looked down at the floor, leaving her to wonder if he was seeking his reflection in the polished wood. "Sometimes, when I glance in the mirror, I'm surprised to discover how . . . old I appear."

"Oh, yes, you're quite the ancient one."

He lifted his gaze to her. "I do feel that way at times."

She eased closer to the warmth of the fire, standing nearer to him, grateful when he didn't dart away. "I believe men grow more handsome with age. I'm not certain women grow more beautiful."

"I can't imagine you being anything except beautiful."

"But when I am wrinkled and withered—"

"Your eyes and your smile are where your beauty lie."

"Here you are being poetic again."

"Truth is its own type of poetry."

She felt the heat rise up from her chest to

her cheeks. "I never realized before how seldom you and I truly talked. We always played word games or gossiped about Lady Sylvia's atrocious attire or Lord Eastland's attempt to cover his balding pate by combing all his hair forward. I prefer our present conversation."

"As do I." Taking her glass from her, he stepped over to the table and set them down. "We should go to dinner now."

"I thought perhaps we should consider entertaining soon," Torie said when they were very nearly finished eating, dinner enjoyed in near-perfect silence, with only the occasional scraping of silver across china to serve as evidence that anyone inhabited the room. He'd always been such an entertaining conversationalist at dinner parties that she was surprised to discover that in the privacy of his home, he preferred not to be bothered with small talk.

He stilled his wineglass halfway to his lips. "Perhaps in a few months—after we've settled into marriage."

"I know you are good friends with the Marquess of Lynmore. Who else would you care to invite?"

He took a sip of wine, seemed to enjoy it, before saying, "The Duke of Weddington was always a close friend."

"That revelation surprises me. You gave him a cut direct when our paths crossed in the machinery gallery at the Great Exhibition."

He looked at her as though she'd suddenly announced that the sun had fallen from the sky. He downed the remainder of his wine and stood. "We'll discuss the particulars of whom to invite at another time. If you'll excuse me, I have some other matters to which I must attend, and I don't wish to be disturbed. I'll see you at breakfast."

He strode from the room, leaving her to feel as though she'd done something terribly wrong—once again.

What the deuce was the Great Exhibition? How great was it? What was being exhibited? Machines obviously, but what else? Where was it? Why was it?

What else had happened while he was imprisoned?

He'd thought his greatest fear had come from not knowing how to talk to his wife, but he could slip up with the tiniest assumption—that the monarchy still existed . . . who the deuce was the prime minister? What colonies did England still possess?

Pacing in the library, he wondered where he'd find all the answers. He couldn't just blurt out, "Oh, by the by, could you share the particulars of all that has transpired during the past eight years?"

Wouldn't that raise his wife's suspicions? Although he stood a good chance of having already done so.

She was gorgeous beyond measure, and he'd not taken advantage of his wedding night. Only a madman would be avoiding her. Wouldn't that be an incredible irony—to survive Pentonville without going insane only to end up in an insane asylum?

His behavior was erratic. He knew it, and he could see her reacting to it. He could see her testing him, weighing his reactions. She was no doubt struggling to understand the reasons behind his strange behavior.

He dropped into a chair, placed his elbows on his knees, and buried his face in his hands. He'd set himself an impossible task. Perhaps he should simply go to the Lord High Chancellor and lay out his case.

Sweet Lord, but he felt as though he were living in the Alexandre Dumas novel he'd begun reading last night in an effort to distract himself from thoughts of his wife when sleep wouldn't come. Only he had no musketeers to save him. He had no one except himself.

And what a dreadful, ineffectual righter of wrongs he was turning out to be.

Torie told herself that she should retire for the evening. Return to her bedchamber and . . . sulk. Only she'd never been much for sulking. It seemed to be a behavior that turned on itself. The more one sulked, the more one felt like sulking. As last night had proven when she'd taken her fateful walk.

Although her husband had indicated that he had no wish to be disturbed, she found herself walking to the library anyway. To find a book to comfort her as she lay in bed awaiting her husband's arrival. For surely tonight, after the near lovely day they'd had, he would come to her. She knew he desired her, so why did talk of Weddington send him from the dining room?

The footman dressed in burgundy livery bowed slightly and opened the door.

She walked into the library. The room seemed to stretch forever from the doorway to the far side where the large stone fireplace dominated the wall. Even as she side-stepped the various tables and chairs, her attention was drawn to the portrait. The duchess before her had been a lovely woman, her sons, even in youth, foreshadowing the charm that would draw Torie to one of them.

Her husband, who had been sitting behind the desk, came to his feet. "I told you that I didn't wish to be disturbed."

"I thought to find a book to read," she told him. "And this seemed to be the room for doing that."

"I would appreciate it if you'd be quick about it so I might return to my affairs."

"And what affairs would those be?"

He looked as though she'd tossed cold water on him. "They are not your concern."

Perhaps not, but still she was curious, more about his behavior than what he was busy with.

She ambled over to the side of the room where the shelves ran from the floor to the ceiling. "Are the books in any particular order?"

"The books were my father's collection. I never paid any attention to how he arranged them."

She peered over at him. “You once told me that you had a passion for books.”

“A passion for books, yes. Arranging them, no.”

She ran her fingers over the spines. “What is your favorite story?”

“I don’t have a favorite.”

“Everyone has a favorite.”

He sighed. “Very well. *The Last of the Mohicans*.”

“How interesting. I suppose it’s the adventure of it.”

“I suppose. What’s your favorite?”

His voice contained less tartness as though he’d accepted that she wouldn’t be put off so easily.

“*Jane Eyre*.”

He shook his head. “I’m not familiar with that author.”

Laughing, she shook her head. “Honestly, Robert, you’re such a tease. Charlotte Brontë is the author. Her sister wrote *Wuthering Heights*. Heathcliff is the terribly tortured hero in that one. He’s the reason the story is one of Diana’s favorites. She loves men who are tormented.”

“And yet your sister struck me as having such a sweet disposition.”

"Oh, she does! Besides, she doesn't torture the men"—she furrowed her brow—"although I daresay she may try, if any want to seriously court her."

She returned to searching the shelves for something to catch her interest. "Oh, look, your father has a copy of *David Copperfield*." Furrowing her brow, she touched the spine. "Only Dickens didn't publish this story until after your father died." She looked over her shoulder at Robert.

He took a step back from his desk, suddenly appearing uncertain, trapped like an animal that realizes too late that it had stepped where it shouldn't have. "Of course I've purchased books since his death, but I leave the arrangement of the books up to the servants."

"Perhaps I should try to catalogue all the books," she offered. "Organize them in a manner that would make it easier for us to locate what we were searching for."

"I rather like being surprised by what I find," he said, leaving her with the impression that he might not be talking only of books.

"I enjoy reading aloud," she told him. "May I read to you this evening?"

"Torie, I really do have things which require my attention."

"Can you not do them while I read?"

He appeared to be on the verge of allowing her in . . .

"I'm lonely, Robert," she added.

He swept his hand toward a chair near the fire. "Please, it would bring me immense pleasure, if you have the time."

"I have nothing but time presently."

Because it was handy, she selected *David Copperfield*. She sat in the chair, and Robert joined her, sitting in the one opposite hers.

"I thought you were going to try to tend to matters while I read," she said.

"I changed my mind."

"What were you doing before I disturbed you?"

He looked into the fire. "Contemplating the merits of writing a letter to Weddington to ask for permission to call on him."

"So we'll return to London?"

"I suspect he is at Drummond Manor, near the coast. It's only a couple of hours from here. But if he's not there, then no, I'm not quite ready to return to London."

"Do you remember when—"

"I thought you were going to read aloud."

She was slightly embarrassed by his tone, not truly chastisement, but it was laced with a bit of impatience. She opened the book and began to read.

Robert didn't know why he'd attempted to dissuade her from reading. Perhaps because the more time he spent with her, the more difficult it would be to let her go when the day came that he had no choice.

He loved the gentle lilt of her voice. He tried to listen to the story but he found himself becoming lost in her. He was becoming hopelessly besotted.

She wasn't flirting with him or playing coy or teasing him. She was simply reading from the book, her head bent. Yet he thought he would be content if the remainder of his years were spent doing nothing except this: sitting in the shadows of her presence.

Torie lay beneath her covers, her breathing shallow as she listened to the creaking floorboards, signaling once again that her husband was pacing.

It had been nearly ten when she'd given in to weariness and set the book aside. Robert had barely moved a muscle from the moment she began reading, his elbow resting on the arm of the chair, his chin propped on his hand, his head titled slightly, his gaze unwavering. Or so it seemed when she would periodically look up to find him intently listening as though enthralled by the story.

So she'd continued on, longer than she might have otherwise. She'd never known anyone to take such a keen interest in her reading aloud.

He'd escorted her to her bedchamber, bid her good night, and she'd heard the door to his room open and close. She'd been so certain that after the day and evening they'd shared, he would come to her. Once Charity had prepared her for bed and left the room, Torie had done her own pacing for a few minutes before finally taking a deep breath and clambering into bed. She'd fanned her hair out across the pillows, then brought the covers up to her chin, lowered them to her chest, then to her waist.

As she'd lain there, as still as death, with the lamp turned low, and her gaze on the canopy above, she'd begun to hear the pacing.

Why didn't he come?

She contemplated getting out of bed and knocking on his door, alerting him to the fact that she was prepared for him. But that action seemed far too bold, and surely the pacing would soon stop and he would join her.

After a while she began to twiddle her thumbs, then to count the squares on the ceiling and the ticking of the clock on the mantel.

Why didn't he come?

When her eyes began to burn and fill with water, she told herself it was because she'd read for too long. When a clock in the hallway announced the arrival of midnight, and the pacing finally stopped, but her husband did not come to see her, she rolled onto her side and let the tears she'd been holding at bay roll silently along her cheek and onto the pillow.

Chapter 13

To the Duke of Weddington—

It has been a while, my friend. I would like permission to call upon you at Drummond Manor.

Sincerely,
Robert, the Duke of Killingsworth

To the Duke of Killingsworth—

I think not.

Weddington

Robert had tucked the missive from Weddington inside the pocket of his jacket, and it felt like a heavy weight sitting there as the coach traveled toward Drummond Manor. He was being a bit of a coward by not going alone, but he thought Weddington might not be so quick to slam the door in his face if Torie was with him.

After she had asked him about his friends, to whom he might be close, and she'd revealed that John had snubbed Weddington, it occurred to him that his old friend might be someone he could trust.

Weddington's curt note told Robert more about the state of their friendship than any longer missive might have. He and Weddington had been friends at school, had yachted together. That the man wasn't willing to see him . . .

Well, he had no doubt that John had been responsible, and it involved more than simply a cut direct. John's actions made perfect, yet irritating sense. Replace his valet . . . replace his trusted friend.

Now if Robert could only earn back Weddington's trust, he might discover some way to prove the facts of his case.

And he needed to do that as quickly as

possible because it was becoming more difficult not to open the door that separated his bedchamber from hers.

Each moment spent with her was pure pleasure, except for those rare moments when he could see doubt surfacing in her eyes, doubt because she required more from him than he could give to her. Countless times he'd convinced himself to tell her everything, but then she would smile at him, and the thought of never having that smile directed at him was enough to make him rethink his decision. It was selfish on his part, and unfair to her, but he'd gone so long without so much that he was like a starving man desperate enough to settle for crumbs and instead finding himself offered a feast.

He told himself that tomorrow he would tell her . . . and when tomorrow arrived, he convinced himself that the next day would be better . . . and now he'd decided to wait until after they visited Weddington. If Weddington rejected him, Robert might very well need the solace that Torie could provide.

"What do you know of his wife?" she asked unexpectedly, breaking into his thoughts.

"Whose wife?"

"Weddington's."

Nothing at all. He hadn't even known he had a wife. Damnation, when had that happened?

"I'm certain she loves him. He is the type of man that I think any woman would adore."

"How long have you and Weddington been friends?"

"We met at Eton. As our estates are only a few hours' apart, we spent considerable time together when we weren't at school. We both took a fancy to yachting, and Weddington's home is almost at the water's edge. I wouldn't be surprised to learn he was boating before he was walking."

"You've never spoken much about your friends."

"I had so few. John and I being so close in age . . . well, he rather filled my need for a friend. And I his, I suppose. But Weddington, well, I trusted him and came to respect him greatly. We've grown apart over the years, and I regret that. Quite honestly, I'm not certain what sort of welcome we'll receive."

"Based upon the incident at the Great Exhibition, I fear we won't receive a welcome at all."

"Perhaps I shouldn't have asked you to

join me. If you're terribly uncomfortable with the notion of going there, I'll have the coach turned about—"

"No." She shook her head slightly. "My place is at your side."

How he wished that sentiment was true.

"I couldn't have selected a finer lady to be my wife," he said quietly.

"Sometimes I have the impression that you're not at all happy with me."

"Your presence fills me with immeasurable joy."

"Why do you pace your bedchamber rather than coming to mine?"

He glanced out the window, not wishing to hurt her and realizing that it was not enough to simply wish for something. "I didn't realize you could hear me pacing."

"It's an old house. The floors creak."

He turned his attention back to her. "Do you want me to come to your bedchamber?"

She lowered her gaze to her gloved hands, resting in her lap.

"You'd mentioned that you had doubts about our marriage the morning of the wedding. I thought perhaps you would appreciate a little more time . . ." Dear God, but the lie didn't roll easily off his tongue.

She lifted her eyes to his. "The doubts are waning. I've seen aspects to you that I'd never before known, and I'm certain I'm married to the man I was destined to wed."

"Torie—"

"My feelings for you have grown, Robert. I know it has been little more than a week, but I care for you much more today than I did yesterday. Do you care for me?"

"Immeasurably."

"You say that as though it is a terrible thing."

It was. To yearn so desperately for something he couldn't have. He was growing weary of worrying that Torie would figure him out, but now was the worst time of all to tell her everything—when they were nearing their destination. So instead, he leaned across the space separating them, took her hands, and told her what he could.

"Torie, I know my behavior at times must seem odd to you—"

"I simply—"

"Shh." He squeezed his hands. "Hear me out."

She nodded.

He brought her gloved hands up to his mouth, held them against his lips, looking deeply into her eyes, hoping that she could see into his soul. "Torie, for quite some time, I've been . . . lost. I think that's the best way to describe it. But at long last, I feel as though I'm found."

A corner of her mouth quirked, her dimple appeared. "Those are words from a hymn I used to love to sing. 'Amazing Grace.' "

"Ah, yes, I remember the words. But in my case, it's more of a returning."

"Returning to what?"

"To what I should have been."

"I've never found fault with the way that you were."

"I wasn't happy, Torie. So much changed the day I married you." He pressed a kiss to her knuckles. "I still can't believe my good fortune. I quite honestly adore you."

He released her hands and settled back against the seat, embarrassed by all that he'd said. He'd gone a bit too far, but he wanted her to have no doubts regarding his affections, especially if she was lying awake at night waiting for him to come while he was busy pacing, trying to keep himself from reaching for the door.

"Ah, we're here," he said, as the familiar drive came into view.

The coach rocked to a stop. Although he

was anxious to be out and to see about business, he waited for the footman to open the door and to help Torie clamber out first. Coward that he was, he'd avoided looking directly at her, not certain what he might see in her eyes, in her face. Thinking it better to live his life in ignorant bliss of her true feelings, because whatever she felt would be for John, not him.

Once outside, he extended his arm, and once she'd placed her hand on it, he escorted her up the steps that led to the grand manor. He felt his stomach clench as he got nearer the door, and when the butler opened it, it was all he could do to force himself to go against his good friend's wishes and enter.

But once inside, calmness settled over him. He'd been as at home here as he'd been at Hawthorne House.

"Welcome to Drummond Manor, Your Grace," the butler said.

"Watkins." He extended his card. "Will you let the duke know that I'm here?"

"Certainly."

His wife had released her hold on him and was studying several portraits hanging on one of the walls.

"Nervous?" he asked.

"A bit."

"He's really quite nice."

"I've heard he's a distant cousin to the queen."

"So am I."

She spun around, her mouth open, her eyes wide.

He cocked his head to the side. "Did I fail to mention that?"

"Yes, you did."

"Don't let it unnerve you. Most of the aristocracy are related in some form or fashion."

He heard the soft patter of footsteps, turned toward them, and knew a moment of gladness as the small, smiling woman held her arms out to him. "Eleanor?"

"Hello, Robert. It's been a long time."

Indeed it had. Eleanor Darling, the Earl of Beaumont's daughter. The first time he'd set eyes on her, he'd considered courting her. But he'd not yet been ready to court, and she'd been only sixteen. That Weddington had not hesitated to woo her didn't surprise him.

He took her proffered hand and placed a kiss on the back of it. "You look marvelous."

She laughed. "You don't. Your complexion looks a bit sallow."

"All the rain, I fear."

"There hasn't been that much, and it's a beautiful day today."

"So it is. Allow me the honor of introducing my wife."

Eleanor was as gracious as always in welcoming her guests, and Robert couldn't help but believe that Torie held her own, and that she would do well as a duchess. Even if only for a short time.

When Eleanor turned her attention back to him, he asked, "Will Weddington not see me?"

"He's not here. He's out on the yacht with Richard."

She gave him a look that seemed to say "Don't give me that blank expression. You know who Richard is."

"Our son," she continued.

"Ah, yes. Congratulations are in order."

"You're five years late."

"Five years." He hoped she heard the regret in his voice, and he was beginning to suspect that where this friendship was concerned, John might have done something that Robert couldn't undo. "Perhaps I shouldn't be here when he returns. I'd sent him a missive and he'd replied—"

"I know what he replied. He and I don't

keep secrets from each other. The fact that you came anyway says a great deal." She reached up and cradled his cheek. "A great deal. And I think he'll welcome it as a start for mending the rift between you. Shall we have some tea in the garden while we wait for him to return?"

Torie liked Eleanor Stanbury, the Duchess of Weddington. She had light blue eyes and a warm smile, and when she spoke of her husband and son, the love she felt for them was evident in every word.

"Richard is so much like his father. You won't believe it, Robert. It's like watching a tiny Weddy walking around. He already has most of his mannerisms. It's uncanny."

"I can't wait to meet him."

She reached across the round cloth-covered table and patted his hand. "I've wanted you to meet him for so long. I'm extremely glad you're here."

Torie found the woman's affection for Robert heartwarming, and she couldn't help but wonder what had caused the rift between her husband and Weddington.

"So tell me about your wedding, Victoria,"

Eleanor said, turning her attention away from Robert.

"Please call me Torie."

"Oh, I rather like that. So tell me, Torie. Was the church packed to the rafters with the curious?"

"I hardly noticed," Torie confessed. "I was so nervous, terrified actually."

"I know exactly what you mean. It was the happiest day of my life and I hardly remember a moment of it. And Weddy was so incredibly patient with me. I did little more than burst into tears every five minutes. I don't know why. Tell me what you wore."

"It was really nothing special."

"You were beautiful, the gown was beautiful," Robert said. "White satin and lace, with flowers trimming the train."

Eleanor smiled. "Like Queen Victoria's. Mine was very similar. You know she changed weddings for all of us. Before her, a girl would simply wear a nice dress and veil. The veil was the adornment that said, Today I'm getting married. But now it's white satin and Honiton lace and pearls and orange blossoms. I've put my gown aside, hoping I'll have a daughter someday. But first I must see to giving Weddy a spare. A bit of a bother, that. Not the having of the children, of course, but that it's so expected that a woman provide two sons. Otherwise, it doesn't matter what she does, she's considered a failure."

"You'd never be considered a failure, Eleanor," Robert said.

She smiled warmly. "So kind of you to think so."

"So you only have the one child?" Torie asked.

"Yes. I haven't given up hope yet, but it's been five years. Actually that's the reason we're here instead of London. Weddy is convinced that the good salt air in summer is just what we need to help the process along."

"And how long have you been married now?" Robert asked.

Eleanor slid her gaze over to him. "I'd have thought you'd not forget that."

He darted his gaze between Eleanor and Torie, and she felt a trifle sorry for him, as though he'd been placed on the spot and wasn't certain why.

"I'm sorry—" he began.

"A little over five years," Eleanor cut in.

"We were married eight months exactly before Richard was born. Weddy and I were under the impression that you were largely responsible for the gossip going about London that I took great pains to seduce Weddy and get myself with child so he'd have no choice except to marry me."

Torie thought her husband looked as though he wished the sea—visible in the distance—would wash up over him and carry him away.

"Were we wrong?" Eleanor asked.

She watched her husband swallow. "I don't know what to say, Eleanor, except that I'm sorry and regret any hurt that words spoken against you might have caused you."

"That's not really an answer is it?"

"No, no, it's not, but it's the best I can offer at the moment."

She reached across the table and squeezed his hand. "You changed, Robert, after the dukedom passed to you. Weddy missed you terribly. He won't appreciate me telling you that—pride and all that rubbish—but there you are." She perked up, a smile blossoming across her face. "And there *they* are!"

She came to her feet and began waving.

Robert and Torie also stood. Torie could see the large, dark-haired man walking, a small, dark-haired boy balanced on his shoulders. Torie saw the man's long strides falter, slow, then he swung the boy down, held him close in his arms, and quickened his pace.

When he was near enough, Eleanor called out, "Weddy, look who's come to visit. The long-lost prodigal friend."

She moved around the table, meeting her husband a few feet from them, reaching up to kiss his cheek, to take their son. The duke's jaw was clenched, his eyes hard as he glowered at Robert.

"Weddington, it's good to see you," Robert finally said.

"Killingsworth."

"Weddy, allow me to introduce Robert's wife, Torie."

Weddington looked at her, and she was vaguely aware of Robert stepping nearer to her as though he thought she might be in danger. Considering the hatred on Weddington's face, she thought she might very well be.

"A pleasure," Weddington said, although it sounded as though he found it to be anything but a pleasure. His gaze slid over to Robert.

"So tell me, Killingsworth, what rumors should I start spreading around London? What can I say about her that will cut deeply?"

"Don't say something right now that you'll regret," Robert warned.

"I already regret that I greeted you, that I've spoken to you at all."

"He apologized, Weddy," Eleanor said.

Weddington cradled his wife's cheek, the love for her reflected in his eyes running so deeply that it took Torie's breath.

"You're owed more than an apology, princess." He shifted his gaze back to Robert. "If you're not in your coach and on your way in less than three minutes, I shall unlock the case holding my father's dueling pistols—"

"Unlock it."

"—and challenge you—"

"Challenge me."

"—to a duel unto the death."

"So be it."

"Are you mad!" Torie cried.

"Weddy, no!" Eleanor screeched.

"You have five minutes to kiss your wife good-bye for eternity," Weddington said, with the ease of a man about to take a stroll. "I'll meet you at the bluff in ten."

He strode past his wife and into the manor.

Eleanor looked at Torie, then at Robert, then at the son she held in her arms. "Oh, my dear, this isn't good. It's not good at all." She started for the house, stopped, looked back at Robert. "Don't worry, Robert, I'll talk him out of it."

"Don't bother, Eleanor. He needs this, deserves it, actually."

"Dueling might be frowned upon these days but firing the pistols at a target isn't. He's a rather good shot."

"I know. He's an excellent shot."

"I'm sorry. This is my fault. I should have sent you on your way—"

"No, Eleanor, it's not your fault. Help him get ready."

Eleanor released what sounded like a whimper of pain before hurrying into the manor.

"Are you insane?" Torie asked her husband.

He gave her a droll look. "I believe you already asked me that."

"No, I asked if you were mad."

"The same thing."

"You can't possibly intend to meet him."

"I do."

"You don't have a second."

"I won't need one."

"Have you ever fired a pistol before?"

"When we were fourteen, we sneaked his father's pistols out and went to the bluff to give dueling a try."

"And what happened?"

"He missed me and hit a rock."

"And what did you hit?"

He rubbed the bridge of his nose. "A seagull. We decided that a seagull was more difficult to hit since it was in motion, even though it wasn't what I was aiming at. Still we declared me the winner."

"His anger was palpable. I don't see him taking aim at a rock!"

"He wasn't aiming at it before—"

"Don't make light of my fears! He could very well kill you."

"If he does, I should like very much for my last memory to be of kissing you."

He cupped her face between his large hands, angled her head, and lowered his mouth to hers. He tasted of sweetened tea and raspberry tarts. His kiss was as tender as anything she'd ever experienced. Bolder than any kiss he'd given her before, hungry, devastating to her heart.

She didn't want this. She didn't want his

thumbs caressing the corners of her mouth, making the kiss more intimate than it should be. Or perhaps it was his tongue creating the intimacy as it swept through her mouth, deepening the kiss. Or perhaps it was the fact that she was leaning into him, reaching for his mouth, his lips, his tongue, spurring him on, adding to the madness of the moment.

He couldn't possibly think that he would actually die. Surely this was some sort of prank. A jest that the two friends went through whenever they came together. Like two ladies exchanging shopping hints, revealing the best place to purchase a fan or a scarf. Only they exchanged bullets.

She pulled back. "This is madness."

"I know."

He returned his mouth to hers with an urgency that belied the calmness of the words he'd spoken. She was referring to the duel, but she had a feeling that he was referring to the kiss. One had spawned the other. So they were linked.

She felt an unexplainable sorrow, as though she'd married a man she thought she knew, only to discover that she was married to a man she knew not at all and was suddenly wishing she knew better.

She placed her hands over his where they cradled her face, and she wondered what it would feel like to have them touch her with the same tenderness that his mouth was now exhibiting.

He'd confessed that for a time he was lost . . . and she didn't know if she should be more frightened. Would he become lost again?

He broke free of the kiss, pressed his forehead to hers. "If I don't come back—"

"You don't truly think that he's going to kill you."

He pulled back slightly, holding her gaze. "The Duke of Killingsworth insulted his wife. I think he might very well seek retribution."

"Death for an insult is hardly equal. Let him blacken your eye or bloody your nose."

He smiled sadly as he trailed his finger over her trembling lips. "It wouldn't be enough for me if I were in his place."

Then he turned and began walking away from her, away from the manor.

She was left forlorn and alone, with the realization that she didn't know this man at all. Not at all.

A few minutes later, Eleanor came out of the manor, holding on to her son's hand.

"Weddy has gone to meet him. Would you like a cup of tea?"

Men went off to battle, and ladies manned the home front. Torie could do little more than nod.

And so they sat at the table in the garden with the breeze stirring the sides of the tablecloth, the tea cooling in the untouched china cups, the sun shining overhead. They discussed the latest dress patterns, the flowers, the weather, and how remarkable it was that Richard so resembled his father, each one pretending to care about any topic the other presented.

A half hour passed before a gunshot sounded in the distance. A few seconds later another shot echoed.

Chapter 14

Robert stood at the edge of the cliff, staring down at the waves washing over the rocks and the shore, not thinking of his impending death but thinking of Torie, his wife.

He'd enjoyed watching her as she'd visited with Eleanor. He had to give John credit; he'd chosen an exemplary lady to serve as the Duchess of Killingsworth. She fascinated him, and he'd seen in her eyes true concern at the possibility of his death. And her kiss of farewell . . .

He could still taste it upon his lips.

She loved his brother. Of that he had no doubt, and he knew a moment of despair that far exceeded anything he'd experienced during the last eight years. She could never be his, he could never hold her heart.

He told himself there were other women. That if he resolved this encounter and managed to hold on to his dukedom, he could release her and find someone else to take her place. But would any other woman exhibit her combination of shyness and boldness? Would another woman have her smile or her laughter? Would he find such pleasure in simply gazing upon another woman as he did looking at her?

It was selfish of him to bring her here, but he couldn't quite make himself not be with her as much as possible.

He heard grass rasping against cloth, boots hitting against ground. The arrival of his opponent. A man he'd always considered his one true friend. John had even managed to strip him of that. He'd taken every blessed thing, and he'd hurt people in doing it.

Even as Robert knew, *knew*, he'd not been in a position to stop his brother, still he felt responsible. He was the true Duke of Killingsworth, and while he'd not been wearing the mantle, still, the responsibilities of righting the wrongs committed by his brother fell to him.

Weddy—otherwise known as Geoffrey Arthur Stanbury, the fifth Duke of Weddington—came to stand beside him. He inhaled deeply. "A storm is brewing."

"So it is." It was more than the darkening clouds, it was the scent on the air.

"Then we'd best get to the task at hand. Your body will be soaked in blood when I carry it back to the manor. I'd rather it not be soaked in rain as well."

"I thought perhaps you'd choose to toss me into the sea afterward."

"Eleanor insists that I carry you back, allow you to have a proper burial." He thrust the open case in front of Robert. "Since we have no seconds, you are free to inspect the pistols and choose your weapon first."

Robert pulled a pistol free from the case. "No need to inspect them. I trust you."

"The rules we used as boys?"

"Of course."

"Do try to aim a little better. No sense in denying the sky its right to be filled with birds."

Weddington grabbed the remaining pistol,

dropped the intricately carved wooden case to the ground, and spun on his heel.

"I do have one favor to ask," Robert said, again staring at the sea.

"No need to ask. I'll put the bullet right through your heart. Your death will be quick. I can't say the same for the embarrassment you caused Eleanor. It lingered for some time."

"That's not the favor." He turned slowly and held the gaze of a man he'd once called friend. "If you should succeed—and I've no doubt that you will—I ask that you go to Pentonville and use whatever influence you have to meet with Prisoner D3, 10."

"And what message do I deliver?"

"I think you'll know when you see him."

"That's a cryptic sort of favor, but consider it done." He angled his head slightly. "Now, shall we?"

"We shall."

They walked out several feet, then stood back to back.

"Ten paces," Weddington announced.

Robert marked off the steps.

One.

He should have told Torie the truth from the beginning.

Two.

She wouldn't be allowed to marry John after having married his brother.

Three.

Hell for John.

Four.

Unfair to her.

Five.

He should tell Weddington the truth.

Six.

But if even his best friend couldn't discern the difference between the brothers . . .

Seven.

Weddington would no doubt call John out once he realized the truth of the situation.

Eight.

Who was next in line for the dukedom if Weddington killed John?

Nine.

Wasn't there a cousin somewhere?

Ten.

Dash it all. It no longer mattered.

He turned. Weddington already had the pistol raised, his aim steady.

"Are you ready?" Weddington asked.

"Yes."

"Fire!"

Robert waited. Weddington waited.

Robert swung his arm out to the side, raising it to the level of his shoulder, and fired his bullet out to sea. He heard a bird squawk. Damnation, he hoped he hadn't hit it, but he wouldn't look, wouldn't avert his gaze from death. He wanted to be facing it when it arrived.

He heard the explosion echoing around him, saw the smoke billowing from Weddington's pistol, but felt nothing other than the wind rustling his clothing.

Weddington took several steps toward him. "Robert?"

"Who the deuce did you think I was?"

"Your coward of a brother. Where the devil have you been?"

"Five years ago, I suspected it was John pretending to be you, spreading the malicious rumors, but I could no more prove it than you can now prove that you are Robert."

They had trudged down the uneven trail from the cliff above to the shore below, until they reached a boulder at the edge of the sea. They sat on it, gazing out at the turbulent waters, and Robert couldn't help but think how much those waves reflected his life.

"So you think he paid a warder to hold you at Pentonville without benefit of trial?"

"I must confess to not having a very active imagination. That's the only explanation at which I can arrive with any satisfaction. Besides, the warder came to the house to tell John when I escaped. He seemed quite distraught by my disappearance and quite relieved to find who he thought was Prisoner D3, 10 returned to his care."

"England's perfect penal system seems to have a few flaws. But to hold you for eight years? Unbelievable. The place serves as more of a holding facility than anything else. Prisoners are only supposed to be there for eighteen months before being shipped off to a penal colony. Why were you never taken to a transport ship?"

"Inside our cells was posted our information: our number, the date we entered our cell, the date we were scheduled to leave. The warder, Mr. Matthews, periodically changed mine, whenever the designated date for my departure grew nearer."

"And no one noticed?"

"He was in charge of my cellblock. Why would anyone question him? And since our faces were always covered with a hood, why would anyone notice that the same man walked the exercise yard? It's not as though we were recognizable."

"I think I would have removed the damned cap."

"You'd think. You'd think we all would, but without having been there, you can't understand the oppressive atmosphere. We did what we were told because we knew it was the only way to survive. Far too many men go insane, Weddington. It's an atrocious system."

"Well, you're free now, back where you belong."

"There is still the matter of John and our moment of reckoning. You can't possibly think he'll accept me as duke without a fight or more treachery."

"I say send a message to his warder and inform him that he's to be placed on a damned transport ship immediately so he can serve out the rest of his life sentence in Australia."

"And constantly look over my shoulder, wondering if he's somehow managed to make his way back here? So he can once more imprison me? Then I turn about and imprison him? No, I need a more permanent solution."

Out of the corner of his eye, he saw Weddington turn his head toward him. "What of your wife? Torie, was it?"

"Yes, Torie. Short for Victoria. She doesn't know. It was John who asked for her hand in marriage, John to whom she gave it. My misfortune was escaping the night before the wedding, not knowing a wedding was to take place." He shifted his gaze to Weddington. "I've not yet consummated the marriage. I'm running out of excuses not to visit her bed."

"Then stop making excuses. Even as angry as I was, I couldn't help but notice how lovely she is. Besides, I have a difficult time believing she'd prefer John to you."

"She preferred him before we married."

"She didn't have you to compare him to. How are you going to prove your claims?"

"Haven't a clue."

"I would be more than willing to announce that you are the Duke of Killingsworth."

"And John would no doubt have Lynmore claim that John is the true Killingsworth. And so it would go, each us of lining up friends to claim we are Robert, in which case he with the most friends would win."

"Not a bad way to achieve success."

"Except that I have been locked away for

several years and am rather short on friends right now. Speaking of which, how did you know it was me?"

"I didn't. Not until you shot the bird. If I hadn't been so incredibly angry with you, I might have realized it when I first saw you. Eleanor didn't deserve what John did to her."

"I'll make it up to her."

"It's too late for that. Besides, it's not your place. God, I thought I could never love her more than I did. We'd been married for eight months when Richard was born. The rumors had begun circulating before then, of course. They escalated when he was born. Eleanor, bless her, stood up to them, though, telling people our son had arrived early because it was the way of Weddington men to be in a hurry to get on with business. Of course, the truth was, she was already with child when we got married. My fault entirely. Could hardly keep my hands off her. Still can't, truth be told."

"Your son looks like you."

"He does. But I can see much of Eleanor in him. He's a smart lad. Speaking of smart lads, you'll need to see about getting yourself an heir."

"Not until I've dealt with John." A shiver

raced through him. "I don't even want to contemplate what he might do to a son of mine—one who would stand next in line to gain everything."

"Have the key to his cell thrown away."

"If only it were that easy. Sitting here, talking to you, I've come realize that it's far more than proving that I'm Robert. I must secure the future for my family. And how do I do that?"

He felt the first drop of rain hit his nose.

"We should head back before we're drenched." Weddington stood up and held his hand out to Robert.

Robert grabbed hold and let himself be pulled to his feet, taking comfort in the fact that their friendship had managed to survive John's manipulations.

"You could always kill him," Weddington said.

"Don't think I haven't thought of that. But what sort of man would that make me?"

Weddington leaned near. "A live one."

"Can you believe it? I still can't. He shot another blasted bird!" the Duke of Weddington exclaimed.

After the gunshots had echoed in the distance, Torie had sat there frozen. "We should go see what happened," she finally whispered.

"I promised Weddy that I wouldn't, no matter what I heard."

Torie hadn't promised anyone anything. But she didn't know the area, couldn't risk getting lost again. And so she'd sat there for nearly an hour, terrified that he might have died.

As the rain had begun to fall, she'd spotted the two men walking with a lively step toward the house, the wind carrying their laughter toward the ladies in the garden. And because the rain had yet to let up, they'd been invited to stay over for dinner.

"You can hardly credit me with the hit," her husband said, sitting at one end of the table while Weddington sat at the other. "I wasn't aiming at the blasted thing."

"You weren't aiming at all!"

"I must say, Weddy, it wasn't very charitable of you to leave me and Torie to worry so when you had no intention of actually going through with the duel. I'm quite put out with you, and I've no doubt Torie is put out with Robert." She looked at Torie, who was sitting across from her. "I think we should deny them our comfort for a few days."

"Oh, Eleanor, don't be cruel. You know how I suffer when you give me the cold shoulder."

"No more than I this afternoon when I thought you might come back slung over Robert's shoulder."

"Oh, princess, have some faith in my ability to place a well-aimed shot."

"We heard two shots, Weddy."

"Well, yes, he only clipped the bird. I had to finish the poor bugger off. It was the gentlemanly thing to do."

"How can you all make light of this?" Torie finally asked. She'd held her silence through the entire ordeal. While the rain had begun to fall, while her husband had finally reached her, while he'd assured her that he was fine, and the men had started laughing again about a bird, then decided that the storm would only worsen . . .

"Let's go clean up then," Weddington had said, "and we'll discuss it all over dinner."

Only they weren't discussing it, not really. They were discussing the stupid bird that had gotten in the way of a bullet—what rotten luck! Ha! Ha! Ha!—and not the fact that

Torie had sat there for an hour not knowing whether her husband was alive or dead!

"Do you know how a gunshot reverberates?" she asked. "Do you know how deafening it is once the bang falls silent? Do you know how terrifying it is to sit there not knowing what happened? And wanting to search for you, but not knowing exactly where the bluff is when there are bluffs all over the place—"

"Torie?" Robert said quietly, calmly, placing his hand over hers where it rested on the table.

But she didn't want calm and quiet. She wanted . . . She didn't know what she wanted except to rant.

"And your wife wouldn't leave because she promised she wouldn't go looking for you and so we just sat there as though everything were normal, sipping our blasted tea—"

"Torie?" Robert squeezed her hand. "It's all right, darling. It *was* very inconsiderate of us."

"Who in the hell duels anymore?"

"Apparently Weddington does."

"You're still joking about it." She clapped a hand over her mouth, mortified that she was screeching like a shrew.

Her husband's chair scraped across the

floor as he stood. "If you'll excuse us for a moment—"

"Of course," Weddington said.

Robert came to stand behind her, placed his hands on her shoulders. "Come on, let's step outside for a moment."

"It's still raining, which is the reason that we're still here!"

"No, we're here because our friends asked us to stay. And by outside, I simply meant out of this room."

She got to her feet, looked at the duke and duchess. "I'm sorry."

"No need to apologize," Eleanor said. "You're leaving gives me the chance to have a few harsh words with my Weddy. I'd planned to do so in the privacy of our bedchamber, but here works just as well."

"You'll upset my digestion," Weddington said.

But when his wife glared at him, he simply sighed, laid down his fork, and said, "So it appears my digestion will be upset. Better that than my wife."

Robert escorted her out of the dining room, and once in the large hallway, took her hand, and led her through the labyrinth of rooms.

"Where are we going?" she asked.

"Someplace with a bit more privacy."

They finally went into a darkened hallway. A footman opened the door, and Robert pulled her into what she realized was the library. At the far end, lit candelabras flickered on either side of the room. This end, however, was shadowy. As soon as the footman closed the door behind them, Robert drew her into his arms.

"I'm sorry, Torie, I'm dreadfully sorry."

She pressed her face to his chest, relishing the warmth, the scent of him. He'd been drenched by the time he and Weddington had finally reached the manor. The servants had shown him to a bedchamber where he'd apparently bathed and changed into some of Weddington's clothes, but through them all, she detected his unique scent, a fragrance she'd feared would be forever lost to her after she'd heard the initial gunshot.

"I know I'm being unbearably silly—"

"No, no." He cut her off. "I'm not accustomed to being married, to thinking of anyone other than myself. I gave no thought to what you might be experiencing, and I should have. Forgive me for allowing my thoughtlessness to cause you such distress."

Pulling back, she studied his face, the

genuine concern reflected within the blue depths of his eyes. She'd not looked into those eyes nearly enough, not a lifetime's worth, and it suddenly occurred to her how very fond she'd grown of him. And how silly she'd been to have had any doubts at all about marrying him.

He grazed his knuckles along her cheek. "Weddington should have known, though. He's been married a trifle longer. If the rain stops tomorrow I believe I'll call him out—"

"Don't you dare!"

He held her gaze only a heartbeat longer before he lowered his head a bit. He was turned toward the candles so she could see his face clearly, could see his eyes darken with desire, beckoning to the wildness in her, wildness she'd not even known she possessed.

"Don't you dare call him out," she whispered, surprised by the raspy quality of her voice. "But do dare to kiss me."

His eyes widened slightly, as though in surprise, before a strange kaleidoscope of emotions she couldn't decipher passed over his face, then his mouth was on hers and all thoughts of deciphering anything went clear out of her head. She was aware only of the scalding heat of his kiss, the enticing lure of his tongue, and the delightful manner in which he plied his skills. And he *was* skilled.

She wound her arms around his neck, scraped her fingers along his neck into his hair. Groaning low, he pulled her closer, his arms like strong bands of steel. She raised herself up on her toes to give him easier access and to improve the angle of his mouth over hers.

He willingly took what she offered, responding with a feral growl and a deepening of the kiss that sent pleasure spiraling through her all the way down to her toes. They curled in response; her entire body seemed to be curling and unfurling, as though each sensation enticed one of greater magnitude.

She plowed her fingers into his hair, scraped her nails along his scalp, holding him nearer, keeping herself tethered. She'd thought she'd lost him this afternoon, only to discover now that she'd never really possessed him: not heart, soul, and body. She'd been waltzing along the outskirts of love as though it were a frozen pond, fearful of stepping out onto it, afraid that it would crack and shatter beneath the weight. Trying to protect her heart, and in the protecting she was causing it harm.

She no longer wanted to be safe, because he wasn't safe. He was a danger to her heart, but he was also a salvation.

She suspected that he was harboring the same fears, and that was the very reason that he had yet to make love to her, because he could sense that she was holding back her heart, and he wanted everything. For the first time since she'd met him, she was willing to give it.

Everything, all of herself.

She slipped her hands inside his jacket, pressed her palms against his chest, and felt the hard, almost violent pounding of his heart.

He skimmed his mouth, damp and hotter than imaginable, along her throat, his tongue swirling over her skin, leaving a trail of dew in its wake. Then he was traveling upward again, latching his mouth onto hers, while his hand slid up and down her side, until eventually he closed his fingers over her breast.

A shudder rippled violently through him, just before he tore his mouth from hers, pressing her face to his chest, while his harsh breathing echoed around them.

Her own breathing was rapid and labored,

and she thought she should object to the position of his hand, but it was as though her breast had swollen to accommodate its size, as though it was drawn to the miracle of his touch.

It was several moments before he finally released his hold and drew back. He studied her briefly before plowing his hands through his hair. "I got rather carried away."

"Rather."

"I shan't apologize, though, as you did dare me."

"Is that the reason you did it? Because I dared you?"

"I kissed you because I wanted to. Desperately." Reaching out, he tucked stray strands of hair back into her bun. "I've mussed your hair."

"Do you think our hosts will notice?"

He shrugged. "I suspect they expect us to come back a bit untidy. We've been gone quite a while." He took a step away from her. "We should return to dinner."

"Yes, I suppose we should."

He took a step away as though he was considering returning to kiss her, rather than returning to dinner.

"I'm sorry I was so beside myself at the table," she said.

A corner of his mouth quirked up in what she was coming to recognize as his kind, indulgent smile, when he sought to make her feel better. "I think we spend far too much time apologizing to each other."

"Do you suppose it's because we're married and have never been before? Sometimes I'm not quite sure how to act, what to say. I'm not completely comfortable with being a wife."

"Nor I with being a husband. I suggest we observe Weddington and Eleanor a bit more closely. They seem to have figured it all out."

"I like them," she told him.

"So do I. I rather suspect, though, that they'd like to finish with dinner."

"Oh, yes." She fairly jumped, startled by the reminder. "I'm sure they would. They're probably beginning to worry about us."

He opened the door, and she followed him into the hallway.

"I hope you remember how to find the dining room."

"I could find it in the dark."

He extended his arm, and she wrapped

hers around it, halfway wishing he'd lead her to a bedchamber.

"You might fool them into believing that the duel was all a grand prank, but not me, Weddy. Never me. You left here with the intention of killing him."

Weddington studied his wife, the uplift of her chin that indicated she'd stand for no nonsense. Dear God, but he loved her so, and he could only pray that his son would be fortunate enough to find a woman that he loved half as much.

"Yes, I had plans to kill him," he reluctantly acknowledged, not overly proud of his initial intent.

"Why didn't you?"

"Because he's not the man who hurt you."

"So it wasn't Robert?"

"No."

"So it was John, as you suspected?"

"Yes."

"Where was Robert when all this was going on?"

"It's complicated, Eleanor, and I don't wish to be in the middle of the explanation when they return. Suffice it to say that Robert has been . . . indisposed all these years. Unfortunately, he has yet to tell his wife the entire story."

"Why?"

"It's complicated."

"You keep saying that—"

"Because it's the truth." He glanced toward the doorway, decided that Robert might be a while calming his wife, so he proceeded to tell Eleanor his friend's tale. She listened without uttering a single word, until he was finished.

"How awful for him. And for her. She's not married to the man she thought she was going to marry."

"No, she's married to a better man."

His wife pressed her lips into a tight line.

"You know it's true, princess."

"Regardless, he must tell her the truth of the situation."

"He will."

"When?"

"When the time is right."

She scoffed. "You don't think he did anything wrong in marrying her."

"She was to marry the Duke of Killingsworth and that's who she married."

"But he's a different man than she expected."

"Their marriage is not our problem, Eleanor."

"I like her, Weddy."

"Then you should be glad that she's married to Robert and not John."

"Men. You always stick together."

"Only because ladies always stick together."

"We're not at war."

"Let it go, Eleanor. There are more important matters at stake."

"Such as?"

He scowled at her. "His titles and estates."

"So typical of a man to have his priorities mixed up. If he feels that they are more important than she is then he doesn't deserve her."

"Eleanor, right now he needs our support and friendship more than anything. Not our censure."

She puckered her very kissable mouth. "Very well. I shall let it go for now, but if he doesn't tell her soon, I shall have to get after him."

"I'll give him fair warning."

"Speaking of fair warning, I'm concerned about this storm, Weddy. It's getting quite fierce. I thought to invite them to stay the night rather than travel through this muck, but I wasn't certain how you'd feel about it."

"I'd like it very much if you'd offer them our hospitality for the night, but do be sure to put them in the other wing. I have plans for you later."

"Do you plan to indulge in a bit of wickedness?"

"Most assuredly."

Her smile withered and her brow furrowed. "Do you think everything will turn out all right for Robert?"

"I'll do what I can to help him, but I fear most of the responsibility for making things right will fall to him. Although there is something you can do to help."

"Tell me what it is. I'll do whatever I can."

"If an opportunity presents itself, you might expound upon his virtues, coax her toward falling in love with the man she married."

"I thought you said their marriage wasn't our affair."

"It isn't."

"Yes, well, what you're asking me to do seems very much to be contradicting that view."

"It will make matters easier for him once

his deception is discovered if her feelings are stronger for him than they are for his brother."

"It seems strange to think of him as the *deceiver* when he is the rightful duke."

"Unfortunately, he doesn't see himself as the rightful husband."

"He is the better husband."

"Without a doubt. So you'll do as I've asked?"

She gave him a sly smile. "Only if you promise to be very wicked when we go to bed."

He leaned toward her. "I shall be as wicked as you like."

"I do love you, Weddy."

"No more than I love you."

Chapter 15

The storm grew in intensity. Torie could hear the wind howling outside. One particularly loud clap of thunder had sent Eleanor rushing upstairs to see to her son in the nursery, even though he had a governess tending to him. She'd claimed to hear the child cry out. Torie hadn't heard anything except the wind and thunder.

She'd looked at Weddington, who'd simply shrugged, smiled, and said, "A mother's ears are very different. I've learned not to question what she claims she's heard."

A few minutes later Eleanor returned with her son perched on her hip. The child was wearing a nightshirt, his little feet bare. He looked much more vulnerable than he had that afternoon when he'd arrived on his father's shoulders.

"Just as I thought, he was having a devil of a time. Storms frighten him just a bit," Eleanor said.

"What was his governess doing if not comforting him?" Weddington asked.

"Oh, she was doing her job, rocking him, cooing to him, but sometimes a child needs his mother."

Weddington leaned toward Torie where she sat on a couch in the drawing room. "And sometimes a mother simply needs her son. 'Tis Eleanor who is frightened of storms."

"What are you whispering about, Weddy?"

He winked at Torie. "Only the truth, my love."

Then Torie saw a side to her husband that she'd have never guessed existed. He rose from his chair near the fire and approached Eleanor, but talked to her son.

"Hello, Richard," he said quietly. "I'm your uncle Robert. We've not met formally, but I'm pleased to make your acquaintance."

"Are you afraid of storms?" Richard asked.

"Dreadfully afraid. Do you know what I think? I think we should have a dog in here to protect us."

"We don't have a dog."

"I do. In my pocket. But I have to warn you that when he comes out to play, other animals come out as well. Do you want to see?"

Richard bobbed his head excitedly. "I like dogs."

"So do I. But my dog likes a lot of light. If your mother doesn't mind, I'm going to move one of the lamps down to the floor."

"Of course I don't mind," Eleanor said. "I'm equally curious about this pet of yours."

As was Torie. She watched in fascination as her husband moved a lamp to the floor, set it near a wall. He sat on the floor and patted the space beside him. "Sit here, Richard."

The boy wiggled out of his mother's arms and without fear walked over to Robert and plopped down beside him. He looked up at Robert with complete trust.

Robert dug around in the pockets of his jacket. "Ah, here he is."

He brought out his tightly closed fists and jerked his head toward the side. "Watch the wall."

Richard shifted his gaze over.

Robert unfurled his hands and placed them in front of the lamp in such a way that they cast the shadow of a dog's head on the wall.

Laughing, Richard clapped. "It's a dog! I see him! Do you, Mummy?"

"I most certainly do," Eleanor said, as she sat on the couch next to Torie. "What a clever uncle you have."

"He's not really Richard's uncle, is he?" Torie whispered, wondering if perhaps she hadn't fully understood the relationship between these people.

"Not by blood, but by his heart. He and my Weddy were once closer than brothers. I suspect they're on their way to being so again."

"Robert didn't tell me what caused the rift between him and your husband."

"Just a bit of nastiness that's behind us now. No point in dwelling on it."

She couldn't imagine her husband being responsible for any sort of nastiness, but based on the anger with which Weddington had greeted him, she had to assume that the fault for their discord rested with him. It nagged at her, wondering what it might entail, but she forced it from her mind, concentrating instead on her husband and his young audience.

"Remember, I told you," Robert said, "that when my dog comes out to play, other creatures come out as well. I think I hear them coming now."

"Where?" Richard cried out, looking around.

"Here," Richard said, manipulating his hands. "Do you know what this is?"

"A tortoise."

"Do you know the story of the tortoise and the—"

He shifted his hands.

"Bunny rabbit!" Richard cried.

"The tortoise and the bunny rabbit. Close enough."

"What else?" the boy asked, getting up on his knees and bouncing up and down.

"Well, let's see. Something exotic, I think." He moved his hands . . .

"An elephant!"

"You are smart."

Torie sat there, watching her husband manipulate his hands, creating the shadows of one creature after another: a goose, a deer, a duck, a pig . . . on and on he went, his repertoire of hand shadows seemingly endless. Torie had never seen him take such delight in anything, and she was almost jealous of the child who commanded his attention.

"How did you learn to do all that?" she finally asked.

Without taking his eyes from the shadows, he said, "I once found myself with a bit of time on my hands, so to speak."

"Some of these are remarkable," she said.

A snail, a horse, two birds.

"I had *quite* a bit of time to practice."

"When was this?" she asked.

"Oh, here and there."

"Teach me!" Richard suddenly piped up.

"With pleasure." He pulled the boy onto his lap, wrapped his arms around him so he could reach the boy's hands.

The sight of Robert's large hands patiently molding the tiny hands of the child tugged at something deep within Torie. Her heart, she thought. And that tug caused tears to burn the backs of her eyes. He might one day give this sort of attention to their children. She'd given a good deal of thought to what he might be like as a husband, but she'd given no consideration to what he might be like as a father. Watching him, she realized that he would be quite remarkable, and she found herself hoping that they wouldn't go too terribly long without being blessed with children.

Eleanor leaned toward her. "I daresay this storm isn't going to let up anytime soon. I hope you'll consider staying the night. You'd have an entire wing to yourself, and as Robert is already wearing some of my Weddy's clothes, we can find others for him tomorrow. As for your clothing needs, you and I are not so far off in size."

"We don't want to impose."

"It will be more of an imposition if we have to go out in the storm and get your coach unstuck."

"If you're certain."

"I'm most certain. We're so glad to have Robert back in our lives. We've missed him."

It was nearly an hour later before Richard, still nestled within Robert's lap yawned and said, "One more."

Torie had lost count of the "one mores" that the child had asked for. She wondered if Robert regretted showing him the first animal that had led to the second and so on.

She watched as Robert twisted around, leaned his back against the wall, the curled child cradled in his arms, while he looked down on him with such tenderness. He obviously adored this boy he'd only just met.

"I daresay I should take him back to bed," Eleanor said, rising to her feet. She crossed over to Robert and bent down to retrieve her son.

"He's a fine lad," Robert said, and she heard something in his voice. Sadness, perhaps loss. Longing.

"We think so," Eleanor said.

"I'll help you put him to bed," Weddington said, coming to his feet.

As the couple left the room, Torie's husband sat there, one leg raised, his wrist resting on his knee, his gaze on the window where the draperies were still pulled aside so they could watch the show put on by the magnificent storm.

Was that a tear in his eye?

With a soft clearing of his throat, he closed his eyes and pressed his finger and thumb on either side of the bridge of his nose, rubbing his nose, his eyes.

"A headache?" she asked.

He lowered his hand and gave her a poignant smile. "No, just speculating."

"On what?"

"On what I'd be willing to do to protect my children from harm."

"And what would that be?"

"Anything and everything."

"I've never understood why men believe women are too delicate to puff on cigars, drink whiskey, and smack small balls around," Eleanor whispered to Torie.

They were sitting in a corner of the billiard room, watching as the men puffed, drank, and smacked. Apparently the men needed quiet to play their game, although their own talking and laughter didn't seem to disturb them. The ladies had been allowed into what Weddington referred to as a man's dominion because Eleanor had insisted. Torie couldn't help but wonder if a time would come when Robert would give as much deference to her wishes.

"How did you meet Robert?" Eleanor asked, completely changing the subject.

"It was at the first ball of last Season. He was the first duke to ask me to dance. I was quite smitten."

"Because of his title?"

Torie heard censure in Eleanor's voice, and she could hardly blame her. The woman was so obviously in love with her husband, she probably expected every woman to look beyond a man's title.

"Only at first," Torie admitted. "But he was so charming and attentive that he fairly swept me off my feet."

"And if he wasn't a duke?"

"I'd still care for him."

"*Care?*"

Eleanor had jumped on the word like a cat to a fly.

"Did you love Weddington before you married him?" Torie asked instead of addressing Eleanor's question.

"Of course."

"I don't know how proper courtship allows room for anyone to fall in love."

"I suppose I must confess that mine was quite improper. So you only care for Robert?"

Torie felt the heat rise in her face. She wasn't certain that she should tell this woman what she had yet to tell her husband. "I feel as though it's only since we married that I've had an opportunity to truly come to know him."

"And you've grown rather fond of him," Eleanor finished for her.

Torie nodded, Eleanor smiled. "I'm glad

your affection has deepened since you married him."

"Why?"

"Because a man after marriage is often very different from a man who is courting. The reality of that difference can be very disappointing. I know any number of ladies who wished the beaus had not turned into husbands."

Torie smiled deeply. "It was just the opposite with Robert. I much prefer the man as a husband."

"And the way he looks at you," Eleanor whispered, "it's rather obvious that he absolutely adores you."

Torie shifted her gaze over to the men. The friendship between them was so evident.

While she considered Weddington handsome, she couldn't deny that she found her husband to be more so. He'd removed his jacket, unbuttoned the top of his shirt, and rolled up his sleeves as though he needed to get serious about this game. She liked to watch the way he concentrated on the ball right before he smacked it, the way he smiled with satisfaction when it landed in a hole, the way he groaned and grimaced with good-natured disappointment when he missed . . .

He was quite simply . . . wonderful.

"I find fierce storms lend themselves so well to romance," Eleanor said softly.

Stunned by the statement, Torie shifted her attention back to Eleanor. "Your husband told me that you're terrified of storms."

Eleanor wrinkled her nose. "I am a bit. But my wariness serves a purpose. Men are quite ignorant when it comes to romance. I'm not certain why, but it takes a bit of training to bring them around . . . like a well-heeled dog."

Torie widened her eyes. "Are you comparing your husband to a pet?"

"Of course not. I'm simply saying that sometimes men must be guided toward romance so that they believe it was all their idea. I've found storms to be the best time for simply holding each other."

"Simply holding each other?"

Eleanor nodded enthusiastically. "People discount the importance of the small things. Simply being held while a storm rages. Being kissed silly. Talking in the darkness about dreams and plans. And snuggling to our heart's content. Men are really rather stupid creatures when it comes to women. It is left to us to educate them that courtship doesn't end when vows are exchanged.

"Just like now. Men think they must sneak away to enjoy their cigars and whiskey, that it offends our sensibilities. But I take much pleasure in watching my Weddy enjoying his cigar and drink. And I daresay on occasion I've even shared the nasty things with him."

"You haven't!"

"I have. Life is to be experienced, I say. And I want to experience it with Weddy."

"You're very lucky, Eleanor."

"I don't believe in luck. I believe we make our own happiness. Right this moment, I could be off in another part of the house. Alone. But I choose not to be. I choose to be where he is. And the wonderful thing about it, Torie, is that there are times when he chooses to be where I am. And that's the reason I love being married to him, and why I love him."

Torie realized that the balls were no longer being smacked around.

"You're out of practice," Weddington said as he and Robert ambled over.

"Decidedly so," Robert responded.

"Did you win, Weddy?" Eleanor asked.

"Of course, princess."

Robert looked at Torie, shrugged, and grinned as though he thought she might be ashamed by his lack of success. She felt a need to comfort him. "It's no surprise that you won, Weddington, since it's your table in your house. You know doubt practice all the time."

"Whenever possible."

"What shall we do now?" Eleanor asked. "A game of charades?"

"I was thinking we could go to the bathhouse," Weddington said.

"I think not."

"The bathhouse?" Torie asked.

"It's a horrendous place. A huge vat of freezing water," Eleanor said.

"It's healthy to take a dip into it," Weddington said. "My ancestors have done it for generations. Besides, it's a ritual for Robert and me. We always do it at least once while he's visiting."

"But tonight, Weddy? It's raining."

"So? We'll get wet anyway."

"Well, then, you can get wet without us."

"If you insist." He bowed slightly. "Ladies, we'll see you in a bit."

Robert looked at Torie. "Do you mind if we go?"

"No. Spend some time with your friend."

"We may be a while. You needn't wait up."

"All right. I'll see you in the morning, then."

He looked incredibly awkward as he leaned down and brushed a kiss over her cheek. "Sleep well."

Watching as they walked out of the room, she couldn't explain the ache of longing that suddenly filled her chest.

"Have you ever taken a dip?" Torie asked.

"Once." Eleanor's cheeks reddened. "Weddy warming me up afterward was quite lovely, but we wouldn't be doing *that* with company about, now would we?"

"I suppose not. I wonder what they find appealing about jumping into cold water."

"Haven't a clue."

Chapter 16

"You're not really going to jump in, are you?" Robert asked, his voice echoing between the stone walls that circled the pool.

"Hell, no," Weddington said as he retreated into what served as a changing room.

The bathing house had been built a good distance from the manor. Stone pillars guarded the entrance to the stone building. In spite of the rain, they'd managed to bring torches with them and placed them in the sconces on the wall. Eerie shadows danced around the inside of the building. A wide flight of stone steps led out of the pool.

Weddington emerged from the room and

held up his hands, each holding a bottle. "I love Eleanor with all my heart, but there is nowhere in the manor where she would not follow, and I thought we needed a bit of time to talk—alone."

"Like old times?"

"Like old times."

They sat on the stone floor, their backs to the wall. Weddington opened a bottle and handed it to Robert before opening the other one for himself. He tapped it against Robert's. "To friendship renewed."

"To friendship that remained."

Robert took a swallow, the whiskey burning down his throat. He gasped, released a harsh breath, and smiled broadly. "Whew! That was good."

"And there's plenty more where that came from."

"Do you think your father ever deduced that we weren't taking dips for our health in here?"

"I think he might have suspected."

Robert took another swallow, raised his knee, and set his wrist on it, the bottle dangling. Dropping his head back, he watched the shadows dancing over the ceiling. "We had some good talks here."

"Yes, we did. I've told Eleanor about your situation."

Robert rolled his head over to the side, so he could see his friend more clearly.

"She asked me why I didn't kill you, and since she knew it was my intention . . ." Weddington shrugged. "I've never lied to her and I don't keep things from her. She won't say a word to anyone."

Robert looked back at the ceiling. "This situation has already hurt you and Eleanor enough. I don't want it to cause any further harm."

"I don't suppose between this afternoon and now that you've determined how best to handle it."

Robert brought the bottle to his lips, gulped the intoxicating brew, lowered the bottle, and licked his lips. "No. But as I was playing with Richard, all I could think was that with John alive, I would never know that my children were safe."

"Perhaps if you reassured him that he would always be provided for—"

"I've been thinking about that. It's not about the money. There was never any question that he would have an allowance that would allow him to live in the manner to which he'd become accustomed. It had to be about the dukedom itself. The title. *All* the titles. The prestige, the power, the respect accorded someone of rank. He's already demonstrated the lengths to which he will go in order to be duke. I can't assume that my being on to him is enough to deter him."

"What are you going to do, then?"

"I don't know."

"I think you might have another problem that you didn't realize you had."

"What would that be?"

"Your wife."

"I'm very much aware that there is a problem there."

"Are you aware that she loves you?"

Laughing at the absurdity of the question, he took another swallow, letting the warmth race through him. "She loves John."

"It wasn't John she couldn't take her eyes off in the drawing room."

He snapped his gaze over to Weddington. "Only because she thought I was John. If she realized I wasn't the man who'd asked for her hand, she wouldn't be giving me any attention at all."

"I think you're wrong. I think she likes what she sees when she looks at you. I think it's *you* that caused her to smile. I think it was the thought of losing *you* that caused the duel to so upset her. And I damned well know that you love her."

"I can't love her."

"But you do."

"But I can't. It was John—"

"Do you honestly believe that she could have loved him?"

"Yes!" He shot to his feet, drinking the whiskey as he went. "The day we married she told me how fond she was of me. *Incredibly desperately.* Only it wasn't me, it was John she was referring to." He dropped down to his haunches. "The morning after I escaped, I woke up to discover I was to marry. By the time I realized it wasn't simply a lady marrying a duke, the deed was done." He looked down at the bottle dangling between his knees. "I don't want to give her up, but when she learns the truth, she will want to be rid of me."

"Robert, I have known her for only an afternoon and an evening, but I cannot for the life of me envision so sweet a woman falling for so unscrupulous a man as your brother."

Robert lifted his gaze. "I don't believe she is aware of what he did. He has all of London convinced that the Duke of Killingsworth's twin brother immigrated to America."

"I'd heard the rumors. Do you remember all the times he talked about going to America? So his finally going didn't surprise me."

"Only he didn't go. He's supposedly written stories about his fantastic adventures."

"I'd heard that as well. I daresay it's quite mad. All the more reason to win your wife over to your side."

Robert took a sip of his whiskey, something Torie said filtering through his mind. "She told me she had doubts about marrying me—or the man she thought was me. It's so damned confusing."

"Consider this. John is a schemer. It is very likely that he never revealed his true self to her. And if that is the case, do you honestly believe she deserves him? You know the truth of him. Why would you condemn her to a life with him? Not that I think you'll be able to grant her one. The law prohibits a wife from marrying her husband's brother."

"But surely if I return her chaste, if I can undo the marriage, make the courts understand that it was through no fault of her own that she married the wrong brother—"

"I think you should consider that perhaps

she married the *right* brother. You shouldn't take measures to stop her from falling in love with *you*, the real Robert Hawthorne."

With a good bit of whiskey sloshing around in his belly, Robert thought that Weddington's view on his current situation made perfect sense. Was damned near brilliant, actually.

He dropped into the chair in the bedchamber that Weddington had led him to, with a wink and nudge that Torie was in the bedchamber next door. Weddington had offered to send in his valet, but Robert had declined the offer. He wanted to be alone with his thoughts.

He'd been so concerned about her discovering that he wasn't the man she knew as Robert that he'd given no consideration to letting her discover the man he was. He still had no plans to bed her. Should the marriage be dissolved, he wanted to take nothing from her that he couldn't give back. Such as her innocence.

But he could spend more time with her, spend money on her. He could even write her sonnets. Well, writing sonnets might be a bit too ambitious since he'd never written one in his entire life and had read them only when the schoolmaster forced him to.

His mind was wandering off in a direction of no consequence. Reaching down, he grabbed his boot and tugged, tugged, tugged until he jerked it off, then tossed it onto the floor.

He fell back in the chair and held up a finger. He needed to return his mind to the plan. Yes, the plan. Sonnets. No, not sonnets. That would be disastrous. He could read her sonnets that someone else had written. Like Shakespeare. As Robert recalled, he'd written a few good ones that might appeal to a woman's heart.

Time, money, sonnets. What else? He knew so little of courtship. When he would have been engaging in it, honing his skills, he'd been creating shadow friends. Not a lot of good they'd be in wooing a woman.

He heard a light rapping on his door.

Damnation. Weddington had sent his valet after all. Robert looked at his forlorn boot lying on the floor and the one still on his foot and decided he might very well need the services of a valet.

"Come in!"

The door opened, but it wasn't the valet. It

was his wife, standing there in a nightgown and wrapper, her bare toes peeking out from beneath the hem.

"I thought I heard you in here."

"I'm sorry. I'll be quieter."

So much for his plans to woo her. Here was the perfect opportunity for him to say something witty, and he apologized. *Give it up, Robert, you'll never win her over.*

"You didn't disturb me. I wasn't asleep yet. I was actually pondering a problem that I thought you might be able to help me with."

He straightened. Straightened? What was he doing still sitting? A lady had come into the room. His lady. He shot to his feet, wobbled a bit, stilled, and realized how silly he must look tilted as he was with one boot making one side higher than the other. Ah, yes, a man as suave and debonair as he was . . . she would have no choice but to fall madly in love with him.

"Your problem? How can I help you with it?" he asked.

With a shy tucking of her chin, she pointed. "Perhaps I should help you first. You still have a boot on."

He glanced down. "Ah, yes, so I do. And here I thought the storm was causing the house to list to one side, like a ship on the sea."

"Are you foxed?"

"No, no. I'm simply feeling very merry."

"Would you like help getting your boot off?"

"Oh, no, I can manage, thank you very much."

Missed opportunity there, Robert. She would have had to get nearer in order to help.

"Your problem?" he repeated.

"Your boot first."

"Very well."

He sank onto the chair, lifted his foot, grabbed his boot, and tugged, tugged—

"You do need help," she said as she walked over.

Her rose and lily scent wafted around him, as intoxicating as the whiskey in which he'd recently indulged. She knelt down, took hold of his boot, and pulled, having no more luck than he had.

"My valet usually has better luck if he . . ." He let his voice trail off. His valet in the position he was going to propose was one thing. She was something else entirely.

She raised those dark brown eyes to his, and he thought he could so easily get lost in them. No, not lost. It was as he'd told her earlier in the day. With her, he could find himself again.

"What does your valet do?"

"Well, he . . . uh . . . I can get it off." He tried to bring his foot up but she refused to relinquish hold.

"You've tried and I've tried. What does your valet do?"

"He gives his back to me. Straddles my leg. I raise it, he grabs hold of the boot, then I place my other foot on his backside and push," he finished quickly.

"I see."

"I thought you might. Let me have my foot back now, if you please."

Instead she straddled his leg, bringing his foot up, holding on to his boot. Her nightgown lifted until he could see her calves. They were lovely. He wanted to reach down and run his hands along them, then sprinkle kisses over them.

"Hurry up and push," she called out. "Your foot's getting heavy."

His gaze traveled up, up to her hips. Good God. Her backside in no way resembled his valet's. His mouth grew dry. He should do this quickly for her sake.

"Come on, be quick about it," she demanded.

Without further ado, he pressed his foot to her firm—it was so firm—rounded backside and shoved. The boot came off and she tumbled forward, caught her balance, and righted herself.

He jumped to his feet. "Are you all right?"

"I'm fine." She clutched his boot to her chest.

"I thank you for your assistance. I much prefer being the same height on both sides."

She released a self-conscious laugh that caused her dimple to form.

"What is it?" he asked.

"Sometimes you seem so very different that I hardly know what to think."

And that was the problem. He was beginning to sober just a bit, and Weddington's notion about wooing her suddenly seemed like an incredibly bad idea. "You said you had a problem that I could help you with."

"Oh, yes." Very carefully she set his boot on the floor and clutched her hands in front of her. "I couldn't figure out how to do the elephant."

He angled his head slightly. "Pardon?"

"The birds and the dog and the deer with the antlers I could do, but the elephant baffled me."

He was no doubt looking equally baffled because she added, "The hand shadows. From earlier. With Richard."

"Oh, yes, the elephant. It's quite simple really." He glanced around, looking for an empty bit of wall. "Do you mind sitting on the floor?"

"No."

"Marvelous." He grabbed a lit lamp from the table and set it on the floor. "Let's try it over here then. Sit in front of me so I can place my arms around you like I did Richard. Makes it easier to shape your hands," he felt obligated to explain. Now that sobriety was returning with stunning swiftness, he realized it was best to avoid her, because holding his passion in check if he gave it any freedom at all was not going to be easy. It was like taking an inmate to the gates of Pentonville, opening them, and saying, "All right now, take a step out, then come right back in." Not bloody likely.

To reach her arms as she held her hands in front of the lamp required that he be very close to her, and that was best achieved by placing his legs on either side of her hips. She exhibited no hesitation at all as she nestled against him. The possibilities caused his heart to thunder and his mouth to go dry. Once he finished helping her with her "problem" he thought he might make a trip back out to the bathhouse and this time jump feet first into the frigid pool. Head first. Sideways. Every way imaginable. And he would stay there until he—and his manhood that was clamoring for attention—had shriveled into nothing.

"The elephant?" she prodded.

"Yes, the elephant."

He took her left arm, could feel her heartbeat fluttering madly at her wrist. Was she as nervous as he?

"Raise your arm, bend your wrist, relax your hand, let it just dangle. You have such small hands. So soft." He skimmed his thumb over her wrist. Satiny. He remembered from their excursion to the library earlier that the skin at her throat, so near his mouth, felt the same.

"The elephant?" she reminded him, sounding rather breathless.

Showing her how to make hand shadows was not the same as showing Richard.

Robert could hardly keep himself focused on the task when such delectable rewards were within reach. He could nibble on her ear, skim his breath over her hair.

"Lower your two middle fingers. They form the trunk, you see. Then raise your smallest finger and your index finger slightly and you have tusks. Your thumb will form the outline of the mouth. Move it down to open it, up to close it."

He took her other hand. "Now cup your right hand over your left until you've created a head. Curve your fingers slightly until a little sliver of light gets through to make the eye. And there you have it. We're in Africa."

"Have you ever been to Africa?" she asked quietly.

"Only in my imagination."

"I've hardly ever gone anywhere. I'd like to travel."

"Where would you like to go?"

"I've always fancied a trip to Egypt. I don't know why, but I'd like to see the pyramids."

"Perhaps we'll go someday. We could journey down the Nile."

"I think it would take a lot of courage to do that."

"It's not so frightening when you have someone with you."

She turned her head slightly, which brought her lips in line with his. He had but to move his mouth . . . he raised his eyes to hers.

"Eleanor says that storms are good for snuggling, that Weddington holds her and kisses her silly—"

"Kisses her silly? I'm not sure he'd find that description of his amorous endeavors flattering."

"She loves him desperately . . . my arms are getting tired."

"Are they? I'm sorry. Rest them on top of mine." He moved his arms until they were beneath hers, supporting hers.

"Have I ever told you that I'm terrified of storms?"

Dear God. Had she? Was he supposed to know the answer or was it a rhetorical question?

"If you did, I don't remember." Insensitive-sounding lout. He thought he'd remember every word that she'd ever spoken since the moment he met her.

"I am," she said. "Especially here, by the

sea. It's so loud and the wind sounds so angry. And I can't sleep, which is the reason that I was trying to draw comfort from the hand shadows, but it would be so much nicer if the comfort came from you—"

And that was all he needed.

Chapter 17

Torie knew a moment of uncertainty when she saw the desire suddenly smoldering in his eyes, as though he'd kept it banked and was now free to unleash it. She'd been unable to ignore the tenderness toward him that his time with Richard had stirred within her. She wanted to know him in every way possible. She was tired of being the patient wife.

She wanted to open her heart completely. Then his hand was cradling her face, his mouth was on hers, and she realized that she might very well be falling in love with her husband.

She'd never known a touch so tender, a

kiss so enticing, both encouraging her to surrender to his seduction. Not with force or insistence, but with the simple act of granting what she'd asked for and taking no more.

Twisting around, she improved the angle, the positioning of their bodies, giving him permission to deepen the kiss, which he did with enthusiasm. She responded in kind, her arms going around his neck, vaguely aware that he was changing their position once again, carefully laying her on the thick carpet beneath them.

He had one arm around her, the other hand still on her face, his fingers inching up, becoming entangled in her hair which one of Eleanor's servants had pulled back and braided before she'd retired for bed.

He trailed kisses along her jaw, down her throat, murmuring her name as though it were a benediction. Then his mouth was again on hers, with a subtle difference.

He was no longer holding back.

It was as though he couldn't get enough, as though she'd never be able to satisfy the desire burning within him. His groans echoed around her while his tongue explored and his lips taunted.

"What do you want?" he asked, his breath mingling with hers, the kiss barely stopped as he asked.

"What do *you* want?" she replied.

"Everything you're willing and able to give this night." He pulled back slightly, his gaze near enough that she could see dark black flecks in his deep blue eyes. She could see the passion and the doubts, but more she could see the fondness, the possibility for love.

"I want your hair unbound," he rasped, "your buttons undone. I want your touch on my bare chest, my back, in my hair. I want to look at you but be so close I can't see all of you. But mostly I want you to want what I have to offer. Give me permission and I will be as gentle as the night falling around you."

Permission? What an odd thing for a husband to ask for. Had she ever given him the impression that she wouldn't grant it, that she didn't want this moment? Wasn't she the one prodding and prompting and urging him on?

She would have never thought her husband, a duke, would be uncertain of her desire for him, that he would doubt that she wanted him. A man who ruled estates and was coming to rule her heart. She smiled warmly, and he dipped his head, kissing her cheek.

"I love when that little dimple appears," he whispered. "I would do anything to keep it visible."

The rasp of his voice sent shivers cascading through her, her stomach coiled and her heart expanded. "Oh, please," she heard herself sighing, "oh, please."

He returned his mouth to hers, and she thought this moment could be the prelude to something grand. He was so very skilled, his tongue swirling, waltzing with hers, an ancient rhythm. She was vaguely aware that he'd tugged her braid from beneath her, while his mouth wove its magic. Then was gone, his breathing labored as he unraveled the thick rope of her hair and spread it out, bunching his hands in the abundant strands near her scalp.

"So beautiful, so soft." He buried his face in her hair as though it were the most marvelous part of her. A tremor traveled through him, his body tensed, and it was as though he needed a moment to recover from a momentous discovery.

Turning his head into her, he kissed her

jaw, her chin, her throat. Each touch ignited a fire that spread through her. Shadows wavered at the edge of her vision. And she thought of how skilled his hands were at creating shadow creatures, how much more skilled they were at eliciting pleasure.

Sitting up, he pulled his shirt over his head, and she found herself reaching out, flattening her hand against his chest.

"So beautiful, so firm." She smiled up at him, he laughed, a sound she was coming to love.

When he returned to her this time, she sensed the joy and the wonder in him as his fingers skimmed over her buttons. He watched as his fingers undid one button, then another. Not in a hurry, not in a rush, but as though he was opening a gift, each part of the journey toward discovering what was nestled inside the box to be savored.

When the last button was freed, she held her breath while he parted the material. The wonder in his gaze brought tears to her eyes. He molded his hand over her breast, moaned softly, and held it with exquisite care. She'd thought she should be embarrassed or frightened, anything but what she was: wishing he might hold it forever.

With a deep groan, he pulled her to him, the heat of his chest penetrating the coolness on her skin. "You can't imagine how desperately I've wanted to be this close, ever since I first saw you making your way up the aisle."

Before she could respond, he was touching her with his hands, his mouth, his tongue lapping over her skin, and she was touching him as well, reveling in the firmness of his muscles, the velvet warmth of his flesh. Oh, yes, this was what it was to be cared for, cared about.

Try having love without it . . .

No, she didn't think so. It was part and parcel of the complexities of a relationship, the seeking out, the enjoyment . . .

A knock sounded on the door. She squeaked as it opened and a footstep sounded. Robert drew her near, her face buried against his chest. She inhaled his intoxicating unique scent, trying to fight back the mortification of being caught in such a compromising position, even as she was aware that he was seeking to shield and protect her.

"Oh, so sorry to interrupt but frightfully glad to see you were taking my advice."

"I wasn't."

"No? Certainly looks like it. Anyway, it's not important. A ship has gone aground in the storm, a ways from shore. I'm off to see about getting the survivors safely to the beach."

"I'll join you momentarily."

"Good. But hurry. The ship's listing and if it goes—"

"I'll be there!"

"Right."

The door banged shut. Robert lowered her to the floor and rolled away from her. "I'm sorry, but I have to go."

Sitting up, she began refastening her buttons, watching as he put his shirt back on before jerking on his boots.

"But you're foxed."

"I've sobered up considerably." He glanced over at her. "Although I daresay I could easily become drunk on your kisses."

She thought she might have become a little drunk on his.

He stood, stomping his feet into his boots.

"You're going to help them?" she asked.

"Yes, of course. Don't look so worried. I've helped before. I know what to do."

Did she look worried? Probably because she was.

"But it's storming—"

"Yes, that's what caused the problem." He reached for the jacket resting over the back of a chair.

"How will you help them? If they're on the boat—"

"We'll row out, bring a few at a time back to shore."

"When did you help before?"

"When we were lads."

She rose unsteadily to her feet, suddenly more terrified of the storm than she'd ever been, terrified of losing him when she was only just beginning to truly possess him. Her body was still humming, seeking something she didn't quite understand. Her lips were swollen, tingling, and carried the taste of him on them.

He suddenly stopped and stared at her.

"What?"

"Your hair. It does flow past your hips, like a velvety curtain, not really brown, but not red, dark like mahogany. Lovely."

Self-conscious with his flattery, she pulled her hair forward, draping it over her shoulder.

"You will be careful, won't you?"

He grinned at her, a devil-may-care air about him. "Of course."

He strode over, placed his hands on her shoulders, and lowered his mouth to hers, the desperation in the kiss nearly bringing her to her knees. She found herself clinging to him, reluctant to let him leave.

He pulled free. "I have to go."

He headed for the door.

"Robert?" she called after him.

He stopped and looked back at her.

"I'll be here when you get back so I can help you take off your boots."

His grin broadened. "If you are, then I'll kiss you silly."

She laughed as he disappeared out the door. Laughed, for goodness' sakes, in spite of the danger into which he was heading, realizing that she would definitely be there when he returned.

Torie sat in the chair for all of a minute before realizing that she couldn't simply wait for him. Surely she could do something to help. She drew her wrap more closely around her and went in search of Eleanor, certain she wasn't sleeping, either. The servants offered her directions through the massive manor, and she found the Duchess of Weddington standing in front of a large window, three flights up, gazing out at the sea, tears rolling down her cheeks.

"Eleanor?"

Eleanor sniffed and wiped at her cheeks. "Sorry. I hate the sea, you know."

"No. I had no idea. Why ever do you live here then?"

"Because Weddy loves it so. It's the only lady with the power to take him from me. And I fear a day will come when she'll take him away forever."

Torie joined her in front of the window. Whenever lightning filled the sky, the sea, the wrecked ship, the storm became frighteningly visible. "I've seen the way he looks at you. Not even the sea has the power to take him from you."

"A Gypsy fortune-teller once passed through the village, and I made the mistake of asking her to read the tarot cards and to tell me my future. She told me that the sea will take from me two whom I love."

"Your Weddy could travel on the ocean to Egypt and that would take him away from you."

Eleanor shook her head. "No. She said that I wouldn't have the one I love for long.

I've thought a thousand times of asking Weddy to move us to one of his other estates, far from the sea, but I would rather have a few years with him happy than a thousand with him sad."

"Eleanor, no one has the power to see into the future."

"Perhaps not. Perhaps I'm being silly. But it's my fear that our time will not be enough that prevents us from engaging in the social whirl that is London this time of year. I want nothing to distract us from each other. I will never be ready for him to leave me, but I will make memories while I can. And now I'm being morose, and we have much work to do. We'll soon have people to warm, feed, and find dry clothes for. You can help if you like."

"Simply tell me what to do."

Fires were lit in the fireplaces throughout the manor. Blankets warmed before them. Hot soup heated in the kitchen. When servants brought the first survivors up from the shore, they were taken to the kitchen where they could remove their drenched clothes behind a screen in privacy and relative warmth because the ovens were going. Torie would hand them warm blankets, and when they were properly covered, she'd escort them to the large dining room where they were served warm soup, reassuring them all the while that everything would be well.

Servants eventually took them to bedchambers where they could sleep. Twenty-seven in all, passengers and crew.

Torie wasn't certain what they would have done if Drummond Manor wasn't so incredibly large. But it accommodated everyone.

At one point, Torie had thrown on a cloak and cautiously made her way down to the shore to watch the rescue efforts, certain she could do more there than she could inside where so many servants were tending to everyone's needs. But she didn't have the strength to row the boat that Robert and Weddington were taking out to the ship. She barely had the stamina to stand against the wind. But she watched her husband putting his life at risk for these strangers, and her love for him swelled as much as the waves from the sea.

She could hardly stand to watch, the anxiety and terror growing that she'd see him killed.

It wasn't until she returned to the house that she realized she would cause additional work for the staff, because now she needed to be dried and warmed. Eleanor brought another nightgown to her bedchamber.

"I'm sorry. I wasn't thinking," Torie said, after she was once again in dry clothes and sitting in front of the fire. "I'll be down to help you in a bit."

"I think the servants have everything well in hand. And I don't blame you for going down there. This is only the second time that a catastrophe such as this has happened since I've been here. But I can't bring myself to bear witness to it so close to shore."

"Was Robert here when it happened before?"

"Not while I was here. I think it happened once before when they were lads. Ships and storms don't often make a good match."

"I don't know him, Eleanor." She held her new friend's gaze. "I thought he would be ordering people about. I didn't realize he'd actually be in the boat, actually go out in the storm. It terrified me to watch him. And yet at the same time he seemed so sure of himself, so unafraid, so determined."

Eleanor knelt in front of her and took her hands. "Weddy once believed that he had no truer friend than Robert. Then the Robert we knew somehow went away. But he's returned now. Trust your heart, and you'll see the Robert that we all love."

Finding Eleanor's comment somewhat odd and cryptic, Torie stared at her new friend. "When you say he went away, do you mean—"

"Ah, there you are."

"Weddy!" Eleanor popped up and ran across the room, straight against her husband's chest, giving him no choice except to wrap his arms around her to keep them both balanced and prevent their tumbling over.

"I'm wet and cold, Eleanor, and you'll find yourself in the same boat if you don't unlatch yourself from me."

"I believe that I'll simply hang on, and we can dry and warm each other."

He looked over Eleanor's head at Torie. "Robert will be here soon. He's borrowing some more of my clothes."

She was in his bedchamber when he returned wearing only a pair of trousers, his feet bare. He appeared exhausted, and she could hardly blame him. He looked at her, looked at his bare feet.

"Weddington's valet helped me," he explained, almost apologetically.

"I watched you out in the storm. It terrified me."

"Terrified me as well."

"Yet you kept going back out onto the sea."

"They needed help, and I was in a position to help."

"And if you'd died?"

"But I didn't. I see no sense in speculating on what might have been."

"Then let's speculate on what is. You are my husband, and yet the intimacy between us has not gone as deeply as it might. Why do you not want me?"

"Oh, dear God, but I do want you, with every fiber of my being."

"Then take me."

Robert contemplated her invitation as he watched her unbutton her nightgown, part the cloth, and slip it off her shoulders. When had women grown so incredibly bold?

And when had he grown so incredibly weak? He watched in amazement and gratitude as her nightgown slithered slowly along the glorious length of her body, revealing it inch by tantalizing inch, until it finally left her completely bare, possibly vulnerable, stunningly beautiful.

She was exquisite, the lines and curves coming together—

Suddenly dipping down, she snatched up her gown, held it to her chest—

"No," he said more harshly than he'd meant, and she froze, her eyes like those of the deer they'd spotted in the woods when it became aware that it was being watched. "Allow me a moment to simply look at you."

She licked her lips, furrowed her brow. "I thought once I was disrobed, things were supposed to happen rather quickly. I thought perhaps you were disappointed."

"What would I find disappointing?"

She moved the gown aside only a little to reveal one perfect breast. "My breasts are rather—"

"Voluptuous?"

"I was going to say large."

"I have large hands."

Her gaze dipped to his hands, dangling uselessly against his sides. At the same instant her eyes rose to meet his, she released her hold on the gown again, and it made its slow journey back to the floor.

She was a temptation.

And he was only a man. Not a saint.

He'd been so strong for so long, holding

the insanity and loneliness at bay. Tonight he was so weary. Weary from battling the storm, weary from battling his brother, weary from battling his desires. So damned weary.

He surrendered to the seduction of her voice, her scent, her presence, the blush of her bared flesh. He surrendered because he had neither the strength nor the desire to walk away.

As slowly as she had unbuttoned her nightgown, he unbuttoned his trousers, watching her face for any signs of fear or doubt or change of heart.

But he saw none. He saw only anticipation, and God help him, desire.

Weddington was right. She wanted Robert. The man standing before her. Not his brother, not John.

But him. And while he might not be able to lay claim to her heart, while all she might desire was his flesh joining with hers, he would take the offering, be glad of it, and make her equally glad that he had.

Taking a deep breath, he shoved his trousers down and stepped out of them, standing before her as bare and vulnerable—

"Dear Lord, but you're beautiful," she whispered, and he saw the appreciation in her eyes. "I didn't know that a man could look so . . . magnificent. Like a warrior or a god."

"I'm not that magnificent," he mumbled, suddenly self-conscious with her praise, tempted to snatch up his trousers and cover himself. In his fantasies, he'd always been in a brightly lit room, both he and his lover bared, but in reality he'd expected the bedding to take place in complete darkness, beneath covers, using hands to see more than eyes.

"You are to me," she said, dipping her head, peering up at him, the dimple in her cheek appearing, then disappearing. "I can't wait to touch you."

Now that the moment was upon them, she was shy, his wife was. And he adored her for it.

"Let me finish having my fill of you," he said, even as he knew he would soon fill her, but he didn't want their first time together to be rushed, and perhaps was even a little shy himself. He'd never had a woman before—or at least if he had, he had no memory of it.

That had been the purpose of his last celebration, the last night before Pentonville, when he and his brother were to cross over into the debauchery of adulthood with wine and women and gambling. The wine and gambling he remembered. The women . . . he was fairly certain he'd been drugged by then, and if he'd performed, he had little doubt that he'd performed miserably.

He wanted this moment with Torie to be perfection, because he suspected that it would be a first for her as well. The blush on her cheeks traveled down to the gentle swell of her breasts. Even as he gazed on her, noting all the dips and curves, he was well aware that she was taking note of his body as well.

"Are you nervous?" he asked.

She nodded.

"Frightened?"

She shook her head.

"I guess it's a good thing that one of us isn't."

"Why would you be frightened?" she asked.

He was terrified, actually, of doing it wrong, of not making it good for her.

"I know a woman experiences some pain. I don't want to hurt you, and I'm afraid in my effort to spare you discomfort that I'll be clumsy and awkward—"

Reaching out, she pressed a finger to his lips, silencing him, while at the same time igniting the fires of his desire. Her eyes were locked on his, and he wondered if she could see clear into his soul.

The dimple appeared in her cheek. "Why is it that you so seldom talk, until now, when I'd rather you didn't. I'm fairly certain that I'm coming to love you."

"Oh, dear God." He thought he might have dropped to his knees, and if he'd not pulled her to him, latched his mouth onto hers, and held her there for support, he very well might have.

How he'd yearned for this moment. For eight long years he'd envisioned it, dreamed of it, imagined it, but nothing had prepared him for the reality of a woman's bare flesh pressed against his from shoulder to heel. And not just any woman. Not a woman he'd paid for or a servant he'd coerced . . . but a woman who possibly cared for him. She was fairly certain. What would it take to make her completely certain?

As certain as he was. He loved her. If she'd never granted this moment, he still would have loved her. He loved her smile and the tiny dimple. He loved her laughter and the wonder in her eyes when she gazed upon a fawn.

She made silence bearable. He was content to simply be with her, but to have more, to have this . . .

It was all his heart desired. And he would protect it unto the death. He would find a way to prove his claims, he would find a way to keep John from being a future threat.

When he could think clearly. When his mind wasn't lost in the sensations of her. Because he was lost, lost in the wonder of her, the silkiness of her skin against his, the softness of her breasts flattened against his chest, the wonder of her hands running over his shoulders, his back as he kissed her and she kissed him.

Without removing his mouth from hers, he tumbled them onto the bed, a tangle of arms and legs that quickly settled around the other, to hold that person near. She was where she belonged: beneath him, her hair spread out across the pillows.

And he thought he might be where he belonged. He lifted his head, gazed into her eyes, and felt his confidence come to the foreground. He would make this good for her. He would.

Torie saw something shift in his gaze. A

determination she couldn't explain. She ran her hands up into his hair, over his broad shoulders.

He was right where he belonged. Nestled between her thighs. Raised up on his elbows, gazing down on her with a feral intensity. Then she could no longer see his eyes because he'd dipped his head, a quicksilver kiss against her mouth before he pushed himself down and delivered a more leisurely kiss to her breast.

His tongue circled even as he suckled, and she thought this was decadent even as she didn't want him to stop. She combed her hands through his hair, holding him close, relishing his touch as much as he was relishing hers.

"You're so beautiful," he whispered as he trailed his mouth from one breast to the other, his fingers stroking the underside while his lips and tongue saw to the needs elsewhere.

He grazed his hand down her side, down the inside of her thigh, then over to the very heart of her womanhood.

She thought she should have been shocked, appalled, but it all seemed so right, so perfect, and so incredibly stimulating. Her body arched against his hand as though it knew better than she what was required to end this aching that had begun deep within her. And it did know better, because all she knew was that she relished his touch, wanted it on every inch of her skin.

His fingers stroked her intimately, and she released a tiny whimper.

He moved up. "Soon, Torie, soon." He kissed her and as his tongue slid into her mouth, so he began to slide into her. She was ready for him, so ready for him.

As he plunged fully into her, the pain she'd always heard she'd experience was nothing as she expected. Just a quick burst of awareness that the barrier had been breached, that she was now well and truly his wife.

He buried his face in the curve of her neck. "You feel so remarkably good," he rasped. "Like hot velvet."

She heard him swallow, felt hot moisture land against her skin. A droplet of sweat, she was certain, because his back had grown damp with the dew of perspiration. Not tears. Not an overwhelming of gratitude that they'd finally come together.

So still, he was so still as though he was absorbing the moment, the sensations, sensations that seemed to be hovering. Was this it, then? A coming together that seemed to require more . . .

He slowly began to rain kisses over her face, her throat, her shoulders. Then he started to move inside her, slowly at first, long strokes that stretched and filled her . . .

He rose above her, quickening his pace. An urgency that hadn't been there before. His face contorted with his concentration, his eyes holding hers, the intensity feral, almost frightening.

She held on to him as he rode her, she rode him, the sensations building, building until she thought she might burst . . .

And when she finally did, the world exploded around her.

Her husband exploded within her.

And she thought that nothing would ever again be the same.

Robert had always known that he'd been denied a good many things, but the true extent of what he'd been without had been an elusive mystery now solved. As he lay with Torie nestled against him, his hand idly stroking her bare side, the reality of his brother's cruelty became crystal-clear.

Prison was for felons, criminals, those who stole and cheated and murdered. Robert had done nothing to deserve his incarceration, and although he'd always known that fact, the anger burning in him now as a result of the injustice was almost frightening.

He wanted swift revenge, and even as he thought that, he grew weary and realized he truly wanted only that it be over. That he be free to live out his life with Torie in peace.

But how to achieve that goal still remained beyond his grasp.

And he had little doubt that John would see the situation very differently, John, who had courted her, asked for her hand in marriage. John, the man she was to marry.

He tried to ease the guilt that now swamped him with the realization of exactly what he'd done. He reminded himself that she'd told him she had doubts about marrying the duke. He told himself that tonight all her doubts seemed to have vanished like fog touched by the sun.

She'd wanted him. She cared for him.

And he couldn't deny that he cared for her. Desperately.

The storm still raged outside, the lightning

flashing, the thunder crashing, but here was a safe haven, comfort and warmth.

"Where do you go?"

He rolled his head slightly and gazed down on his wife. "Pardon?"

"I can see from the look on your face that you're no longer here with me."

"I was just thinking about how very fortunate I am to have you in my life. And everything I would do to keep you there."

"It shouldn't be that hard of a task—keeping me here. I'm fond of chocolates, flowers, and pearls."

He grinned. "So you can be bribed."

She snuggled up closer against him, trailing her fingers over his chest. "Did I never mention that?"

"I don't believe you did."

"I must have at some point or else you know me very, very well. You gave me the pearl necklace and bracelet I wore the day I married you."

He was grateful her face was down so she couldn't see the look that must have crossed his face. Always, always there would be things he didn't know. Always there was the chance she would discover the truth.

He should confess now, while she lay

sated and content in his arms. Tell her he was not the man she thought he was. But he couldn't bring himself to utter the truth, to ruin her contentment—or his.

Tomorrow, tomorrow he would tell her everything.

Chapter 18

"Despite your protests to the contrary, I can tell that you jolly well did take my advice last night."

Standing by the coach, waiting as his wife said good-bye to Eleanor, Robert blatantly ignored his friend.

It was mid-afternoon; the rain had cleared off and the gray skies had turned blue. After all the rescuing they'd done last night, he and Weddington had slept until only an hour or so ago. Robert would have gladly never left the bed because Torie had been in it, sleeping beside him. He loved watching the way she slept.

She had a little habit of rubbing her feet together throughout the night. He wondered if that was the reason husbands and wives slept in separate beds, although he had to acknowledge that he'd welcome any evidence of her nearness, had found her small actions comforting.

"No comment?" Weddington asked.

"I'd never realized what a vexing friend you are."

"A helpful one as well. I want you to take these with you."

Robert glanced down to the wooden box Weddington was extending toward him. "I don't see myself engaging in any more duels, thank you very much. They upset Torie too much."

"Not a duel, necessarily. A means of protection. You escaped Pentonville. Your brother could as well. He's just as clever as you are."

Robert couldn't deny that. In some ways, perhaps more so.

"Did you tell her the truth of your situation?" Weddington asked.

Robert grimaced, not proud of the answer he was forced to give. "No."

"I doubt it would matter to her," Weddington said.

How could it not? Robert wondered.

"Eleanor likes her," Weddington said.

"She likes Eleanor."

It wasn't long after that Torie was finally ready for them to take their leave. Robert bid Weddington good-bye and climbed into the coach after Torie, sitting beside her. She gave him a shy smile. He took her hand. The coach began its journey along the road leading away from Drummond Manor. Robert held off as long as he could. Then he could hold off no longer.

Torie was beginning to recognize when unbridled desire was taking hold of her husband, but after last night he had no more reason to hold back, and so he didn't.

His mouth was on hers, insistent, demanding, but not frightening. There was such goodness in him, such care. And such passion.

It began like a match held aloft, the flame just a flicker of light, but then it blazed into a conflagration, like a bonfire on a winter night that burned so brightly there was no holding it back. She wanted his kiss, his touch. She wanted everything.

He dragged her onto his lap so he could have easier access to her, holding her close, deepening the kiss, his hands making a mess of her hair. And she didn't care.

He tossed her hat to the other seat, and she assumed the pin went with it, and thought of his reaction when he'd sat on it before. Only she didn't laugh. She couldn't laugh, because she barely had the breath in her to survive the onslaught of passion.

She wanted him, wanted him desperately.

She heard pins clinking as they hit the floor of the coach, then her hair was tumbling around her.

"Oh, God, Torie, I shouldn't have begun what I can't finish." He was breathing harshly, his mouth burning along her throat as he popped buttons free.

"You can finish."

"No, not here, not in a coach. I want you in a bed, beneath me. I want us completely naked. I want it all. But it will be sweet, sweet torture to wait."

She so agreed. She was hot, and everywhere he touched blazed hotter.

"How much farther?" she asked, her voice raspy with desire.

"An hour, I think. No more. Perhaps a bit less."

"Then let's just torment each other until then."

And he was exquisite at tormenting her. He peeled back her bodice, kissing each bit of flesh that became visible, touching, stroking, holding. When he lowered his head and closed his mouth over her breast, she nearly came off his lap.

She wanted him to stop, wanted him to continue, wanted him to find them a bed. Now! Right this instant.

She returned the favor, unbuttoning his shirt, kissing his chest, tasting the saltiness of his skin. He moaned her name, and his fingers tightened on her breasts. She could feel the hardness of him against her hip and she thought if she just hiked up her skirts, if she just twisted around, simply straddled him, that the intimate part of her that was screaming for attention could find it with the part of him that was demanding it.

It was instinctual, this wanting to come together. As though she would perish if they didn't. And yet even as she considered all the gyrations that would be required to make it happen, she realized that he was right.

Not here in the coach, all twisted about, bouncing along.

The coach began to slow. He jerked away from her, glanced out the window.

"Thank God, we're here. Let's get you put back to rights."

She'd just finished buttoning her bodice, he'd just finished buttoning his shirt, when the coach stopped and the footman opened the door. The man's expression changed not one iota as he helped his disheveled master and mistress alight from the coach.

Torie's hair was still undone, her hat on the seat, but she didn't care. Robert reached down, lifted her into his arms, and headed toward the house. She buried her face against the warmth of his neck. "I can walk, you know."

"I like carrying you."

He hurried up the stairs, his steps sure. The door opened before he was there.

"It's good to have you home, Your Grace," Whitney said.

"Good to be home," he replied, without stopping, heading for the sweeping staircase that would take them to the family wing. "Tell Mrs. Cuddleworthy the duchess and I shall eat in our chambers this evening, but until I ring we don't wish to be disturbed."

"Very good, Your Grace."

"Robert, the servants are going to talk."

"Let them."

"Why do you always close your eyes when we make love?"

Lying atop her husband, Torie pressed her face to his chest so he wouldn't see her embarrassment. "I don't *always*."

"Nearly always."

"Don't you close your eyes?"

"No."

"Never?"

"Hardly ever."

Once they'd divested themselves of their clothing, neither had been in a mood to put anything back on. They'd been in his bedchamber all afternoon, all evening. They'd had dinner brought here and eaten in decadent nakedness.

"Why?" he asked again. "Why do you close yours?"

Raising her head, she dug her chin into his chest bone.

"Ow!" He slipped his hand beneath her chin to stop the pressure. "What did you do that for?"

"Because your question is too personal."

"Too personal? How can anything between us be too personal after all that we've done this afternoon?"

She couldn't deny that he made a rather compelling point. He was quite the adventurer. She didn't think they'd yet made love in precisely the same position twice. He'd slipped pillows beneath her to raise her hips to alter the angle of his entry. Once they'd made love sitting in a chair. Once standing up.

He seemed insatiable, her husband.

Holding the ends of her hair, he tickled her nose. "Come on, Torie. Tell me why you close your eyes."

She released a quick, impatient burst of breath. "Because it's too personal to actually watch what we're doing. I can tell what we're doing without looking."

"I like watching."

"You're perverted. I've married a pervert."

"I'm not perverted. I'm interested. I'm curious. If I closed my eyes I wouldn't be able to see the blush that creeps over you from your hairline down to your tiniest toe when rapture sweeps over you."

"Oh, yes, I'm sure it's my blush that holds your interest."

"I want you to watch next time."

"Is there going to be a next time?"

He gave her a wicked grin, and she felt a nudge against her backside.

Returning his smile, she said, "Well, yes, I suppose there will be."

"Watch this time."

"Why do you care?"

"I don't know. Just the thought of you watching, though . . . well, you can feel how it affects me."

"I don't think I can watch. Besides, my eyes aren't always closed."

"They are once I'm inside you."

"How can you say that so casually?"

"How would you prefer I say it?"

"I'd prefer that you not."

He reached down and patted her bottom. "Get up."

"I thought we were going—"

"We will. I need to do something first."

She rolled off him and pulled the sheet up to her breasts.

"No, you can't have that," he said. "I need it."

He tugged the sheet free of her and began tying one corner to the top of the bedpost.

"What are you doing?" she asked, drawing up her knees and wrapping her arms around them.

"You'll see." He tied another corner to the other post.

A wall of white was to her right by the time he came around, shoving a table in front of him, moving the bedside table forward, positioning lamps . . .

Then he stood, his feet spread, his hands on his hips, a look of keen satisfaction on his face. "That should work."

She turned her attention to where he was looking and saw the shadowy silhouette of a woman sitting on the bed.

"Oh, no," she said, releasing her legs and scrambling for the end of the bed.

He grabbed her ankle, stilling her before pulling her back to him. Grabbing the other ankle, spreading her legs, wrapping them around his hips, he lowered himself, pinning her in place. "I thought you liked shadow games."

"I like watching what you do with your hands."

A look of pure masculine triumph reshaped his features. "Oh, I shall definitely do something with my hands."

"That's not what I meant." She sounded

breathless, unable to believe that she was already so incredibly aroused.

Flattening his palm against her cheek, he urged her, "Look, Torie, it's not so wicked."

She followed his gaze, wishing she had the strength to resist, but her curiosity getting the better of her. And there they were: two shadows, a woman on her back, a man raised up above her.

"It looks like you're inside me, but you're not."

"Noticed that I'm not inside you, did you?"

"It's a little hard to miss when you are."

He grinned. "Why can you tease me with words, seem so comfortable with the banter, but have no interest in watching?"

"I don't know."

She looked back at the shadows. "It seems rather boring, doesn't it?"

She watched as the shadow above lowered itself, then she felt Robert nipping at the sensitive flesh below her ear.

"Still boring?" he asked in a low voice that caused her body to tighten.

She felt his tongue lapping at her skin.

"Still boring?"

"No," she breathed, her eyes slowly closing.

"Don't close your eyes. Just watch the shadows."

Watch the shadows. Watch the shadows.

She watched as the man rose up on his knees, his shoulders back, his sword at the ready. She watched as the lady eased up slightly, ran her hands up the man's thighs, up his stomach, up his chest, and down, down, laying claim to that which he offered.

The shadow quivered, the man's head dropped back, and his throaty growl reverberated between them. He raised his fists, and she watched as the woman's hands glided over him, cupping him and stroking him, some aspects clear, others blurred, shadows wavering, the lines indistinct.

She became lost in the shadow dance as the man reached for her arms, pulling her up as he fell back, tugging her forward until she was straddling his hips. She stretched out over him like a lazy cat about to lap up the cream. And she did lap at him, her tongue traveling over his bare skin, licking, tasting, relishing. Groaning low, he wrapped his hands around her arms, bringing her up until her breasts hovered above him.

Then he was doing to her what she'd done to him. His tongue taunting and teasing, circling her nipple while his mouth closed over her breast and his hand slid down between them, to stroke and drive her mad with desire.

She turned her gaze away from the shadows on the canvas and looked at her husband. His head was turned to the side, his gaze riveted by the dance of seduction unfolding. Watching him, watching them . . .

She felt pleasure coil so tightly . . .

He grabbed her hips, brought her up, brought her down . . .

She cried out, her release instantaneous, more intense than anything that had come before it, but hovering within reach . . .

Another.

She whimpered as he began pumping himself into her, controlling her movements with strong hands that bit into her hips.

Now she was the one throwing her head back, turning her head to the side, watching as she glided her own hands along her stomach, cupped her breasts, taunting him with her wickedness as she touched herself in the same manner that he often touched her. It was exhilarating to abandon her reserve, to express her desires with such freedom . . .

He released a feral growl, his back arching up, his hips making a final thrust even as he drove her down to meet him. Pleasure, intense beyond belief, shot through her, and once more she found herself crying out.

She watched the shadow lady grow limp and melt into her shadow lover.

"Now you can close your eyes," he said with a satisfied chuckle, as his arms came around her, holding her close.

Turning her head, she smiled at the sated couple lying in shadows. Smiled before drifting off to sleep in contentment.

Chapter 19

The mornings that followed were filled with Robert secluding himself in the library or the study while Torie saw to the management of the house. The afternoons were filled with walks and rides, tours of the countryside, long heated kisses beneath the boughs of trees where they took a rest, picnics, and walks along the river.

The evenings consisted of a lovely dinner, reading afterward, her reading to him, because he so loved the sound of her voice. She'd never known any man to be so enthralled with a woman's talking, as though he could never get enough.

The nights . . . they never seemed long enough. They made love, and slept, awoke to make love again. With each time that they came together, the fluidity of their lovemaking increased.

Torie came to know his body almost as well as she knew her own. And she knew beyond any doubt that he knew hers equally well. He knew how to touch her to create the wonderful sensations that spiraled through her. When to pull back and drive her crazy, when to push forward and grant her release.

He was quite simply remarkable.

My darling sister,

I have thought of you often in the days since I embarked on my wedding trip to my husband's estate. Or I should say that I've thought of the conversation you had with Mother the morning of my wedding. Although I have been married only a month, I daresay that I shall never tire of the dish I'm being served.

I thought I knew so well the man I was to marry, and yet each day

brings a new discovery and a deeper love. It's been a marvelous revelation to realize that I shall never grow weary of being with this man. No matter that we stroll along the same path through the garden each evening before dinner, something always catches my attention to delight me. The rumble of his laughter, the timbre of his voice, the sight of his smile, the warmth in his eyes, the heat of his kiss.

Oh, dear sister, his kiss. It lasts forever and is over too quickly. I must confess that I disagree with Mother's assessment that slow lovemaking is to be endured. Rather, I find it is to be relished.

I write to tell you this only because I wish to assuage your fears that a woman would find discontentment if she settles on only one man, for even though he is but one man, he has many moods and he is a constant mystery to be slowly unraveled.

I take joy in knowing that it will take me a lifetime—

At the sound of a gentle knock on the door, Torie stopped writing, glanced over her shoulder, and bid entry. The butler opened the door and stepped into the room.

"I apologize for disturbing you, Your Grace, but the duke wishes a moment of your time in the library."

"He's returned already? I wasn't expecting him until nightfall." She rose to her feet, wondering if he finished with his business at the village more quickly because he didn't like being away from her any more than she liked his being away. "Tell him that I'll be there in ten minutes."

"Yes, ma'am."

After he closed the door, Torie walked to the dresser, gazed in the mirror, and assessed her appearance. As he'd returned early, she had little doubt that there was no need for her to take much time in preparing herself. She suspected he'd soon have her hair mussed and her gown pooled on the floor.

Strange that he'd asked to see her in the library, rather than coming straight here to spend time with her. She hoped all was well. A sudden sense of foreboding traveled through her, and she feared that perhaps something was amiss.

She hurried into the hallway and down the stairs. At the bottom of the stairs, she headed toward the library.

When the footman opened the door for her, she waltzed into the room and saw her husband standing at the window, staring out at the gardens. She didn't recognize his clothing. It wasn't what he'd been wearing that morning when he'd left. But she'd recognize him anywhere, the way he stood, the tilt of his head, the shape of his back.

She was surprised that he didn't turn to face her, that he didn't acknowledge her arrival.

"Whitney said you wished to see me."

Still he didn't turn. Fighting back her trepidation that something was wrong, she crossed the room, walking over thick rugs. Slipping her arms around his waist, she pressed her cheek to his back. "I missed you desperately."

"Did you?" he murmured.

"How could you possibly doubt it? Didn't you miss me?"

"More than you can possibly understand."

He took hold of her hands, moving them

away so he could face her. She took a step back, not certain why, only knowing that she felt an overwhelming urge to do so. Something was different. Something she couldn't identify or explain. His eyes, she thought. There was something different in his eyes, something different in the way he looked at her. The fine hairs on the nape of her neck prickled.

She took another step back. "You're not my husband."

"Unfortunately, no, I'm not."

She tried to smile, to laugh, to understand. "Oh, you were playing a prank, telling Whitney the duke was here, wishing to see me, but you're John. You've come to surprise Robert. He'll be so pleased. He was terribly disappointed that you weren't able to make it over for our wedding. Still, I do wish you'd told us you were coming."

He scrutinized her as though she was the village idiot, rambling along, making no sense, and she realized that she was indeed rambling. She couldn't explain his unexpected appearance or his odd behavior. But he certainly wasn't acting like the prodigal brother returned.

"I just realized why you're looking at me

so oddly. You have no idea who I am. I'm Torie. Your brother's wife."

"I know who you are."

"John, please allow me to—"

"I'm not John."

"Are you a cousin then? What a striking resemblance—"

"Torie, my sweet, I'm not John, nor am I a cousin."

His voice carried a hint of warning, like a dog that growls if one gets too near its bone. She found herself taking another step back. "Then who are you?"

"I'm Robert Hawthorne, the Duke of Killingsworth."

Torie stood there, staring at the man, trying to make sense of his words. She shook her head, unable to decipher their connotation, even though she was well aware of what the words meant. They made no sense. He made no sense.

She shook her head. "I know Robert. He . . ." He had kinder eyes, a gentleness, a vulnerability. His soul possessed traits that this man's didn't. Just from gazing at him, she recognized that he was at once familiar and yet a stranger. She shook her head more vigorously. "You, sir, are not Robert Hawthorne. You're not my husband."

"No, I'm not your husband. He stole that honor from me, just as he has sought to steal everything else." He took a step toward her. "Look closely, Torie. Look into my eyes. You've looked into them before. For six months while we planned our wedding, for six months before that while I courted you—"

"No." She took another step back, wanted to run screaming down the hallways. "I don't know you, sir. I married the man into whose eyes I gazed—"

"No, you did not!" Reaching out, he grabbed her arms and shook her, his face contorting in agony. "That's what I'm trying to tell you! You didn't marry Robert. You married John!"

Chapter 20

Twisting and wrenching herself free of his grasp, Torie backed away, the horror of his words settling in the pit of her stomach.

"That can't be. I . . . I . . ." She pressed a hand to her mouth. In the beginning, hadn't she thought countless times that it was as though she was married to a stranger? Hadn't she wondered at his reticence?

Yet she'd fallen in love with the man she married. She'd discovered a gentleness, an extreme kindness. She enjoyed his company, enjoyed every aspect of being with him.

"You know I speak true, Torie. I can see it in your eyes."

She thought what he saw in her eyes were tears, because her eyes and throat burned. She felt the moisture roll over onto her cheeks. He was familiar, a familiarity that reached far beyond the shape of his nose, the fullness of his lips, the blue of his eyes. She had spent time in this man's company. Why did she recognize the truth of it now and not when she'd first seen him standing before the window?

"It's possible," she rasped. "I recognize you, not as a stranger, but as someone I've known."

"Someone with whom you've danced while you wore a white gown decorated with pink roses and lace?"

Her heart thudded at the reminder of what she'd been wearing the night she first met the Duke of Killingsworth.

"Someone who fed you strawberries dipped in sugar while you picnicked by the Thames?"

Her chest tightened to the point that she could barely breathe.

"Someone who asked you to honor him by becoming the Duchess of Killingsworth?"

She released a strangled cry. Oh, dear Lord, he could only know those things if he was the one who'd experienced them. Her trembling legs weakened, and she found herself dropping into a nearby chair.

"I don't understand," she whispered, hating the doubts and fears she heard reflected in her voice.

"There's no reason that you should." His tone was kind. "For as long as I can remember, John has coveted what was mine by right. As the firstborn son, I stood to inherit everything. It is English law, entailment—"

"I am exceedingly familiar with English law," she snapped, losing patience, desperate for him to get to the crux of the matter. She held out slim hope that perhaps it was all a horrible joke. Part of her felt violated, and yet a larger part of her simply wanted to see her husband, to have him hold her, to have him tell her that everything would be all right.

Only it wasn't her husband standing before her now. It was someone else, from another lifetime.

He gave her a wry smile. "Of course you are. But as my brother wanted my titles, my estates, it stands to reason that he would also want to possess my lady."

Only he hadn't. Not really. He'd tried to avoid her. She was the one who'd traipsed after him like a puppy in need of comfort, until he'd finally given in.

"You tempt me beyond all endurance," he'd whispered.

"But he didn't even know me," she reminded him. "He was in Virginia—"

"No. His being in Virginia was a carefully crafted lie, to protect the family."

"But his letters—"

"I wrote them myself."

"Why?"

He pulled a chair forward so that he could sit facing her. So close that she was hemmed in, imprisoned. Her heart beat erratically, her palms grew damp. She felt like a cornered animal, not at all certain that escape was possible.

"Where is"—she didn't know what to call him—"my husband?" she dared to ask.

"Out seeing to the affairs of the estate, I imagine."

"And when he returns?"

"You and I must decide on a plan of action."

She pressed the heels of her hands against her temples. "I don't understand how any of this has come about."

"I'm trying to explain as best as I can." He took hold of her wrists and brought her hands down to her lap. "As incredible as it seems, my father recognized that John couldn't be trusted to honor my place above his. On the night that we turned eighteen, he had John carted away to Pentonville—"

"Pentonville? It's a prison."

"Yes. The alternative was Bedlam. My father thought that Pentonville, being a modern facility, was a kinder choice."

"But it is a place for criminals. Your brother committed no crime."

"But he would have. My father was sure of it. So he paid a warder handsomely to keep my brother imprisoned within the walls of Pentonville."

"And you knew of this injustice?"

"Yes."

She studied her hands, then lifted her gaze to his. "Is that the reason that you stopped to look at it on occasion?"

"Yes. I hated the thought of my brother being incarcerated there. I was trying to determine if it would be safe to have him released. As it turns out, his freedom meant my hell." He came up out of the chair with such force that Torie reeled back against her chair, fearful that he might strike her.

He swung around and stood behind the

chair, his hands gripping its back until his knuckles turned white, his jaw clenched as he continued. "My brother escaped. His timing couldn't have been worse: the night before you and I were to wed. He came to the house in London and had me carted off to Pentonville in his stead." He squinted at the ceiling as though the memories resided there. "I was placed in solitary confinement, so it was some time before I was able to talk with the warder and convince him that a mistake had been made. I was released quietly three days ago."

He turned his attention back to her. "Then my real hell began. I made discreet inquiries and learned that my brother had gone through with the ceremony. That John was masquerading as Robert, and had taken not only my titles and my estates, but my lady as well. And judging by your earlier reaction, I assume that he has also taken your heart."

As well as her body and her soul.

At that moment, he looked as though he hated her down to the tips of her toes. She dropped her gaze back to her hands, finding his scrutiny difficult to bear, as though he could see everything that his brother had done with her, every kiss, every touch . . .

"Your story is incredible."

"It's not a story, but the truth."

She dared to lift her gaze back to him. "Your father's solution to what he perceived as a problem seems cruel." She shook her head. "No, it doesn't seem cruel. It was cruel. There had to be another way to protect what you claim is yours."

"What I claim? It is mine, Torie. It was to be yours as well. Has my brother bedded you?"

She felt the heat rush to her face.

"Has he bedded you?"

She nodded. He spun around, giving her his back.

"I could kill him for that alone," he muttered.

"No." She rose to her feet. "He doesn't deserve to die. If what you say is true—"

He jerked around. "You doubt me?"

She swallowed hard. "I don't know what to believe."

"Believe this. Not a single night went by when I didn't think of you. Not a single moment passed when I didn't worry over what might become of you. Not a single second ticked by that I didn't see your face, hear your laughter, remember your smile."

It was insanity, and she was beginning to doubt her own, his, and her husband's. "But how could I not know the difference? Even if you looked the same—"

"Do you still doubt that I am the man who courted you?"

She felt the tears stinging her eyes, burning her throat. She thought she might be ill. In the beginning she'd felt as though she'd wed a stranger. In fact, she had.

The chair toppled to the floor as he shoved it aside, knelt before her, and took her hands.

"Who am I, Torie?"

Her mouth was too dry to speak, her throat knotted with emotion.

"Am I the man who courted you?"

She studied his face, his eyes . . . She nodded.

"Am I the Duke of Killingsworth?"

Was he? She didn't know. She only knew he wasn't the man she married.

"I need to see"—she wanted to say Robert, but what if she was this very second staring into Robert's eyes—"my husband."

"Do you believe that I am the Duke of Killingsworth? That I am Robert?" he insisted.

"Why would he lie to me?" she asked, instead of answering his question.

"I told you. He wanted what I possessed."

"If what you say is true . . ." Tears blurred her vision, rolled onto her cheeks.

"It's true, Torie. You must believe me. Why would I create such an elaborate story?"

"What is it that you expect of me?"

He squeezed her hands. "You must understand that in all likelihood, even when faced with the truth, he will still claim to be Robert. I fear he *believes* he is Robert. Worse than that, however, I fear he is insane. The night he escaped—"

Because he was holding her hand, she felt the tremor ripple through him.

"What? What happened the night he escaped?"

"He bound and gagged me."

She could see the horror of what he'd endured reflected in his eyes.

"He struck me to render me unconscious. When I awoke, I was alone. Completely alone in a dark place."

She was still having a difficult time believing, and yet she couldn't deny the man she'd married wasn't the man she'd agreed to marry. She could see it so clearly now. Her husband's initial hesitations . . .

"Are you going to send him back to Pentonville?"

"No. I never agreed with Father's solution to the problem. I was trying to honor his wishes, but I can see now that he treated my brother most unfairly. Still, I cannot risk his trying to again take from me what is mine."

She could do little more than nod her understanding of the situation. "What would you have me do?"

"I want to meet with him, to speak with him—"

"He should be returning home any moment."

"Not here. I want to meet with him away from the house where the servants can't hear. I have no doubt there will be a good deal of shouting, until we can sort the matter out. He won't like hearing what I have to say, but if he will only acknowledge that he is John, then perhaps there is hope for us all, for a way out of this mess."

"I don't understand why you can't just meet with him here."

"Because he is likely to get violent."

"He doesn't strike me as a man of violence."

"Does he strike you as a man who is living another's life?"

"No."

"There are numerous things about my brother that you don't know. But remember, Torie, by taking you as his wife, he betrayed you far worse than he did me."

Robert so enjoyed the twilight strolls he took with Torie. It had become their habit before dinner to spend this time together, allowing the burdens of the day to fall away. This evening she'd met him at the stables as soon as he'd returned home, and while she'd seemed most anxious for their walk in the beginning, now she seemed particularly solemn, unlike her usually pert self.

He knew he couldn't continue the deception any longer. He had to tell her the truth. And once he told her . . . he had to maintain faith that her feelings toward him wouldn't change.

He'd not planned to fall in love with her. And yet he had. There was nothing about her that he didn't treasure. Nothing he didn't adore.

He'd spent the afternoon riding aimlessly around the countryside, trying to determine how best to break the news to her. When the best time would be. Before he made love to her again? For surely he would. He had no willpower where she was concerned. Perhaps he should tell her afterward, when she lay lethargically in his arms, the glow of her release highlighting her skin.

He should tell her over dinner—so she could ban him from her bed if she chose.

Or in the morning, so he'd have one more night with her in his arms.

And he'd use the same excuses tomorrow and the day after that. It was the very reason that he was now in this unconscionable predicament. Because he'd not wanted to hurt her, and in the end, he feared he was going to do exactly that.

"Is everything all right, Torie?" he finally asked.

She glanced up at him, giving him the smile, the dimple he adored. "Of course. I'm simply distracted."

"Isn't that one of my habits with which you continually find fault? My drifting off into my thoughts until I'm no longer here."

She nodded, and he thought he saw tears spring into her eyes before she averted her gaze.

"Torie?"

"I'm fine. I was wondering when you thought we might return to London."

He did need to return to London. He had

to determine how best to handle the situation involving John, which was the very reason that he could no longer put off telling Torie.

He'd considered that perhaps there was a way that he could manage to release John without anyone being the wiser, but the problem was how to ensure that John didn't cause any more mischief. Robert would put Torie at risk if he didn't tell her the truth, and if John ever came to visit, she might very well recognize him as the man who had proposed to her.

He'd never meant for it to come to this. He'd simply wanted to regain what was his by right.

They were a good distance from the house now, walking through the area of the gardens where the hedges were high and the foliage dense.

"I've been giving a good deal of thought to that, actually. I thought perhaps—"

He heard a rustling of plants. Even as he turned, Torie scampered away. The two men who grabbed him were huge, brawny, and even as he struggled against them, he knew he had little hope of escape. One delivered a forceful punch to his gut, and he dropped to the ground as the air rushed out of him. His arms were wrenched back—

"Don't hurt him!" Torie shouted.

—a rope bit into his wrists. Fighting to draw—

"Get him on his feet."

—in a breath, he peered up at the sound of a voice he recognized. He was jerked upward and fought to stay on his feet when his legs desperately wanted to crumple beneath him, not so much because of the pain still radiating just below his ribs, but that centering where his heart beat.

Torie stood there, not surprised at all to see the appearance of a man who looked exactly like her husband. And he realized that she'd known John would be waiting there, John and his henchman.

The pain of bitter betrayal sliced through him.

"Torie—"

"She knows the truth now, brother," John said. "Knows you are John and I am Robert."

Ignoring his brother, he focused his attention on his wife. "Torie, you must believe that I am Robert. You must."

"Why didn't you tell me the truth from the beginning? Why did you pretend—"

"I wasn't pretending!" His words echoed around them. "I'm Robert."

"You pretended to be the man who courted me, who asked me to marry him. You knew all along that I thought you were someone else . . . I trusted you with my heart."

"And I trusted you with everything."

"How poetic, John."

He glared at his brother. "I'm not John and well you know it."

"Of course you are."

He fought futilely to break loose of the hold these men had on him. "I'm Robert Hawthorne, the Duke of Killingsworth." He shifted his gaze to his wife. "You must believe that, Torie."

"Why didn't you tell me? If it is true, why didn't you tell me?"

"You doubt the truth of it."

"How can I not when you have deceived me from the moment we met?"

"Deceived and betrayed her as well as betraying me," John said. "Take him to the mausoleum."

"Why the mausoleum?" Torie asked.

"Because it is the only building that he

wouldn't dare desecrate in an attempt to escape."

"Torie—" Robert tried one more time, but she turned away from him, and he saw the look of triumph in his brother's eyes.

"Be sure and bind his feet once you get him there," John said. "I don't want to take any chances that I might have misjudged what he will not desecrate. After all, he stole my titles, my land, and my love."

The pain ripped through Robert's chest as he watched Torie welcome John's arm going around her in a comforting gesture, and he realized that she was well and truly lost to him.

Torie thought she would forever remember the look of devastating betrayal that had crossed her husband's face when he realized that she'd knowingly led him into an ambush. Only she hadn't known it would be like that. She'd been as surprised as he was, but she'd also still been in a fog after the revelations of the afternoon.

Now she wasn't certain what she was supposed to think, what she was supposed to do. She sat in a chair in her bedchamber, gazing out into the darkening twilight.

Utterly and completely exhausted from the ordeal, confused about her feelings, worried about . . . the man she'd betrayed.

Two men claimed to be Robert Hawthorne.

One she had promised to marry.

The other one she had married.

One she had liked.

One she loved.

Did it matter if she was married to John? Her heart didn't care if she was a duchess. But if he was John, he needed help. Desperately.

She heard a door open, the door separating the duke's bedchamber from hers. She'd been so looking forward to his coming to her tonight, and now she wished only that this man would leave.

He came to stand beside her, pressing his shoulder against the window casing. She could feel his gaze fixed on her.

"What are you thinking?" he asked.

"I'm trying to decide if I am married to the man with whom I exchanged vows or the man whose name appears on the marriage license."

"I've been wondering the same thing. However, until we know whether or not you carry my brother's child, it is a moot issue."

She turned her attention to him. "I don't understand."

"I shall not visit your bed for a month. If after that time, we determine you are not with child, then I shall take you as my wife—as we originally agreed. However, if you are with child . . ." His voice trailed off.

"What then?" she asked.

"I can't risk that it would be a boy, an heir. I would have to divorce you on grounds of adultery."

"You would divorce me when you never married me."

"The fact that I was not at the altar does not change the fact that my brother exchanged vows with you and that you in good faith thought you were marrying *me*."

"We'll simply explain that your brother"—she couldn't quite bring herself to call her husband John—"was pretending to be you."

"No. I won't have that sort of scandal rain down on my family. What has happened will be kept between us."

"You think it better for London to believe your wife was unfaithful?"

"Let's hope it's not a decision we must make."

"What are you going to do about . . . your brother?"

"I've yet to decide."

"What if I could convince him to give all this up, and he and I could go away—"

He released a brittle laugh. "He'd not give all this up, not even for you."

"He told me that he loves me."

"He also told you that he was Robert, the duke. Lies flow from his lips like wine from a bottle. You can't trust him, Torie."

"I don't know why you had to lock him in the mausoleum."

"It was either that or the village jail."

"What will you do about him? You can't leave him there forever. It's a cold, cold place."

"He'll only stay there until I decide how best to handle him."

He shoved himself away from the window, reached down, and cradled her chin. "He had no right to you. The dukedom, I could forgive him for taking that from me. But you. That I shall never forgive him for." He leaned down, his face close to hers. "Because you see, I love you as well."

Releasing his hold on her, he straightened. "Now let's go dine."

He said it as though her heart hadn't been devastated, her world crumbled.

"I'm not hungry."

"You must keep up your strength. Our ordeal has only just begun."

Robert barely felt the biting cold or the hunger gnawing at his gut. His bound hands and feet had grown as numb as his heart.

He lay on his side, where he'd been unceremoniously dumped by his brother's henchmen—how was it that John could always manage to find the dregs of society?

At least there had been light at Pentonville. Now there was nothing but the bleak darkness of despair.

Torie doubted him, and the pain of that doubt was like a finely honed sword stabbed through his heart. It had taken more strength than he'd known he possessed not to cry out his anguish as he'd watched John lead her away.

If Torie doubted him, what did it matter if he proved his claims?

The dukedom, the estates, the titles . . . none of them seemed important anymore.

He caught sight of light wavering on the

stained-glass windows at the front of the mausoleum. He heard a grinding of the key into the door. It opened, and he heard his wife's soft voice.

"Thank you, I'll be fine. The duke told me to tell you to go up to the house and have yourselves something to eat. I'll stay until you return."

Torie stepped into the chamber and closed the door. In one hand she held a lantern, in her other arm a bundle of blankets, as though she didn't realize that physical comfort no longer mattered to him.

He cast his gaze downward to the floor, preferring to stare at it rather than her. He heard her footsteps echo hollowly around him, then a clatter as she set the lantern down.

"I brought you some blankets," she said quietly, as though she feared disturbing him.

He shifted his gaze over to her, then turned his attention back to the floor.

"Would you like me to help you sit up?" she asked.

"No."

"I hate the thought of you being kept

here," she said, "but your brother fears that you'll try to usurp his authority—"

"As well he should, as he has none." He glared at her. "He tells you stories and you believe them."

Hugging the blankets closer to her chest, she knelt on the hard stone floor. "I was in shock. Do you have any idea what it is like to discover that you're not married to the man you thought you were?"

"You thought you were marrying the Duke of Killingsworth and that is exactly who you married."

"Not according to your brother."

"He lies, Torie. Why are you so quick to believe him and not me?"

"Because he never deceived me—"

"But he did deceive you, he deceived all of London, pretending to be me."

"And you could have righted that by telling me the truth in the beginning, but you didn't. You knew you weren't the man who proposed to me. Why didn't you cancel the wedding?"

"Because I couldn't fathom that it would be anything other than a marriage of convenience. That you wished to marry a title, not a man."

"A title can't warm me at night."

"At the time, I didn't know you well enough to know you felt that way."

"And now?"

"I know you very well, but you apparently don't know me."

"So tell me what I don't know."

He didn't want to tell her anything. He wanted her to believe him based on what she did know now. That should be enough. If she truly loved him, it should suffice. But he also recognized that in her mind, her request appeared reasonable—because it was.

"I've decided I'd like to sit up after all."

She set the blankets aside, took hold of his arm, and struggled to pull him into a sitting position until he was resting his back against his mother's tomb, his knees raised for balance as much as comfort.

"Would you like me to wrap a blanket around you?" she asked.

"No, I'm fine."

"You're trussed up like a holiday hog and yet you state that you're fine."

"Trussed up thanks to your suggestion that we take a walk farther into the garden."

She looked down at the floor. "I didn't

know he was going to—" She shook her head. "He told me he wanted to talk."

"And yet still you believe he is the true Duke of Killingsworth."

She raised her gaze to his. "Tell me what I should know."

"You should know without me telling you that I am Robert."

"Let's say you are. You still deceived me. You're not the man who asked for my hand in marriage."

He sighed. "You're right. I'd not planned . . ." *To come to love you.* But he left the words unsaid for they, too, no longer mattered.

"You asked me to tell you what you don't know. I don't know what you *do* know so I'll simply tell you what I know.

"Shortly before we were to turn eighteen, John suggested that we have one long celebration that would begin at dusk on my birthday and end at dawn on the day of his. We mapped it out: the establishments we would visit, places he assured me we would be welcomed. I should have suspected something then. I'm not sure why, but I should have.

"We traveled around London, drinking whiskey in the coach. We went to a house on the outskirts of the city. I wasn't familiar with it, but apparently John was because everyone seemed to know him. Inside there was more drinking, revelry, and ladies. I remember John giving me a glass of whiskey, slipping a lady's hand into mine, and telling me to drink up and leave the work to her." He shook his head.

"I remember going up the stairs, going into a room . . . my next memory is waking up in a cell, wearing prison garb, calling out for help, and receiving a beating because of it. I was Prisoner D3, 10. And when I realized that I was at Pentonville Prison, I knew I was in a great deal of trouble.

"I thought perhaps John was there as well, in another cell. That we'd stumbled onto some sort of slave trade or something. Or that the people in the house we'd visited were using us to replace their friends who were to be sent to prison. Any and all explanations seemed ludicrous, but then so did the entire situation. I was stupid, naïve, and unable to comprehend why any of this was happening.

"As you know, we had to wear hoods when we walked in the exercise yard, but I would try to look in the prisoners' eyes, find eyes similar to mine. Sometimes I tried to whisper to the man in front, but that only got me complete isolation for a time.

"Then one day, I have no idea how many days had passed, but one day I received a letter. Inside was a clipping from the *Times*. It was the obituary for the Duke and Duchess of Killingsworth."

"Your parents," she whispered.

He nodded. "The letter simply said, 'Thought you should know.' It was signed by Robert Hawthorne, the Duke of Killingsworth. And that's when I knew that I wouldn't find John in the prison. That our birthday celebration had been an elaborate ruse to get rid of me."

"But why that night when you weren't yet duke? And surely someone would have noticed that one of the sons wasn't around."

"Countless times John had told our parents that he wished to travel to America. I think, pretending to be Robert, that he might have told them that John had followed his dream and gone across the Atlantic, following our birthday celebration. Maybe he'd told them that he'd gotten a bit drunk and taken off. But that is only a guess on my part."

She began briskly rubbing her arms, and

he didn't know if she was cold from the air surrounding them or his chilling tale.

"You don't believe me," he said.

"He said your father had made the arrangements because he knew you would try to take what wasn't yours."

"What did my father stand to gain by doing that?"

"What did your brother stand to gain?"

"The dukedom."

"But not for years. He had no way of knowing that your parents would succumb to death so soon."

Robert swallowed hard, forcing himself to say the one thing that had haunted him the most all these years. "Unless he knew that the dukedom would soon fall to me."

She stopped rubbing her arms. "But the only way he could know . . ."

Robert nodded. "Was if his plan included killing our father."

Torie suddenly felt a chill that had nothing to do with the cold marble surrounding her.

"Why didn't you cancel the wedding?"

"I'd thought about it, but you must realize that I'd been isolated for so long, unable to share my thoughts with anyone save myself, and I found myself standing at the altar trying to determine the best course of action. I didn't know how to prove I was Robert, and I feared that if I didn't go through with the ceremony, questions would be asked that I wasn't yet prepared to answer. After the ceremony, I couldn't tell you the truth because you told me that you cared for me desperately, and I thought confessing would result in your going to the authorities before I had a chance to determine how best to prove my claims.

"I planned to never touch you, and once John could be freed, then I planned to find a way to undo the marriage and some way to circumvent the law—even if it required an act of Parliament—to see to it that you were able to marry the man you'd planned to all along."

His voice held such sincerity, such desperation to believe him, to trust him, to understand.

"How did you escape?"

She listened in silence, spellbound and fascinated as he described his daily routine, the continual isolation, except for the walk in the exercise yard and the walk to chapel. But even during worship the isolation was there, the silence surrounding them except when they sang. And how he'd worked to loosen the floorboard and make his escape.

He told her about Mr. Matthews and how he'd had John returned in his place.

"Although it really wasn't my *place*. I should have never been there to begin with."

She saw the tears spring to his eyes, watched as he blinked them back. He averted his gaze, and she saw the muscles of his throat working.

"Torie"—his voice was rough and scratchy—"you can't imagine what those eight years were like. To never be touched, except when being shoved, to never be able to talk to someone about the most inconsequential of things—the weather, the color of a woman's eyes, the grace with which she walks—let alone the momentous yearnings of your heart, your hopes, your dreams."

"And yet you held your distance, until the night of the storm when I asked you not to."

"You were not mine to touch."

"And yet you did."

"If you want an apology—" He shook his head. "Whether or not you want it, you deserve it. I'm sorry, Torie. For whatever hurt I caused, whatever damage I've done that can't be undone—"

"How will you prove your claims?"

"Do you believe me?"

His voice contained such hope, such desperation to be believed.

"I know only that I love you," she admitted.

Releasing a deep sigh, he lowered his head. "That's not enough."

Her heart twisted painfully with his admission. But she suspected that her reluctance to recognize him as the duke was equally painful to him. If she loved him, shouldn't she believe him?

Searching through the blankets, she pulled out the knife she'd hidden within the folds. "Regardless of who you are, you don't deserve this treatment." She began sawing on the rope binding his legs. "Go to London and find out to whom lords are supposed to talk when there is a dispute over their claims."

"The Lord High Chancellor."

With his feet freed, she stilled and glared at him. "If you knew, why haven't you already spoken to him?"

"Because I can't prove my claims. It is John's word against mine."

"And you think this is better? To play a game of tag imprisoning each other?"

"No, you're right. I must trust the courts."

She scooted up while he twisted around, giving her access to his hands. When she'd cut the bindings, he groaned and began rubbing his wrists, flexing his fingers.

"Go to London," she ordered.

Reaching out, he cradled her cheek. "Will you go with me?"

When her love wasn't enough for him? With tears burning her eyes, she slowly shook her head. "I can't."

Hearing the door open, she spun around, her heart leaping into her throat at the sight of the other man who claimed to be Robert.

"Thought I'd find you here," he ground out. "Imagine my surprise when I saw my guards trudging toward the manor."

Torie's husband grabbed the knife from her hand and struggled to his feet.

"What are you doing to do with that, brother?" the man by the door asked.

"It depends on what you *force* me to do with it."

"It seems we are at an impasse. I'm curious, though. How did you manage to escape from Pentonville?"

"Through the flooring in the chapel."

"Ah, clever."

"And you?"

"I didn't escape. I was released. Once they let me out of solitary confinement, I insisted on speaking with Mr. Matthews—"

"The warder."

"Yes. Fortune smiled on me the night I met Matthews. He liked his drink and he liked his gaming hells. Unfortunately, cards seldom favored him. He owed a few unsavory men a good deal of money. He was only too willing to take what coins I offered. He also has a secret he wishes kept—the fact that I knew what it was caused Matthews to realize he'd made a dreadful mistake. He arranged for my release. And now he's on his way to America."

"Convenient. The only witness to your scheming is gone."

John smiled. "I must do what I must do."

"What of Mother and Father? Did they never question only one of us returning that night?"

John rolled his eyes. "Brother, they never knew only one of us returned. It was quite tricky, my pretending to be both of us . . . never at the same time, of course. And only for a few days, only until *John* convinced them that he would be leaving for America to seek his fortune."

"And Weddington?"

"He was a bit of a bother. Always hinting that he thought I might be John—you. I had to sever that friendship. It was some time before I could sever it completely, though. Not until he got involved with that little trollop."

"You've been so diabolically clever."

"I had no choice. You kept claiming to be the heir apparent."

"Would you have ever released me?"

"I don't know. Matthews was terribly good at the task I gave him. I'd only expected you to be there for a few months. Until you were to be transported, but he feared moving you out of isolation would bring with it the risk of his actions being discovered." John shrugged. "Or so he confessed when faced with his benefactor. And now you are once again trying to usurp my place."

"You have me at a disadvantage, but I'm willing to let you have it all."

"Including your wife?"

"No, not her."

"But if I am Robert, then she is married to me—"

"Grant her a divorce."

"A divorce is so scandalous. Besides,

even if she's free of me, she can't marry her husband's brother."

"In America she can."

John arched a brow. "Are you going to America?"

"Yes, I think we shall."

"Will you send me letters? I so like reading of your adventures. I think you should travel west, though. Virginia's growing boring."

"I shall write you letters from wherever you like."

Torie watched as the man by door slowly shook his head. "Unfortunately, brother, I don't trust you."

She watched in horror as he leveled a gun—

"No!" she shrieked, rising to her feet, lurching in front of her husband. She felt fire pierce her body and explode within her, heard an echoing bang that she thought might cause the ceiling to cave in, found herself back on the floor, darkness creeping in along the edges of her vision.

Had someone extinguished the lantern?

"Oh, dear God. Torie? Torie?"

She felt warm fluid seeping out of her, pooling around her. Everything around her was fading to black; even the voice calling to her was growing distant. She felt herself being wrapped in blankets, felt herself being lifted into strong, steady arms.

"For God's sake, man, don't just stand there! Get to the village and fetch a physician. Now!"

As she succumbed to the welcome abyss of oblivion, she realized she'd just heard the voice of the true Duke of Killingsworth.

Chapter 21

She sat in a field surrounded by raspberry bushes in bloom, the tiny flowers calling to her. Her husband was stretched out beside her, his head resting in her lap. He plucked a flower free of the thorny bramble and handed it to her. Resting in her palm, she watched as it miraculously turned into a raspberry. She placed it against the lips of the man she loved . . .

Torie fought through the darkness, her body aching as though someone had tossed her off a cliff. She shifted slightly, pain slicing through her side. She moaned.

"Shh, rest easy now."

She felt fingers combing her hair back from her brow. Opening her eyes, she saw the man sitting beside her bed, so much love and concern for her reflected in his eyes that she thought if a hundred men who looked exactly like him were lined up in a room, still she would be able to pick him out.

He'd been there each time she opened her eyes, giving her a reassuring smile, bathing her brow, spooning broth into her mouth, urging her to get well, as though the choice were hers.

"Robert?"

"Shh," he urged again, taking her hand, pressing a kiss to her fingertips. "You've been through a horrible ordeal. You need to rest."

He looked as though he'd been through a similar ordeal, and she couldn't imagine that hers had been any worse. He had several days' growth of beard, his hair was disheveled, his eyes rimmed in red, his shirt unbuttoned at the collar.

"I know how to prove you're Robert," she whispered.

"Dear God, Torie, you almost died. Do you honestly believe I care about the damned dukedom?" he asked, his voice rough with emotion. "More than I care about you?"

She could see tears in his eyes, which he was furiously blinking back. His hand was trembling when he laid it against her cheek. "I spent eight years alone, but when I thought I might lose you, that I might never again see your smile, or that tiny little dimple, that I would never hear you laugh . . . loneliness is not a big enough word for what swept through me. Despair so deep that I would give up everything, my titles, my properties, my name, everything for one more moment of holding you. Just one more moment."

Tears burned her eyes. She wished she had the strength to reach for him, to wrap her arms around him.

"I can't abide the thought of a world without you in it." He averted his gaze, and she watched his throat muscles as he worked to regain control of his emotions.

When he looked back at her, she was surprised to see that fury reigned.

"And if you ever again put yourself at risk . . . what were you thinking to leap in front of me like that?"

She placed her hand over his where it still cradled her face. "That I couldn't abide the thought of a world without you in it."

He released a sob that seemed to come

from the depths of his soul. He laid his head on her bosom, and she threaded her fingers through his hair to hold him close.

"I never want to lose you," he said.

She wanted to tell him that he wouldn't, that she'd figured it out, but she began growing weary, her eyelids heavy. She needed him to know how to prove his claims. Just before she drifted back off, she whispered, "Raspberry . . ."

Raspberry.

Torie had been going on about the silly fruit for two days now.

Robert felt Torie's hands relax in his hair, lifted his gaze to see that she'd drifted back to sleep. But at least she'd been awake for a moment. Tomorrow perhaps she'd awaken for a few minutes more.

He'd thought Pentonville had been hell, but it was nothing compared to the agony of the past three days. He'd never felt so helpless. Realizing what she'd done, what John had done, seeing the blood pooling around her . . . an emotion he couldn't describe had welled up inside him, and he hoped to never experience it again. Terror, cold and relentless. And when it had passed . . .

Gingerly he moved himself off his wife, only to discover that she was once again awake, watching him, her eyes clear, the tiniest of dimples visible, a slight smile when he'd feared to never see one again.

"Raspberry tarts," she said softly.

Smiling, he leaned nearer. "Would you like me to have Mrs. Cuddleworthy bake you some?"

"No, they're how you prove you're Robert, the Duke of Killingsworth."

"Pardon?"

"The first morning here, Cook told me that as a boy Lord Robert loved raspberry tarts."

"Yes, that's true."

"John doesn't like them. I don't know why I didn't remember sooner—"

"Torie, darling, it doesn't matter."

"But it does. You're the duke and proving it is so simple."

"With raspberry tarts."

Her dimple appeared, deepened. "So simple," she said wearily, her eyes warm with love, not fever.

He brought her hands to his lips, held them there. So while her fever had raged and her body had fought to heal, she'd been dreaming of saving him yet once again.

"It's even simpler than that," he told her. "I simply have to *be* Robert, the Duke of Killingsworth."

"I don't understand. How does that prove—"

"Torie, I realized that I don't need to prove who I am. Not to anyone. When John shot you"—he shook his head, trying not to remember the blood soaking through her clothes onto his, the terror he'd felt—"when you lunged in front of him, when I saw you on the floor, for the first time since I escaped Pentonville, I truly became the Duke of Killingsworth. I wasn't going to allow anyone on God's green earth to get between me and what I knew had to be done to save you."

"I heard you," she whispered in wonder. "In the mausoleum. And I thought, Whichever man is speaking, he *is* the duke."

Robert smiled at her. "No one questioned my orders. Not even when I ordered them to restrain John."

A look of worry passed over her features. "Where is he?"

Reaching out, he combed the stray strands of hair from her brow. "Where he will never harm me or mine again."

"Where?" she insisted.

"There is an asylum, in the countryside, not too far away. I had him taken there. He's not a well man, Torie. There are times when I think he truly believes he *is* me."

"Whatever happened to make him—"

He pressed his thumb against her lips. "I don't know. I don't know if we'll ever learn the truth of John Hawthorne."

What he did know was that John's parting words as he'd been led away haunted Robert.

"She loved me first!" he'd screamed.

Robert had responded like a child taunted by a bully. "I only care that she loves me last."

When she was strong enough, he would have to test her love . . . and his.

Chapter 22

As she regained her strength, Torie couldn't help but be aware that her husband was ever so attentive to her needs, but also cautious as he saw to those needs. He brought her meals on a silver tray as though they possessed no servants to do so. He would watch her eat as though he thought it was the most amazing activity in the world.

In the afternoons, he would wrap a blanket around her and carry her out to the garden so that she could benefit from the sunshine. Much to the diligent working gardener's dismay, Robert would spend several moments plucking the brightest of the blossoms from the gardens until her lap was filled with an assortment of colors and fragrances. Then he would sit beside her and ply her with questions about the Great Exhibition and the many inventions and changes that had occurred since he'd been out of society. That was how he'd begun to refer to the time he was in Pentonville, not as his incarceration, or his imprisonment, or his brother's dreadful act, but as the time during which he was out of society. He never wanted anyone to know that his brother had swapped places with him for a time. He wanted her to explain all the modern inventions so that he could carry on as though he'd never been away.

As she told him of one thing and another, she was amazed at how much progress could be made in eight years.

In the late afternoons, he would leave for a time, and while he always told her that it was to see to estate business, and while she knew that he had a good many duties that required his attention, she suspected that he was visiting with his brother. She knew Robert was saddened by the fact that his brother was locked away from society, more saddened by the fact that he didn't know why John had turned against him or why John believed he was Robert.

And doubts had surfaced surrounding the deaths of his parents. Arsenic was easily obtained, available for purchase from any chemist, a favorite among ladies who used it to enhance their complexions. The law did require that a person sign the *Poison Book*, but what happened to it after that . . . well, not everyone used it on her complexion. It was becoming a favorite murder weapon among married ladies who wished to dispose of their husbands. Robert had hired a man to travel throughout London, searching all the apothecaries' books. Robert's signature had been found in one of them, the arsenic purchased a month before his eighteenth birthday. And as Robert had never purchased poison, he had to believe that once again the act was carried out by John pretending to be Robert.

But all that could be proven was that arsenic had been purchased. Not that John had actually used it. Although Torie had never thought that his complexion needed righting.

She knew the knowledge her husband had gained haunted him, so she was relatively certain that he was spending some time with his brother, trying to discern what had shaped him into such a different man, but it was a hopeless task. He would return in the early evening, more somber and solemn, reflective. And she would seek to cheer him by sharing portions of the letters that Diana wrote to her, telling her of her exploits to find a man who wouldn't bore her after a day or two.

After Torie retired for the night, he would join her and simply hold her, as though she were delicate, too fragile for anything else. And they would talk.

"I want to understand the kind of man you are. What you endured. How it might have shaped you."

"You are a morbid little thing, aren't you?"

"Were you beaten? Flogged?"

"No. It wasn't as bad as all that. Oh, a guard might strike you if you talked or didn't put your peak on to cover your face. But they had a worse punishment: solitary confinement."

"I can't see how that was different from what you were already asked to endure."

"At least in my cell, I could hear activity. So although I was alone within myself, I wasn't completely alone. I knew others were about. I could hear them stirring as I worked my loom. I was fortunate in that regard. My job was to work the loom in my cell all day, to make cloth."

"I don't see how you could consider any aspect of your experience fortunate."

"I survived. That was fortunate. And they would bring us a book to read from time to time. The worst part was at night, because everything got truly quiet."

"Is that when you learned to do your hand shadows?"

"Yes. Each cell had a gas light to see us through the early hours of the night. Until the guards came through turning off our gas at nine, I would spend the time manipulating my hands, seeing what sorts of creatures I could create. And I would let them carry me away beyond the walls in which I lived. Elephants in Africa and camels in Egypt. I tried to create every animal I'd ever heard of. And people as well. I can create a hag and an old bearded man."

"I can't imagine how lonely you must have been."

"I don't want you to imagine it. I don't want you to imagine any of it."

Then he would say, "Tell me about your

life, what you enjoy, the things you like. I want to know everything about you."

"Well, let me see. My favorite color is red. My favorite season is spring. I enjoy long walks and . . ."

But as she grew stronger, a part of her feared that it wasn't her recovery that prevented him from making love to her, but a realization that he hadn't chosen her to be the Duchess of Killingsworth. Rather his brother had. And she was a constant reminder of his brother's treachery.

The doubts bombarded her with increasing frequency and strength, like waves bashed up against the shore during a tumultuous storm. Especially late at night, as she prepared for bed, wondering if her husband would assume his role as her lover.

Sitting at her dressing table, she was barely aware of moving the brush through her hair as she pondered her place in Robert's life. She supposed any woman would be content with the attention he gave her, but it was difficult to settle for less when she'd once had more. And perhaps that was the source of her growing discontent. She'd considered it while she'd taken a luxurious bath. Thought about it while Charity had helped her with her nightgown. Thought about it after Charity left her for the night and she awaited her husband's arrival.

Divorce was the solution she kept turning to. He'd been a young man when he'd been imprisoned. He'd attended few balls, few dinners. He never had a chance to look over the debutantes, to select the one who might appeal to him most. He'd married her because she was the one who joined him at the altar.

"You promised that someday you would allow me the privilege of brushing your hair."

Lifting her gaze to the mirror, she saw her husband's reflection as he stood behind her, in a blue silk dressing gown that matched the shade of his eyes.

"I didn't hear you come in," she said.

"You seemed far away in thought, as you often accuse me of being, there but not really there. Where were you?"

"It's of no importance," she lied. Tomorrow she would ask him for a divorce, but not tonight. She wanted one more night with him . . . and even as she thought that, she thought perhaps she'd ask him the day after . . . or after . . . How many days could she postpone facing the truth?

Coming to stand behind her, he reached around and gently took the brush from her hand. "Everything about you is important." Slowly he glided it through her hair. "I remember the first time I saw your hair loose, spread out over the pillow of that bed."

She watched him in the mirror, the intensity with which he gazed down on her. "My first night here, the night of the storm. When you brought me warm cocoa."

"I thought I would crush the bones in my hands, because I had to hold on to them so tightly to keep them from reaching for you."

"I wanted you to reach for me."

"But you thought I was someone else."

Something occurred to her.

"The pox," she whispered. "That first morning in the library, you said you had the pox, not a fox."

He appeared remarkably embarrassed. "I was trying to determine a satisfactory excuse for not fulfilling my husbandly duties. I wanted you to realize that the reason rested with me, not with any shortcomings on your part."

"But you don't have the pox."

"No."

"But you were trying to find a way to avoid being with me."

"Not avoid being with you. Avoid making love to you. I had this insane notion that I could return you to John untouched."

Nodding in understanding, she swallowed. "That's what I was thinking about earlier, when I was lost in my thoughts. How unfair to you it is that you found yourself with a wife whom you didn't choose."

"My thoughts have been running along a similar path. As John was being dragged away, he had the audacity to remind me that you loved him first."

"No." She twisted around and gazed up at him. "No, I told you that night in the coach, I had doubts . . ."

He cradled her cheek. "I remember. But when you look at me, do you *see* the man who asked you to marry him?"

She slowly shook her head. "No, I see the man I came to love."

He fell to his knees and bracketed her face between his large, powerful hands. "You see Robert Hawthorne, the Duke of Killingsworth."

"No. I don't see a name or a title. I see only a man. A man who held me through the night while sitting in an uncomfortable position in a coach. A man who tried to hide the fact that he wept over the loss of his parents.

A man who took a child on a shadow journey through the jungles of Africa and the sands of Egypt. A man who risked his life to save others in a storm. A man who was treated unbearably badly by his brother, yet still seeks to help him. A man whose wife betrayed him, and yet still he reads to her in the garden. I'm so sorry for doubting your name, but please believe me when I tell you that I never doubted my feelings for you. I love you more than anything."

"Oh, Torie." He crushed her to him, bringing her down from her chair, positioning her on his lap. "You can't imagine how unbearable it is to not feel love, to be isolated and alone with only your thoughts for company."

"And shadow creatures."

He drew back, holding her head, his hands tangled in her hair, his gaze riveted on her. "I thought I would go mad there. I had all these plans for revenge, how I would make John suffer, then you walked into my life and all I wanted was you."

She watched as his throat muscles worked, felt him tighten his hold.

"I love you beyond all reason. I fought against the temptation of kissing you, of making love to you, of being with you. Victoria Alexandria Lambert Hawthorne, will you honor me by remaining my wife, by becoming the mother of my children, the lady of my heart?"

She felt her tears resurface and spill over onto her cheeks. The look he bestowed on her was as heartfelt as the words, love pure and true. Beyond all reason.

"Yes," she rasped, her word choked, her throat clogged. "Yes."

He blanketed her mouth with his own as though he wanted to seal the word for all eternity. He kissed her as though he thought he might never have the opportunity to do so again. Kissed her as though his life depended on it. Kissed her as though he would never have enough of her. Kissed her as though he loved her with all his heart, all his soul. As though she was the reason he existed.

And she returned the kiss with equal measure. She loved him.

Within her arms, she held her heart's desire. Everything she'd ever wanted. To be loved, to be cherished, to be seen as worthy. He was everything to her because she was everything to him.

"How is your wound?" he asked, nipping at the tender flesh along her neck below her ear, before allowing his tongue to circle the shell of her ear.

"It's completely healed."

"Perhaps I should inspect the scar."

She leaned back slightly, smiling at him as she wiped away the tears that had begun to dry. "Do you think?"

He nodded solemnly, and she thought perhaps he wasn't teasing her, but was serious about his need to see it.

Easing off him, she sat back on her heels and undid the first button—

"I'll do that," he said, moving her hands away before he took over the task.

She could feel the tiniest of tremors in his fingers and she remembered the first time—

"You were locked away for eight years."

He lifted his gaze to hers. "Yes."

"You'd been a long time without a woman."

"I'd been *forever* without one."

She stared at him, in stunned disbelief. "Was I your first?"

"And you shall be my last."

She again felt those irritable tears. "I can't believe that you . . . showed such restraint. Legally—"

"I had the right, Torie. I know. But it wouldn't have been fair to you. I wouldn't use you as a means to slake my lust. When I finally came to you, it wasn't lust that drove me there." He angled his head slightly. "Well, I suppose it was a bit. I'm not sure men are ever completely devoid of lust."

"You were so skilled that I would have never guessed that you'd never before—"

"I had eight years to ponder the possibilities. I shall have to share with you sometime some rather unconventional shadow images."

"Are they wicked?"

"Decidedly so."

Now she was the one left to ponder the possibilities as he turned his attention back to her buttons and released them one by one. He slid his hands inside the parted material and slowly peeled her gown back off her shoulders until it pooled around her hips. His eyes closed, his brow pleated, as though he were in great pain. When he opened his eyes, she saw that the pain ran deeper than she could have imagined.

"You should have let the bullet strike me," he said, his voice hoarse with emotion. He dipped his head and pressed his lips to the nearly healed scar at her side that marked the entry of the bullet, which had miraculously not struck anything of significance.

She wove her fingers into his hair, kissed the top of his head. "How could I? Losing you would have been far worse than any physical pain I might have suffered."

"If one of us must suffer, I prefer it be me."

"Which is my point. If you'd died, I would have been the one suffering."

He narrowed his eyes. "I believe your reasoning is convoluted."

"Let's see to it that neither of us ever suffers again."

"All right. I promise. You'll never suffer again."

He rose to his feet, reached down, and drew her up, her gown slithering down her legs to the floor. Bending down, he slid an arm behind her knees and lifted her into his arms.

"I can walk, Robert," she murmured even as she wound her arms around his neck and nestled more closely against him.

"I need you to conserve your strength."

"Why?"

"Because you're going to need it for what I have in mind."

What he had in mind was absolute pleasure that began the second he placed her on the bed and divested himself of his robe.

He was magnificent as he came to her, ready and eager.

They became a tangle of limbs, his mouth on hers, his hands caressing, stilling each time they passed over her healing wound.

"It no longer hurts," she said, when he again stopped as though waiting for her to cry out with pain.

"I never want you to hurt again."

"Then kiss me."

An inquiry seemed to pass over his face, as though he was wondering what one statement had to do with the other, then it was as though it no longer mattered. He latched his mouth to hers, kissing her deeply, thoroughly, a man hungry, a woman starving for what had too long been denied.

She stroked his shoulders and back. She kissed his throat, his chin, his jaw, relishing the echo of groans, as he rose above her.

He was nestled between her thighs, looking down on her with an expression of complete adoration. She hoped that he could see that she felt the same as she rubbed the soles of her feet up and down his calves.

Threading his fingers through her hair, he held her head in place while he kissed her forehead, her nose, her lips, her chin. "You were an unexpected gift, and now that I have unwrapped you, I think I should enjoy playing with you."

"What are you going to do?"

He winked at her before scooting down, his mouth paying homage to one breast with a circle of kisses, before he blew a cool breath over her nipple. She felt it pucker and harden, drawing up tightly, even as the sensitive area between her thighs coiled tightly as well. She arched slightly, pressing herself against the flat plane of his stomach, searching for release while he continued to torture her by denying it.

He ran his tongue over the peak before closing his mouth around it entirely, suckling, stroking, suckling again.

"Robert," she rasped.

"Mmm?"

"You've enjoyed your gift enough. Come to me, so I might enjoy you."

"Not yet."

He journeyed to her other breast, leaving a path of dew-kissed flesh in his wake. He gave the same attention here as he had there, so his hands skimmed along her sides, her hips, her thighs. Marvelous hands, large hands.

And she returned the favor, stroking

where she could reach: shoulders, back, chest, sides. She loved the feel of him, the tension building, the urgency she sensed in him even as he tried to tamp it down, to go leisurely.

"You're driving me mad," she murmured.

"It's only fair," he said, his voice low and throaty. "You do the same to me every hour of every day. God, how I love you, Torie. I would be content to spend the remainder of my life here with you in bed."

He eased farther down, kissing her stomach. Farther still, brushing his lips over the inside of her thighs, sending delicious tremors racing through her. How could a touch at one point create sensations at another? And yet they did. Over and over.

Then he became decidedly wicked, looking up at her, his eyes blazing with desire just before he lowered his mouth to her most intimate place. With his tongue, he stroked and swirled. He slipped his hands beneath her hips, lifting her slightly, an offering to him that resulted in exquisite pleasure for her.

She dug her fingers into the sheets, holding them tightly, fighting to keep herself tethered even as he was urging her to soar above the mundane, to take flight. She squeezed her thighs against his shoulders, ran her feet over him, heard her tiny cries escalating, quickening . . .

Then she was calling his name, begging him to stop, begging him to continue. Her body convulsed with the force of release, lethargy spreading throughout her like molten lava flowing down a hillside. As her breathing slowed, she was vaguely aware of his resting his cheek against her stomach, as though he thought she needed a moment to recover from the cataclysm that had overtaken her.

She threaded her fingers through his hair. "Come to me," she whispered, surprised to find that she seemed to have no energy. But it was a wonderful lethargy.

And when he rose up above her, she discovered her energy renewed. And when he entered her with the surety born of love and acceptance, she thought nothing on earth could give her greater satisfaction.

He began to move like a man obsessed, a man with a purpose, his movements not solely for him, but for her as well, rocking, stroking, pressing home his point that he'd not take this journey without her. Groaning low, he kissed her as she felt the tension building within him, felt it building within her.

She'd not expected this second rising, thought the first had done her in, but it was there, rushing over her. She dug her fingers into his shoulders, seeking some sort of purchase from the storm that was about to overtake her, overtake them—

And when it washed over them, it lifted them both, took them under, lifted them back up. She felt him pumping his seed into her, felt her body closing around him. When the spasms stopped, she thought she might never move again. Still raised up on his arms, he buried his face against the curve of her neck and shoulder.

She could feel the slight tremors still passing through him. She rubbed his dew-coated back. "Relax."

"I'll crush you."

"No, you won't."

"Give me a moment."

"I'll give you a lifetime."

His chuckle sounded as though it came from the depths of a weary soul as he rolled off her and brought her up against his side. "I'll gladly take a lifetime."

Epilogue

He'd promised her that she'd never again suffer, but he could hear her cries of anguish, despite the fact that he knew she was fighting desperately not to be heard. Would her agony never end?

"Will you stop pacing, for God's sake? You're making me dizzy."

Robert glared at Weddington sitting on a bench in the hallway outside the duke's bedchamber door. Every heir to Killingsworth had been born in the duke's own bed. It had been near midnight when Torie had awakened Robert and informed him that she needed to be moved to his bed. He'd gotten into the habit of sleeping in her bedchamber. He preferred it over his own. After all, it was where he could always find her, hold her near, and hear her gentle breathing during the night. It was where they made love, whispered secrets, shared dreams. It was where he drifted off to sleep, loving her more each day.

"It's been over eighteen hours."

"Relax, it's not as bad as it sounds."

"Easy enough for you to say. Eleanor's only done this once. Torie has done it twice already today and it's not getting any easier!"

Robert regretted his words as soon as he caught a good look at Weddington's face.

"I'm sorry, Weddington."

"It seems you are to have an embarrassment of riches, my friend, all delivered within the span of a single day. Enjoy them. Eleanor desperately wants another child. Perhaps you can give us one of yours."

"I don't think so, and I apologize for my harsh words. It's just that—"

Torie went silent, but there were other sounds.

Then the door opened and Eleanor looked out. "It's over."

Robert released a great sigh of relief. "So there were just two then?"

"No, there were three."

"Three?"

She nodded, an impish smile on her face. "We'll have them all ready in a bit to meet their father."

"What about Torie? When can I see her?"

"In a bit. She needs to be readied as well."

"Is she all right?"

"She's doing remarkably well, considering."

"Considering what?"

She laughed. "Considering that she just delivered three babies. Weddy, tell him to relax and not worry."

"I've tried, princess, he won't listen to me."

Eleanor shut the door in Robert's face. Robert leaned against the wall, his legs barely able to support him any longer. "Three," he repeated.

It seemed to take forever before the physician made his exit and Eleanor motioned for Robert to come into the bedchamber.

Torie was lying on the bed, three small bundles nestled against her side, her arm somehow around all of them. Robert knelt beside the bed.

"Oh, Robert, look how tiny they are."

"There's three of them," he said, awed by their presence and their remarkable beauty.

Even with their tiny pinched faces and their pink skin, they were beautiful. He'd long ago stopped counting all the things his brother's deception had denied him. Rather he'd begun to be thankful for all the things it had brought him: Torie and now three daughters.

"Yes."

"All I can say is, thank God they're daughters. Not a single heir among them."

He had no desire for his firstborn son to have a twin. He never wanted his heir to endure what he had. He never wanted a second son to lose his way as John had. Robert continued to visit with him once a week, but it was always difficult and disappointing, because John was still convinced that he was the rightful heir, that Torie belonged to him. Robert hadn't a clue how to reach him, how to help him.

Strangely, Torie's sister had taken to visiting with John as well. "He fascinates me," Diana had said on one occasion. "He's never quite the same man."

She had patience with him that others didn't, and Robert couldn't help but wonder if perhaps she would be the key to his salvation, because his dearest wish was that the brother he'd known as a boy would return.

"I'll right that mishap next time around," Torie assured him.

He leaned up and kissed her briefly. "Thank you for having daughters this go round."

"I didn't think dukes were supposed to be happy with daughters unless they already had sons."

"I'm happy with anything that you give me."

"I *will* give you a son next time."

"If not, we'll keep trying until we get it right."

She laughed. "Even when we get it right, you'd best keep trying."

"I will do that, I promise."

And he knew it was one promise he would definitely be able to keep.

In the years that followed . . .

It was said of Robert Hawthorne, the Duke of Killingsworth, that no man fought more diligently and with more purpose for the rights of prisoners and prison reform than he.

It was also said of the duke that no man loved his wife or his children more.

Author's Note

Dear Reader:

From the moment I saw an engraving depicting the inmates of Pentonville Prison walking about the exercise yard, peaked hoods covering their faces, I knew this prison was destined to play a role in one of my stories. The Man in the Iron Mask Meets Victorian London **was how I thought of it.**

Built in 1842, Pentonville was considered the first "model" prison. Substantial planning went into its

design and management. It was built during a time when convicts were transported to Australia. But they were first sentenced to serve eighteen months at a "model" prison before deportation, so they would have time in isolation and silence to reflect on their crimes. For Robert to have been placed in the prison without first being sentenced in the courts, and not to have been transported after eighteen months, required considerable manipulation on John's part.

While there are no indications that any of the warders at Pentonville were as unscrupulous as Mr. Matthews, I hope you'll grant me a bit of literary leniency in depicting him and the situation in which Robert found himself. But with faces never seen, it seemed to me that the possibility could exist for a man to be imprisoned unjustly and indefinitely, which is the beauty of writing fiction, after all. One has the liberty to explore the possibilities and is limited only by imagination.

As for Robert's escape from Pentonville, it is based on the true account of a prisoner named Hackett. His was not the only escape, but I thought it one of the more daring and ingenious ones.

And while I'd always planned for the story to involve an American heiress, I couldn't quite make the timing work to my satisfaction.

A report issued in 1853 indicated that far too many prisoners were being carted off to Bedlam, an insane asylum, rather than Australia. Pentonville was not intended to be a cruel place, and the report made recommendations for reforming the prison system yet again, the first order of business being to dispense with the use of the "peak" or scotch cap, as the hood was called. And unfortunately, American heiresses didn't begin making an impression on the English aristocrats until the early 1870s when Jenny Jerome married Lord Randolph Churchill in 1874.

I was fascinated by my research of Pentonville. Much of it came from

The Victorian Underworld **by Donald Thomas, as well as a website hosted by Lee Jackson, www.victorianlondon.org/prisons/pentonvilleprison.htm. I'm grateful to both for making their findings available.**

Most sincerely,

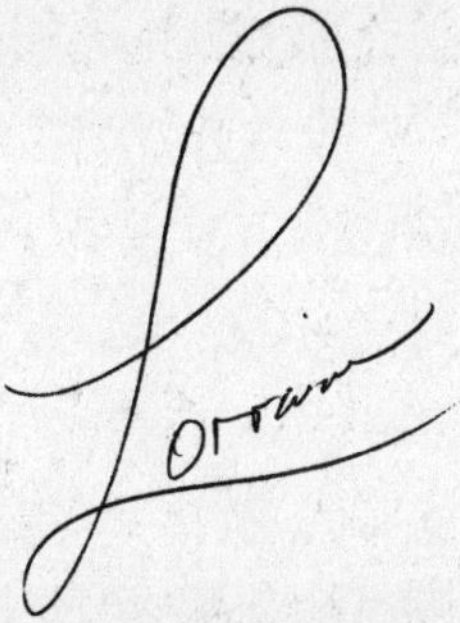